Seduced by the suspect...

Jon knew the woman to be a schemer and a killer, and yet, the moment he'd gazed into her eyes, his defenses had vanished. He could have sworn he saw genuine appreciation and sweetness in her expression. He must have lost his mind. The woman was a hardened seductress, and Jon Everett was nobody's fool.

As she arched against him, Jon summoned every ounce of strength in his character, reached into his pocket and hauled out his handcuffs. Clamping one on her wrist, he fastened the other to his own arm.

"Sorry, Gloria," he said. "You're a wanted woman. And not only by me."

ABOUT THE AUTHOR

Born in the small town of Mannered, Texas,
Jacqueline Diamond grew up in Tennessee and
Southern California, locales that are often
reflected in her writing. Unlike her heroine, she
isn't an heiress and can't remember the last time
she put polish on her nails.

Books by Jacqueline Diamond

HARLEQUIN AMERICAN ROMANCE

Don't miss any of our special offers. Write to us at the
following address for information on our newest releases.

Harlequin Reader Service
U.S.: 3010 Walden Ave., P.O. Box 1325, Buffalo, NY 14269
Canadian: P.O. Box 609, Fort Erie, Ont. L2A 5X3

JACQUELINE DIAMOND

THE COWBOY AND THE HEIRESS

Harlequin Books

TORONTO • NEW YORK • LONDON
AMSTERDAM • PARIS • SYDNEY • HAMBURG
STOCKHOLM • ATHENS • TOKYO • MILAN
MADRID • WARSAW • BUDAPEST • AUCKLAND

ISBN 0-373-16631-1

THE COWBOY AND THE HEIRESS

Chapter One

When two sedans pulled out of their end-to-end slots in the beach parking lot, the sports car driver saw his chance.

He didn't care about the motor home already heading toward the extra-large opening. He didn't care that his sports car could squeeze into any space, while the motor home might circle for hours without finding another place large enough.

The hot-rodder knew he could get there first. Maybe some people would consider it cheating, but that was life and they'd better learn to deal with it. Why should he let some rube with Texas plates beat him to a spot at his favorite Southern California beach?

He stepped on the accelerator. The souped up car leapt around the lumbering motor home and shot into the first space.

En route, the hot-rodder glimpsed the RV driver. He got the impression of a tall, sun-bronzed man wearing a Stetson, like some kind of cowboy.

The rodder stopped, testosterone pounding, and smirked into his side-view mirror.

The motor home kept coming.

It wasn't moving fast, but he didn't hear even the slightest creak of brakes. Nervously, the hot rodder idled forward into the second space. Didn't the idiot see him?

The motor home inched toward him. So the guy wanted a game of nerves. The rodder folded his arms and lifted his chin.

Then he glanced in the side-view mirror again.

He could see the driver better now. Mid-thirties, with a few sun-etched wrinkles around the eyes. The set of the firm jaw announced that this guy didn't kid around.

The cowboy's grip on the wheel tightened as if bracing for impact. The corners of his mouth twitched in a hint of a smile, the kind of smile that belongs to a man who has bumpers of reinforced steel.

The hot-rodder muttered angrily, already smelling defeat in the air. It wasn't worth a crushed fender just to steal a parking space. Besides, he remembered in a rush, his license had expired and he owed enough speeding tickets to put his wallet into hock until the millennium.

With a string of curses, he stomped the accelerator and zoomed away in a cloud of exhaust.

The motor home eased to a stop. A moment later, the door opened and the cowboy got out.

Tall and rangy with the broad shoulders of a former high school quarterback, he wore a blue work shirt, jeans, embossed boots and an air of concentration that made it clear he'd already forgotten the hot-rodder.

The cowboy stared toward a red convertible parked a few spaces away. From his shirt pocket, he pulled a small photograph and examined it.

The woman in the picture, half turned away, had a dramatic flow of blond hair and, from what he could see, babydoll features. A real beauty, and real poison.

Gloria Hess had a hundred thousand dollar bounty on her head. As soon as she returned to her convertible, the money would be as good as his.

MADDY ARMAND flashed along the Beachside boardwalk, her blonde hair flying. With the expertise born of many hours' practice on in-line skates, she zipped between two Japanese tourists and a woman shepherding her children.

Hearing a mumbled protest, Maddy swung around and skated in reverse. "Sorry!" she called, and smashed backward into a bicyclist.

Down they went across the sidewalk in a crunch of spokes and skates. The cyclist, one of those racer types so dedicated he shaved his legs to reduce drag, filled the summer air with blue phrases.

"Are you hurt?" Maddy responded with genuine contrition. "How's your bike? I'll pay for the damage."

The man glared as he straightened his high-priced racer. "It's dented. And you're messing up my workout."

Despite his knee guards, he had suffered some scrapes. Scrambling to her feet, Maddy said, "Here's my card. You can send me the bill."

The man waved it away. "I repair my own bike. I won't let anyone else touch it." Adjusting his helmet, he remounted and took off, as if losing even a few minutes' practice might cost him an Olympic medal.

Maddy knew what her father would say. *Thirty years old and you can't find anything better to do than knock people over at the beach.*

It wasn't for lack of trying, she reflected as she checked her scrapes and decided they didn't require first aid.

Citing her showgirl looks, friends had urged her to try acting. A couple of performance classes, however, had convinced Maddy she could never project herself into someone else's personality.

She'd then labored for three years in her father's business, helping build and operate shopping centers. Maddy possessed an aptitude for public relations, but her father kept such close tabs on her that she felt smothered.

Handing in her notice, she went to work for a couple of years at an animal rescue shelter, not minding the minimum pay in light of the not-so-modest fortune she'd inherited from her mother. That lasted until Maddy realized her supervisors were more interested in coaxing a large donation out of her than in the love and care she showered on the animals.

Maddy made the donation and quit the job.

Now, skating past a row of bikini and surf shops, she wondered what her life would be like if she hadn't been born an heiress. Maybe she would have found a meaningful career; maybe she would have met a wonderful guy instead of fending off fortune hunters.

On the other hand, she had to consider the downside. Maddy tried to picture herself working long hours at a dull job, shopping at discount stores and sharing a tiny apartment with roommates. Her imagination, usually active to a fault, failed miserably.

What she needed was an adventure to provide a whole new outlook on life, Maddy reflected. And anything seemed possible on this splendid June day.

The usual California coastal smog had yielded to sea breezes. Bright umbrellas polka-dotted the beach, and children laughed as they raced in and out of the surf.

A boy of about fourteen wandered along the strand, wearing designer shorts and a crisp T-shirt that read Beachside in front and Backside behind. His gaze shifted from sunbather to sunbather, finally fixing on a woman who lay half-hidden beneath a sun shield. A few feet away, her wallet spilled from an open purse.

The boy edged toward her. "Hey!" Maddy called. The boy glared at her and strolled away.

She wondered if he really needed money. She might have offered to help, but his air of cold calculation put her off. Besides, his precision haircut and new clothes made her suspect he wanted the money for a boom box or computer game, not for essentials.

Then something caught the corner of Maddy's eye, far out to sea, and she forgot the would-be thief.

Pausing in front of a boarded-up store, she stared over the ocean toward Catalina Island. Near the horizon, something sparkled ruby red, then vanished.

A teenager, padding by with a surfboard under his arm, asked his companion, "Did something fall out of the sky? Like, you know, a UFO?"

"A pink UFO?" scoffed the other young man. "More like fireworks."

"Yeah, right," snorted the first surfer. "Maybe the sea lions are setting off sparklers." Then he caught sight of Maddy and his lips pursed into a whistle. "Wow! What a babe! You free for lunch?"

She eyed his boyish features. "Thanks, but come back when you grow up."

"Promise you'll wait for me," he teased.

"I don't wait for anybody." She tossed her hair.

The boy paused as if to say more, but his companion tugged him away.

Maddy supposed she ought to be flattered when guys noticed her, but she'd grown tired of being treated like a toy in a shop window. Still, the young man hadn't meant any harm.

On the sand, sunbathers stopped peering to sea and flopped back on their blankets. There was no further sign of the ruby sparkle.

That had been the most excitement she was likely to encounter today, Maddy decided glumly. She knew some women would envy her choices for the afternoon: having her hair done, shopping, taking in a movie. To her, it spelled boredom.

Then she noticed something odd. Something even stranger than the red sparkle.

Maddy could have sworn she'd been standing in front of an abandoned store. But now, preparing to resume her skating, she saw that the shop was neither empty nor boarded up.

Quaint was the word that sprang to mind. Multipaned bay windows, one on either side of the doorway, reminded Maddy of a scene from Dickens's *A Christmas Carol.* The gabled roof rose above the flatness of neighboring establishments, while a sign over the door read: Curios For the Curious.

Trying to peek in, Maddy discovered that she could see nothing. The windows had a smoky tint and although the door stood ajar, the interior lay in shadow. She got the irrational impression that it lay in another dimension, as if to step inside meant to enter another world.

Her heartbeat speeded up.

Maddy knew she must be letting her desire for adventure run away with her. How foolish, to think a shop could materialize out of nowhere, and that entering it meant—well, anything more than checking out the merchandise.

She examined the windows for the usual stickers and placards announcing the presence of a security system, warning against smoking, and banning food or beverages. There were none.

Maddy decided she would go in. It wasn't as if she had anything better to do.

Yet, for an instant, unaccustomed caution held her back. She couldn't shake the sensation that she would be taking not an ordinary step but a giant one that might change her life. That once she entered, things would never be the same.

Well, good. I don't want them to stay the same.

Maddy lifted her foot over the threshold and skated into the shop.

The shadows vanished, and she found herself in a well-lit emporium, with a wealth of merchandise crowding odd-size tables of varying heights. Although Maddy found it easy to move around as she examined the stock, there were no defined aisles.

She'd never seen such delicate items: flower-filled glass paperweights; thin, colored bottles wrought with silver filigree; a scene of animals entering Noah's ark, carved from a single antique tusk that could have been a museum piece.

"I have something that might interest you."

Maddy's head jerked up at the unexpected voice addressing her. Until this moment, she hadn't realized there was anyone in the shop, although of course there must be salespeople.

An elfin couple sat behind a counter piled with gemstones, carvings and porcelain dolls. The pair both had pointy chins and inquisitive eyes, as if they were a matched set.

The man wore a green cloth hat, a tan fringed jacket and leggings, and green pointy shoes propped on the counter. Beneath a tiara of daisies, the woman's wavy ginger hair fell to the shoulders of her filmy gown. The cloth shimmered, changing colors from green to amber.

At first glance, Maddie thought they were teenagers. As she focused her attention, however, she realized they must be middle-aged, or even older. Perhaps much older.

The sense of strangeness that had touched Maddy in the doorway returned now, much stronger. The room lay in silence; she could hear neither waves nor playing children, only the faint hum of blood in her arteries. The sunlight that filtered around her bore a tawny tint, as if she stood inside a sepia-toned photograph.

"Who are you?" she asked. "What is this place?"

"My name is Ariel," said the woman. "This is my husband, Tuck. Please come here. I have something you will like."

Confronted with this otherworldly pair, Maddy became aware of her all-too-earthbound appearance in a short halter top, fashionably ragged shorts and booted skates. "I don't think— I mean, you must be expecting someone else."

"Come and look." Ariel's cupid's mouth quirked in amusement. "You won't know until you see it, will you?"

With dreamlike slowness, Maddy skated to the counter. The woman lifted a velvet-lined jewelry box into view.

"Oh!" The word sang from Maddy's mouth. "How lovely!"

Inside rested a pair of gold wedding rings. Each had been worked as a dove with folded wings and diamond eyes. The richly burnished surface of the gold invited Maddy to touch it, and when she did, she felt a faint pulsing and heard the rapid flutter of the bird's heart.

"That's amazing," she said.

"And reasonably priced," offered Tuck. His voice, tenor with a hint of a brogue, reminded Maddy of a player in some traveling Shakespearian theater company.

"But I'm not getting married," she said.

"You will be," murmured Ariel.

Her husband gave her a quelling glance. "What my wife means is that the rings bring good luck," he said. "Particularly in matters of the heart. You need buy only one. In fact, we could only sell you one."

Without intending to, Maddy slipped the smaller ring onto the third finger of her right hand. For an instant she felt light-headed, almost as if she would faint. When the dizziness passed, she saw that the bird had nestled into place.

"But what use is one without the other?" she asked. "Surely most customers would want to buy a matched set."

"Not our customers," said Ariel.

Maddy had never seen a store like this. She couldn't picture Ariel and Tuck marching downtown to secure a business license, or submitting to a fire inspection. There was something decidedly unorthodox about the whole situation.

But the ring felt so good on her finger, as if it belonged there. And it *was* beautiful.

"Well, all right," she said. "Do you take credit?"

"Whatever." Tuck glanced at the card she removed from her pocket and wrote down the number and the amount. Maddy had to remind him or he would have forgotten her signature.

How did these two ever manage to stay in business?

"Oh, dear." A note of alarm darkened Ariel's tone. "Now who is this?"

Maddy turned to see the boy from the beach, the one with designer shorts and larcenous eyes, amble into the shop. She could hardly warn the couple about his dishonest nature, not with the boy so close at hand. Besides, Tuck already watched him sharply.

The boy approached the counter, regarding Maddy with a sly arrogance that made it clear he remembered her and intended to proceed anyway. "I'm looking for a present for my mother," he said.

"We have lots of nice things." Ariel glanced dubiously at her husband.

"What price range?" asked Tuck.

Too late, Maddy saw the boy's gaze fix on the man's ring in the velvet box. Before she could speak or reach out, he snatched the ring and raced out the door.

"Oh, my!" Ariel's cry pierced the air. "Not that!"

Tuck glanced helplessly toward the threshold. "We can't go out there."

Stuffing her credit card into her pocket, Maddy skated for the exit. "I'll catch him," she said. "You guys call the police." And away she went.

Behind her, the two elfin people stared at each other in shock.

"This is terrible," said Ariel.

"She'll get it back." Tuck's fingers moved restlessly across the counter.

"But she doesn't know the danger," said Ariel. "If he puts it on . . ."

"He won't. It's too big for him." Tuck tickled one of the porcelain dolls, which gave a tiny squeak of laughter.

"He might try," said his wife. "And you know what will happen if he does. We should never have come here!"

"We wanted to give true passion a chance," Tuck reminded her. "If people have turned away from it in our world, perhaps their hearts are still open here. Now we must trust that the rings will find the right owners."

"That boy may outgrow his selfishness someday, but for now..." Ariel shook her head. "If he puts it on and they fall in love, then what?"

"It won't happen," said her husband. "The magic—I mean, I don't think it would allow—surely two people so unsuitable couldn't fall in love, even wearing magic rings."

"I wish I could be sure." The daisies in Ariel's hair drooped. "Oh, Tuck, I'm so worried."

"Don't be," he said, but tiny crease lines deepened in his forehead as long minutes passed, and no one returned.

"IT'S REALLY A BARGAIN." The boy waved the ring in the sunshine. "Them diamonds is real. A hundred bucks—that's less than my mom paid for it, but like I said, we need the money."

"It's probably stolen." The cowboy didn't even glance at the ring. He was watching the red convertible.

The boy shifted uncomfortably. "Look, Mister, honest, my mom lost her job and hurt her leg and we need the airfare back to, uh, Arkansas." He pronounced it Our Kansas. "So she sent me out to sell her ring."

"Yeah, right," muttered the cowboy.

"Okay, fifty bucks," said the boy. "You got a girlfriend? She'd love it!"

"Haven't got time for a girlfriend."

"With this ring, you'll get one!" The boy's voice took on a desperate note. "Thirty bucks. It's a steal, mister."

"I don't want—" The cowboy froze. A striking woman with long blond hair was heading in this direction along the sidewalk. She would have to pass the motor home to get to the convertible.

Those Texas plates might alarm her. He didn't want her to notice him or anything about him. If only the kid would stop yammering!

"Just take a look. I mean, it's almost alive. You've never seen anything like it!"

Another few steps and she would hear the boy's jabber. With an impatient motion, the cowboy pulled a twenty-dollar bill from his shirt pocket. "Take it or leave it."

The blonde was approaching fast. From her smooth motions, she must be wearing skates. Not Gloria's usual style, but then, how much did he really know about her?

"Yeah, okay." Disgruntled, the boy took the bill and dropped the ring into the cowboy's palm, then vanished into the maze of parked cars.

She was almost here. Impatiently, the cowboy stuck the ring onto his finger. Shrugging aside a momentary dizziness, he crouched to strike.

MADDY COULDN'T FIGURE out how the boy had disappeared so quickly. She'd spotted him heading in the direction of the parking lot, but he was too young to drive. Maybe he'd hidden inside an unlocked car, but who would be foolish enough to leave a car unlocked at the beach?

She couldn't give up. That sweet old couple had seemed so distressed at the theft, and she didn't blame them. The rings were magnificent.

Of course, she didn't believe jewelry could hold magic powers, or bring luck either good or bad. Yet she *had* sensed she was entering a new world when she stepped into the shop, and she *had* felt light-headed when she put on the ring.

It must be the effects of exercising in the heat.

Circling the perimeter of the lot, she asked a parcel truck driver if he'd noticed a boy in a Beachside T-shirt. Instead of answering, the man examined her boldly and invited her to hop into his van.

"I don't want a ride! I want to catch the little creep!" Maddy snapped and skated furiously away.

Just her luck! Instead of helping, the first man she met propositioned her. Why couldn't she meet a guy who had something more important to do than ogle her skimpy clothing?

Maddy allowed herself a moment of longing for Mr. Right: a fellow who would bring her flowers, and take her to the theater, and value her opinions. And not care about her inheritance.

You're asking the impossible. Now pay attention or the thief will get away.

Then she saw him, darting along the far side of the lot near a red convertible. If she didn't hurry, he was going to climb into a bus slowing along the adjacent street, and she'd lose all chance of catching him.

Teeth gritted, Maddy left the sidewalk and stroked her skates hard across the pavement. Hips and arms shifted into a swaying motion that lent speed to her movements.

The kid couldn't run as fast as she could skate. The bus was wheezing to a stop, but it hadn't opened for passengers yet. Another few dozen feet and she'd have him.

Maddy flew past a motor home, her attention riveted on the boy beginning to bang on the bus. "Stop!" she yelled, and then something slammed across her waist as if she'd hit an iron bar.

It was an arm, she realized as the wind burst out of her. A large, muscular arm, and before she could grasp what was happening, the man attached to it jerked her into the motor home and slammed the door.

Chapter Two

Maddy's cry of protest died in her throat as she stared into the man's face. She caught a whiff of tantalizing maleness and sun-warmed skin, and felt herself prickling with awareness of the man in a way she'd never experienced before.

In a rush of emotion, she sensed the size of him, a large taut frame, long legs, arms corded with muscles. She could feel the blood thrumming through his arteries and the mixture of hunger and admiration flooding his synapses.

In his brown eyes, she caught a glimmer of honed intelligence mixed with surprise at his reaction to her. And he certainly *was* reacting, breath coming quickly, pupils dilating, cheek brushing hers as he inhaled her perfume. He seemed to be soaking up her essence and drawing it into himself, the same way she was doing with him.

Even as she yielded to her feelings, Maddy searched for an explanation. She didn't know this guy. He'd assaulted her; he might be a kidnapper, or a prison escapee in search of a hostage. She had no reason to trust him.

And yet she did. More than trust; she desired him. She wanted to merge with him, succumb to him, drive him wild, tease him and fulfill him.

And then she wanted to do it over again, day after day, year after year.

Vaguely, Maddy remembered that she'd had some urgent task to accomplish, but she couldn't recall the details. Surely it could wait a few minutes. Or hours. Or a lifetime.

The man bent his head, his lips probing her mouth as he carried her through the motor home and laid her on a couch. Maddy curled against him, wanting more, wanting it all instantly, and wanting it slowly so she could relish every moment.

The man tossed his cowboy hat upside down onto a chair and surveyed her with a puzzled expression, as if he were fighting his own instincts. Why? she wondered as she peeled off her skates.

A shudder ran through the man, as if something primitive had seized control. Maddy felt him ease her halter downward, baring her shoulders and upper chest.

His lips traced the exposed skin and his tongue tasted the valley between her breasts. An intense sensation rioted through her nervous system, drawing out a long, delicious moan.

The stranger poised over Maddy, stroking the length of her body with hands that brooked no refusal. She grasped his shoulders and drew him down, her tongue tangling with his in something like a duel.

Maddy had never met a man like this before. She knew she never would again. They were meant to be together, and however oddly it had come about, she wanted him to claim her now and forever.

JON KNEW THE WOMAN to be a schemer and a killer, and yet the moment he'd gazed into her eyes, his defenses had vaporized.

Now he understood how a man could fall hopelessly in love with the wrong woman. He needed her with a primal drive so strong it wiped away self-control and common sense.

Maybe once he possessed her, she would cease to possess him. But he didn't think so.

Jon Everett had his own code of ethics, one that didn't always suit other people. A bounty hunter couldn't worry about his targets' guilt or innocence, although he assumed most of them were guilty. In the case of Gloria Hess, he had no doubt at all.

So why was he tearing her clothes off, panting like an overgrown adolescent? And why was she unbuttoning his shirt and running her fingers across his chest?

Maybe she intended to plant a knife in his heart while he was lost in ecstasy. But where could she be hiding a knife in this scant outfit?

He could have sworn he saw genuine appreciation and a certain sweetness in her expression. He must have taken leave of his rational mind. The woman was a hardened seductress, and Jon Everett was nobody's fool.

As she arched against him, Jon summoned every ounce of strength in his character. With the sense of struggling through a sea of molasses, he reached into his pocket and hauled out his handcuffs. Clamping one on her wrist, he fastened the other to his own arm.

"What are you... hey!" The woman sat up, blond hair sweeping across her shoulders. The sight of her wrenched Jon right to his masculine core, and it took all his power to refrain from resuming their delicious horizontal tango.

"Sorry, Gloria," he said. "You're a wanted woman. And not only by me."

"Gloria?" Azure eyes blinked at him in shock. "Who the heck is Gloria?" She tugged as if to break free of the cuff, and then stopped, staring at his hand. "Where did you get that ring?"

"Some kid sold it to me." Jon pulled it off and dropped it into his shirt pocket.

The passion drained from his body, leaving a residual warm buzz. Studying the woman again, he couldn't deny her obvious charms, but the uncontrollable passion had gone. Thank goodness.

"It's stolen," she said, and held up her hand. "See, I've got the other one." Jon frowned, trying to make sense of the fact that she wore a matching ring. "I was trying to catch the thief. Who are you, anyway?"

"My name is Jon Everett and I'm a bounty hunter," he said. "There's a hundred thousand dollars on your head, Gloria, my friend. And I'm going to take you back to Texas to stand trial for murder, if I have to drag you screaming and half-naked across three states."

A tiny smile warmed her face. Damn, but she *was* pretty, not cold and nasty as he'd expected. "Sounds like an adventure. Do we have to go the whole distance handcuffed? Don't you think we might get distracted?"

She was the first prisoner he'd ever taken who had a sense of humor, Jon had to admit. "You'll be handcuffed, all right, but not to me."

The woman sighed. In her skimpy clothing, every breath rippled across her golden skin, with a predictable effect on Jon's libido. The initial frenzy might have abated, but he was still a man and she was the most gorgeous woman he'd ever set eyes on. Then she added, "You know, I'm really not Gloria. My name is Maddy. If you'll reach in my pocket, there's ID in the wallet."

Since the pocket she indicated lay on the same side of her body as the handcuff, she obviously couldn't reach it herself. Feeling like a contortionist, Jon angled his opposing hand into her pants.

As he did so, his arm brushed her soft curves, and he felt himself growing hard with desire. Who would know the difference if he took her now? Gloria herself obviously wouldn't mind.

She was so supple, so willing and so deadly.

His fingers found the wallet, made of smooth, expensive leather. It didn't fit with the ragged shorts and the beach bunny image.

Jon reminded himself to stay alert. If he didn't, this luscious, cheerful young woman could render him very dead, very fast.

Fishing out the wallet, he was about to flip it open when a motor started nearby. Straddling the woman, Jon flipped open his curtains and peered out.

The red convertible was backing out of its parking space. A mass of blond hair floated around the woman at the wheel, and as the vehicle straightened, Jon caught a clear glimpse of her face.

She had the pert nose and mouth of a baby doll, and the flat soulless eyes of a cobra.

He cursed and tried to leap up, forgetting for an instant that he was still handcuffed to a stunning and totally unknown blonde. The effort brought Jon back down right on top of her.

"Does this mean you love me, or do you do this to all the girls?" she asked.

"Don't ask stupid questions," he said. "Come on!"

The woman let Jon drag her forward and made no protest as he turned on the ignition. In his haste, he'd clamped his right hand to her left. Ordinarily, that would have been a major mistake, but now it meant he could drive as long as she didn't resist his movements.

Out of the corner of his eye, he noticed that she'd done a poor job of straightening her halter. One shoulder was bare, and the bodice kept slipping down to the right in a tantalizing way.

This was no time to worry about playing peekaboo. Jon jerked the motor home into drive and lumbered after the convertible.

MADDY KNEW WHAT her father would say.

I've always suspected you were irresponsible, but I didn't know you were a certified lunatic. Insist that this man let you go, at once!

But she wasn't ready for the man to let her go. Not until she figured out who he was and what was really going on. Not to mention how the guy managed to stir up emotions in her she hadn't known existed.

Taking a sidelong look at him as they barreled through a yellow light, she conceded that Jon Everett would attract Texas-size feminine notice in any state of the union. A hunk, as Bitsy would put it.

Bitsy was Maddy's housekeeper. Okay, so she was a former manicurist laid off for getting a little too creative with color choices. Her idea of fixing dinner ran to ordering pizza, and she dusted the furniture with a broom. But she needed work, and Maddy had grown tired of starchy housekeepers who spied on her comings and goings for her father.

Besides, Bitsy did a great job on her nails.

Bitsy would approve of Maddy's current situation: handcuffed to a big, masculine tough-guy in hot pursuit of a criminal. She'd give extra credit for the disarranged halter and bare feet.

No matter what her father might think, Maddy wasn't about to demand that the man leave her anywhere. She hadn't had this much fun in a long time. Maybe ever.

"Are you going to give me the ring?" she asked as Jon followed the convertible onto busy Beachside Avenue.

"What ring?" he growled, peering through the windshield.

"The one in your pocket, with the dove."

"Cost me twenty bucks," he said. "Who's going to pay it back?"

Maddy couldn't believe the man was making such a big deal about it. "I could have you arrested for receiving stolen property. Not to mention kidnapping and assault!"

"Assault?" He gave her a glance so fiery it could have flamed out a brigade of tanks. "I know encouragement when I encounter it, lady."

"Then how would you explain the handcuffs?" She knew she had him there. "Excuse me, I think I see a police car." Maddy started to lower her window.

"Hey!" The man flipped a switch and the window popped back up. "I'll set you free as soon as I get a chance."

Over the traffic, they could see the convertible half a dozen vehicles ahead. "You can pull over here," Maddy suggested, banking on the likelihood that he'd refuse. She didn't want to get out, not until she saw the conclusion of this chase.

"By the time we get the darn cuffs off and you collect your in-line skates, she'll be long gone."

"I suppose so." Pretending to acquiesce reluctantly, Maddy said, "The least you could do is to explain what's going on."

"I already did."

"You're a bounty hunter after a woman named Gloria Hess," Maddy summed up. "I got that part. What did she do?"

"Murdered her husband." Jon jerked the wheel and the RV swerved around a stalled car with more agility than Maddy would have thought possible. The handcuff pulled her off-balance and she fell against Jon, unable to brace herself because of the manacled arm.

He righted her with a nudge, just enough force applied at precisely the right point. "You're good at that," Maddy marveled. "Do you travel this way often?"

"Any horseman knows when to apply pressure and when to let the animal's instincts take over," Jon replied.

She couldn't believe his arrogance. "You're comparing me to a horse?"

"Not a very well-broken one, either," he said.

The RV paused at a stoplight, one lane over and three cars back from the convertible. Maddy could see Gloria's dark roots, along with a pile of packages in the back seat. The woman should have spent her money getting her hair touched up instead of shopping the beachside boutiques, but Maddy didn't suppose Jon would be interested in that observation.

Not that she much cared whether he was interested or not. "I suppose you like your women docile and 'well-broken,' to use your term," she said.

"Just for the record, I don't have any women and if I did, I'd choose one who already knew all she needed to know about horses." Jon punched the accelerator as the light changed, but the convertible shot forward until it was almost out of sight down the block.

"We should have taken my car," Maddy muttered.

"And exactly where would we stow Gloria in a car?" Jon returned. "This is absurd. My pursuit of the suspect doesn't involve you or your car."

"Oh? Thanks to your convenient one-size-fits-all handcuffs, it most certainly does involve me!"

"We'll take care of that in a minute."

"The sooner the better." The handcuff was beginning to chafe. In order to ease the rubbing, Maddy had to edge closer to Jon, and then the gearshift threatened to put a permanent crease in her leg.

"Sit up straight," he growled.

"I'm trying to get comfortable."

"You're also giving me and every passing truck driver an eyeful." He gave her another of his expert nudges. "Pull your strap up. That beach bunny outfit might be okay to flaunt in front of a bunch of surfers, but it looks ridiculous here."

Maddy bristled at his nerve. "Who appointed you a fashion critic? Besides, for your information, the Western look is out of style and has been for at least three generations."

"A generation meaning the length of your attention span?" Jon nosed toward the rear bumper of a lagging sedan, which took the hint and moved aside. "Which I'd guess must be about, what? Half an hour?"

Maddy was getting tired of arguing with the man. He didn't take it in the right spirit, that was the problem. He ought to be flirting and reacting to her the way most men did. Instead, he couldn't seem to think about anything except catching that Gloria woman.

"You didn't finish telling me about Ms. Hess," she said. "Why did she kill her husband?"

"Why else?" he retorted. "For the money."

"How can you be sure? Maybe he was rotten. Maybe she killed him in self-defense."

"By smothering him with a pillow while he slept?" Jon wrenched the wheel, and Maddy barely had time to clamp onto her seat. She hadn't realized they were so close to the freeway until they veered up a ramp and entered it.

The red convertible sped along, nearly a quarter of a mile ahead. If heavy midday traffic hadn't hampered it, it might have escaped already.

But then, Gloria didn't appear to know she was being followed.

"You want to hear the story?" Jon asked.

Maddy nodded, then realized he wasn't looking at her. "Yes."

"Reach into my pocket."

"Why?"

"Don't you ever do anything without asking a million questions?"

"Why should I?" said Maddy.

"Just do it."

She twisted in her seat, so she could reach across with her free hand, then discovered that Jon's jeans fit so tightly that she could hardly get into the pocket.

As she wedged her fingers inside, she could feel the tension in Jon's thigh. Was this a way of getting a cheap thrill? It didn't fit with his indifferent manner.

Then she felt the key. With a tug, Maddy pulled it out and worked it into the handcuffs. When the metal parted, she rubbed her wrist with an odd mixture of relief and disappointment.

"My turn." Jon rattled his cuff.

"You haven't told me the whole story."

He turned toward her, cold fury animating his high-boned face. "I said I would tell you. You have no cause to doubt my word."

With an apologetic shrug, Maddy leaned over to unlock his cuff. "Sorry. It's hard to know who you can trust any more. Especially when they handcuff you."

"You shouldn't trust anyone," said Jon.

"Then why were you offended?"

His eyes narrowed as he considered how to answer, or maybe he was just squinting into the afternoon glare. "I'm an honest man, more or less."

"What do you mean, more or less?"

"I'm only untrustworthy where large amounts of money are concerned," he said.

"I'll remember that." Maddy finished removing the cuff and turned her attention to tucking her clothing into place. The halter had done a landmark job of revealing cleavage without quite slipping into indecency; it was almost a shame to restore it to boring old normalcy.

As she looked up, Maddy noticed that they were heading north. "Wonder where she's going."

"She just checked out of her motel," Jon said. "Could be headed anywhere. Maybe even out of state."

The thrill of adventure began to fade as Maddy considered the fact that she hadn't brought along so much as a lipstick, let alone a change of clothing. And she wasn't overjoyed about leaving her expensive sports car unattended at the beach.

Well, she would deal with harsh realities later. Maddy had learned long ago that with enough money, few problems were insurmountable.

"Okay, buster," she said. "Let's hear the rest of the story."

Gloria, Jon explained, had met wealthy rancher Sid Owens at a cattle show in Dallas. None of Sid's family knew exactly how they'd met or what Gloria had been doing there.

Sid's grown children from his first marriage hadn't been pleased when he arrived home with a bleached-blond wife thirty years his junior. They'd been even less pleased when Sid changed his will, leaving the lion's share to Gloria.

Two nights after the will was signed, Sid died in his sleep. The local doctor declared it a heart attack.

When Gloria set about trying to sell the ranch as rapidly as possible, Sid's children hired a pathologist to perform an autopsy and an investigator to look into Gloria's past.

The autopsy indicated that Sid had been smothered. The detective discovered that Gloria had been married twice before to rich, older men, both of whom had died under suspicious circumstances. One was electrocuted when a radio fell into his bath; the other succumbed to shock when he accidentally ate food cooked in peanut oil. He was allergic to peanuts.

Gloria escaped charges both times by the skin of her teeth.

"Each time, she ran through her inheritance pretty fast," Jon said. "Apparently she likes to gamble."

This time, luck had turned against her, but not fast enough. The woman had fled with what valuables she could carry, and ten thousand dollars from Sid's bank accounts.

"I'm surprised she'd squander it at the boutiques," Maddy said.

"Has to keep up appearances," Jon muttered. "I suspect she's already got another victim in her sights."

When the family put a price on Gloria's head, Jon explained, he'd joined the chase. "I'm the detective who traced her roots in the first place. Actually, I'm a bounty hunter-bodyguard-you-name-it. Whatever pays the best. Besides, I'm from ranch country myself, and hearing about Sid's murder kind of offended me."

"Glad to know you've got a heart." Maddy didn't really believe it, though. This man obviously would do anything for money. Hadn't he admitted he was untrustworthy? "How did you track her here?"

"Wasn't easy." They switched freeways without slackening their pace, heading toward the mountains beyond Los Angeles. "It's been six months of hard digging.

"She's been heading west all her life. First murder was in New York, second in St. Louis, third in Texas. To catch herself another rich target, she had to head for a big city, so I figured it would be either California or Nevada."

At a car dealership in Las Vegas, Jon located her white Cadillac, which she'd traded for a red convertible. As her address, Gloria had given a rent-by-the-week motel near a convention hotel.

Jon tracked her there, to find she'd checked out the previous week. Her departure coincided with the end of a boat show, a real estate seminar and a psychological convention.

"That covers a lot of ground," Maddy said.

"There's something else that makes me nervous," Jon admitted.

"What's that?"

"Something she bought," he said. "Right before she left."

"A gun?" Maddy guessed.

"Nope."

"A ticket to South America?"

"Wrong again," he said.

Maddy was out of ideas. "I give up."

"A dress," said Jon. "The kind with white lace, a veil and all the trimmings."

"She's getting married?" Maddy gasped.

"She didn't buy it to play roller hockey," he said.

Chapter Three

From Maddy's worried expression, Jon gathered that she now understood the urgency of capturing Gloria before she killed again.

He hoped that meant his dizzy blond passenger wouldn't object when he dropped her off at the first convenient spot. He'd put himself in an awkward position by virtually kidnapping her, but maybe he'd finally penetrated that beach bunny brain so she wouldn't make trouble for him.

The more he thought about it, the less Jon understood his initial reaction to Maddy. Even a fool could see she was pretty, but the woman would drive any man crazy in short order with her nonstop questions and mulelike stubbornness.

Besides, Jon had always preferred to go his way alone. His type of woman was fiercely independent, the kind who stayed for a few days or weeks and then headed out for her own adventures.

Maddy possessed spirit, sure, and maybe in time she would develop the maturity to stand on her own. But right now, Jon got the feeling she would prove a liability in an emergency.

He would finish his story, as promised, and then it would be *sayonara, Maddy.*

"Gloria left Vegas in a hurry, before the alterations were complete," Jon went on. "She arranged to have the gown shipped to an address in Beachside, another residential motel. When I got there, she'd just checked out, but the manager showed me her car. Apparently she decided to do a little last-minute shopping before she left."

He didn't bother to point out the obvious, that Gloria was buying her trousseau. Jon would be willing to bet that wherever they were heading, they'd find a wedding on the agenda.

No point in piquing Maddy's interest any further. Women loved weddings, or so he'd heard. He didn't want her even to think about sticking around.

The freeway stretched ahead of them, wide open now that they had passed beyond the city. Jon allowed more room between the RV and the convertible, to avoid arousing suspicion.

He had expected Gloria to head for some wealthy enclave like Beverly Hills. But now that he thought about it, it made sense that she would choose someone who lived in a remote area.

That decreased the likelihood of anyone getting suspicious of her. And it would make her getaway that much simpler after she sent her new husband to an early grave.

During the months in which he'd tracked her, Jon had given a lot of thought to what might motivate a woman like Gloria. She couldn't expect to escape forever, but he doubted she gave much thought to the future.

The woman was addicted not only to money but to attention. With her looks and ability to charm men, she could have landed herself a solid position in society. The only conclusion he'd drawn was that, deep inside, she must know herself to be a fraud. The illusion couldn't be sustained, so each time Gloria cut her losses and ran.

To her, the men she killed must be nothing but objects. He wondered if she felt even a glimmer of tenderness or passion for any of them.

Passion. Instinctively, Jon glanced at the woman beside him. Maddy was chewing her lip and leaning forward as if willing the motor home to overtake the convertible.

He wished he didn't find her so appealing. Even now, with the initial heat dissipated, he couldn't help admiring the smoothness of her skin, the soft curves of her body and the liveliness that sparkled in her eyes.

But he couldn't disregard the perfectly groomed fingernails and sculpted hair that spoke of a pampered life. This was not the kind of woman who would make herself at home in an RV, roughing it on beans and wieners.

On the other hand, if he caught Gloria, he wouldn't have to live on beans and wieners anymore.

A hundred thousand dollars. Jon hadn't allowed himself to dwell on what he would actually do with that much money. Even before his family had been cheated of their ranch—well, virtually cheated—there had never been more than a modest income. Certainly not enough for luxuries.

He didn't fancy wearing duded-up clothing, or hanging around the glittery emptiness of Las Vegas. Maybe he'd buy a piece of land somewhere and develop it, make it into something he'd be proud of. Make himself and his family so financially secure that no one could ever force them out again.

"Can't you catch her?" Maddy demanded. "You could force her over on this straightaway."

"And get us both killed?" Jon couldn't believe the woman's naiveté. "This isn't a shoot-'em-up movie, kid. I have no legal right to assault her, and certainly not to cause an accident on the freeway. Have you considered what would happen if we hit other vehicles?"

"Well, no." The woman fluffed her hair, an instinctive gesture that reinforced her pampered image. "But it doesn't pay to be too cautious. We should catch her while you've got me along to help.''

"As a matter of fact," Jon said, "I was thinking of dropping you at one of these call boxes."

"What?" She swiveled to face him. "You'd leave me on the freeway?"

"At a phone," he said.

"Big deal!" Her blue eyes took on stormy depths. "That's the most despicable thing I've ever heard of!"

"Worse than Gloria killing her husbands?" he muttered.

"Almost." Maddy pressed her lips together in determination. "Look, don't throw this chance away. You need my help."

"I do?"

"If that woman catches sight of you, in that cowboy hat and those boots, what's the first thing she's going to think? Right! That some cowboy from Texas has shown up to arrest her! She'll run so fast you'll never see her for the dust."

Jon had to admit, the difficulty had occurred to him as well. That was why he'd felt so lucky when he nabbed Maddy in the parking lot, in the belief that she was Gloria. It had all seemed so easy—and it had turned out be such a waste of time.

Come to think of it, if not for Maddy, he might have caught the real Gloria back there in Beachside. Silently, Jon cursed his luck. "She might pull over at a rest area. I'll catch her then, when nobody's around."

"A rest area?" Maddy snorted. "A woman traveling by herself wouldn't think of stopping at a rest area. She'd go to a tourist shop where there'll be a zillion people. Or maybe she won't stop until she gets to her fiancé's house. Wherever we're going, you need me as a cover."

"You're not a detective," he said. "You haven't got a clue what you're doing."

"And for precisely that reason, no one will suspect me!" Maddy chortled.

The woman's twisted logic actually made sense, Jon conceded silently. But he couldn't shake the feeling that, in the long run, Maddy would prove more trouble than she was worth.

"I'll leave you at the first gas station," he announced. "That should be safe enough."

"Then how will I ever know whether you catch Gloria?" Maddy demanded. "You're the one who got me involved in this chase, Jon Everett. You can't just dump me off. I won't let you!"

"You won't let me?" he repeated in disbelief. "And who exactly are you? A woman who hangs out at the beach on a Friday when other people are working! For all I know, you were looking for some guy to glom on to, just like Gloria, except you probably aren't vicious enough to kill them!"

Jon supposed he had no right to pass judgment on a woman he hardly knew. Maybe she worked nights, or this happened to be her day off. But with her in-line skates and her mane of blond hair, Maddy didn't strike him as the nose-to-the-grindstone type.

She bristled in indignation. "And what are you? An adventurer! You chase some poor woman across the country on the mere allegation that she might have killed her husband, when probably his children framed her! Or something!"

"His children didn't smother Sid Owens."

"Okay," Maddy acknowledged. "Maybe she is a killer. But you're not motivated by concern for her victims, are you? You just want the money!"

"Is that it?" Jon refused to let her take a high moral tone. He'd discovered long ago that honest hard work didn't mean much in the face of ruthless business practices.

He had also determined long ago that, if he was going to come out on top, he had to pursue his goals with no holds barred, and he refused to let anyone insult him for the path he'd chosen. "I'll bet the real reason you don't want to leave is the hundred thousand dollar reward. You think you can claim half of it, don't you?''

Maddy folded her arms huffily. "I don't need your money!"

"You don't need fifty thousand dollars?" Jon challenged. "Funny, I can't see your halo in this light."

"Who needs a halo?" she sniffed. "I'm Madeleine Armand. Does that name mean anything to you?"

"No. Should it?" The odd part was that her name did ring a bell, but Jon couldn't place it. "What are you, some TV actress?"

"I'm—" She stopped in midsentence. "Uh—I mean—I'm nobody."

"That's not what you were saying a minute ago." His curiosity was aroused now.

"I wish I hadn't brought it up," she admitted.

"Why not?"

"Because I don't need any more—well, people who just want—" She took a deep breath. "Really, it's nothing. I used to play the, uh, the neighbor, the little girl on 'Lassie.' The snotty one."

"I don't remember any snotty little girl on 'Lassie.' Wasn't that 'Little House on the Prairie'?"

"That was somebody else," she said.

Jon barely heard her. His brain was whirring and spinning like the Wheel of Fortune, finally coming to a rest on the Big Jackpot.

Madeleine Armand. Charles Armand's daughter. The heiress to Armand Incorporated.

Jon knew everything he needed to know about Armand Inc. The company developed and operated shopping centers. In particular, they were planning one right outside Vaughan's Gap, Texas.

A big regional shopping mall, it would open in a year's time and make Charles Armand yet another fortune. All at the expense of Jon Everett's family.

The Everett ranch had been in the family for over a century. Twenty years ago, the hard times began when the oil wells ran dry and the cattle fell victim to an exotic disease.

Jon, his parents and his brother had labored to keep the ranch afloat, but everything conspired against them: the weather, the economy, the interest rates. Still, the local bank valued its longtime customers, and cut them enough slack keep them going.

Ten years ago, Armand Inc. made an offer for the ranch that seemed, to the Everetts, pathetically low. They refused.

Charles Armand had looked elsewhere, but ultimately came back. This time, he didn't bother negotiating. He simply bought the bank and foreclosed on the property.

Too exhausted to fight, Jon's parents retired to a small house in San Antonio. His younger brother joined the Marines. Jon attempted to fight the foreclosure in court, but legal expenses soon exhausted his small savings.

And now here he sat with Charles Armand's spoiled daughter demanding to accompany him on a quest.

Maybe she was right, that having another woman along would help him catch Gloria. In any case, Maddy might prove well worth knowing, in the purely financial sense.

Not that Jon would harm the girl. He would never stoop that low. Besides, there was a sweetness and determination about Maddy that he liked.

That didn't mean he couldn't get a little of his own money back, if the opportunity presented itself. Charles Armand could certainly afford it.

"Hey! She's getting off!"

Aroused from his reverie, Jon saw the convertible veering along an exit ramp. He cut across three lanes and followed.

"Think she noticed us?" he asked as the red car pulled onto a surface road.

Maddy shook her head. "She was freshening her lipstick in the mirror."

"Then we must be near her destination."

Maddy tucked her feet beneath her. "You aren't really going to dump me somewhere, are you?"

"I suppose not," Jon said. "The least I can do is take you back to the beach when we're finished."

Instead of expressing gratitude, or even relief, Maddy said, "I hope those old people aren't worried."

"What old people?"

"The ones who own the curio shop. The one the ring was stolen from."

"Mail it back," he said.

"I couldn't!" Maddy gasped. "It's a special ring. At least, they seem to think so. As if it were magic or something. You should see that place."

"What place?"

"Their shop." She hesitated. "Gee, that's funny. I can't remember it clearly. It's kind of like a dream that fades when you wake up. I remember this little man wearing green curly shoes and—that's all."

"Green curly shoes?" Jon shook his head. "Help me watch for the convertible, will you?" He indicated a flash of red on a curve of road above them, barely visible through the pine trees. "I don't want to lose her."

"You won't," said Maddy. "I'll keep her in sight."

Jon pushed the accelerator as they rumbled up a slope in the convertible's wake, and the motor responded with a sluggish groan. They were in the mountains now, with steep grades and narrow roads. If the car didn't stop soon, he would lose it for sure.

MADDY HAD ALREADY forgotten what she'd been talking about a minute before, except that it had something to do with her ring. She'd bought it at the beach, hadn't she? The name and location of the store didn't seem important any more.

Mostly, Maddy felt relieved that Jon had dropped his idea of leaving her at a gas station. She'd never get an opportunity like this again to have an adventure. Wait until her friends heard about Maddy Armand helping catch a murderess!

Maddy's brain played out possible scenarios.

Setting: a remote house in the pines. A middle-aged man emerges, his eyes lighting up at the sight of Gloria. Suddenly the RV barges through the trees and Jon leaps out, clapping the handcuffs on Gloria. As the fiancé races to her rescue, Maddy springs into view, crying, "Stop! She's planning to kill you!" Surprise melts into gratitude in the man's eyes.

Setting: a ski lodge full of beautiful people. A well-dressed man bearing an unmistakable resemblance to Pierce Brosnan leans in the doorway. As Gloria approaches, he steps forward with a broad smile. Jon races from the trees, handcuffs at ready. About to protest, Pierce notices Maddy. "Good heavens! That's the woman I really want!"

Well, okay, maybe she was letting her imagination run away with her.

Besides, Maddy wasn't entirely sure she wanted a suave Pierce Brosnan-type. Peeking at Jon's intent face, she realized that sun-streaked hair and honest brown eyes were sexier than she could have realized.

Her memory might have fogged over the shop on the beach, but it hadn't erased the sensation of Jon's body pressed against hers. Not to mention the ferocity with which his mouth and hands had aroused her.

Of course, he wasn't her type, Maddy reminded herself. Too rough, too opinionated, too much of an outsider. Normally, she wouldn't have given him the time of day.

But it couldn't hurt to have a little fun. Maybe the guy would even acquire a certain measure of polish, hanging around a sophisticated lady like herself. She wouldn't count on it, though.

He was simply a way to amuse herself for a few hours, or a few days. Obviously, he wouldn't care when she departed, and she couldn't imagine herself bringing this cowboy into her sleek home and introducing him to her trendy pals.

Still, for the moment, they needed each other. Maddy grinned when she realized her father would probably learn about all this through the headlines. Heiress Captures Murderer. Or something like that.

He'd rant and rail, but secretly, he'd be proud. Maybe he would finally realize that Maddy was her own person and not just a shadow of himself.

Any way you sliced it, she was likely to come out of this adventure as a heroine.

The road got narrower as they climbed. "Are we almost there?" Maddy asked.

Jon stared at her in disbelief. "Excuse me? Are you under the impression I know where we're going?"

"Oh," Maddy said. "I forgot."

"Now listen." He twisted the wheel and they swung onto a side road. "When we get there—wherever 'there' turns out to be—you stay in the motor home."

"I won't get in the way," Maddy promised.

Jon shook his head. "Not good enough. You stay right here in the vehicle."

"What if you get into trouble?" she asked.

His mouth quirked as if he were debating something. "There's a gun in the glove compartment. I don't suppose you know how to use one?"

"I've had shooting lessons." Maddy's father had insisted she learn to protect herself, even bought her a gun, but she hadn't practiced in years. Although there was always some risk of a kidnap attempt, a policeman had advised

Maddy that she was more likely to be injured if she had a gun than if she didn't.

But if Jon was staring death in the face, she could at least get off a few warning shots. That might be enough to scare Gloria and her fiancé.

"Let's hope it doesn't come to that," he said.

They bumped along the track, hoping no cars would show up going the opposite way, since there wasn't room to pass. "This must lead to private property," Maddy guessed.

"Very private." Jon pointed to a sign. "Trespassers will be prosecuted."

"Are we trespassing?"

"If anyone asks, we're lost," he said.

"What if they order us to leave?"

"Do you hear something knocking in the engine?" he asked.

"No," said Maddy.

"I do." Jon frowned. "A very strong knock. In fact, we might have to stop for repairs."

"Oh," Maddy said. "I see what you mean."

Jon sighed as if doing his best to suffer her ignorance patiently. "Anything I say, Maddy, you're to go along. Got that?"

"I think so." Unused to knuckling under to anyone, Maddy felt a spurt of rebellion. Then she chided herself. This was part of playing the role of an undercover agent.

"It's going to storm any minute," Jon murmured.

Through the towering trees, the sky glowed an unsullied azure. "You must be crazy. There isn't a cloud in sight."

"Wrong!" he said.

Embarrassed, Maddy realized he was testing her. "You're right. It's going to pour."

She sucked in a breath of pine-scented air and felt the altitude nag at her temples. Well, she wouldn't let a little thing like a headache bother her.

"I hardly ever pick up hitchhikers," Jon said. "But you were standing there in that skimpy outfit and I couldn't resist. Besides, you winked at me."

"I would never—" Maddy caught herself. She knew he was baiting her, but she had to play along. "I had a fight with my boyfriend and he pushed me out of the car. I was desperate."

"Better. You never know what story we'll have to come up with." They rounded a bend and slowed. Before them stood a lowered gate and a guardhouse. Beyond it, the road wound farther into woods that hid whatever buildings the property contained.

There was no sign of the red convertible.

A uniformed guard held up his hand in warning as they approached. When the motor home stopped, he came alongside, and Maddy saw that he held a clipboard.

The guard, a well-built African-American man with short hair and a square jaw, wore a tag proclaiming his name as Blair Chesley. On his hip, a king-size revolver jutted from a holster.

"Hi, there." Jon rolled down his window. "What can we do for you?"

From Blair's complacent expression, they must have met his expectations. "You folks here for the Magical Marital Weekend?"

Jon appeared to be struggling to swallow his laughter. "The, uh, magical . . . ?"

"Got your registration forms?" asked the guard.

"Honey?" Jon turned to Maddy.

For a moment, she couldn't think of a response. Then she realized she had to cover the absence of forms. "Oh, dear! They're in the back somewhere! Or maybe I packed them!"

"Doesn't matter." Blair tapped his list. "Just give me your names."

"Mr. and Mrs. Jon Everett."

"Now, I don't see—"

"We sent the forms in late," Jon improvised. "Don't tell me they didn't arrive!"

Behind them, a pickup truck with a cab-over camper stopped and waited patiently.

"I'm not supposed to let anyone in who isn't on the list," Blair advised. "But I hate for you folks to have driven all the way up here for nothing. Especially since, well, I assume you want to work on your marriage, and that's important."

"That's right." Jon reached over and patted Maddy's cheek. "My wife and I need to work things out. You can't turn us away now."

Blair made a notation at the bottom of the chart. "Everett, you say? I'll put you down. Check in at the office and they'll straighten you out."

"Thanks," Jon said. "Thanks a million."

He was about to roll up the window when Blair added, "You two enjoy the massage-in tomorrow! If that doesn't save your marriage, I don't know what will!"

"Sure thing." The gate rose and they drove through. The pickup truck rolled forward and stopped, drawing away Blair's attention.

Maddy released her breath. She hadn't realized until now that she'd been holding it. "So we grab Gloria and leave, right?"

"I wouldn't expect it to be that simple," Jon said. "For one thing, they've got security on the grounds."

"You mean that guy Blair?" Maddy asked. "He's just the gatekeeper."

"Maybe," Jon said. "Maybe not."

"You think he's Gloria's personal bodyguard?" Maddy frowned. "That doesn't seem very likely."

"We don't know who hired him," Jon said. "And we don't know where his loyalties lie. Making assumptions is a good way to get yourself killed."

"Killed?" Maddy said.

"Oh, I doubt we're in any immediate danger. But we'll take this one step at a time," was the laconic response.

"Exactly how many steps will that be?" Amusing herself for a few hours was one thing. Maddy had no intention of sticking around any longer than tonight.

"As many as we need," he said.

They emerged from the woods into a clearing. Directly ahead of them sat a low, modern building that appeared to be a conference center. Beyond it, roughly a dozen motor homes, trailers and pop-up tents sat parked at a scattering of campsites, half-hidden among bushes and low-growing trees.

In front of the modern conference center sat the convertible, a splash of scarlet against the sheltering greens and browns.

"Let's go get her!" Maddy urged.

"Not so fast." Jon indicated the rearview mirror.

Craning her neck, Maddy saw the pickup truck sputtering behind them. In its wake rolled a four-wheel-drive vehicle with Blair at the wheel.

"They must be the last couple to arrive," Jon said as he parked in front of the low building. "Guess he closed the door."

"You mean we have to break down the gate to get out?" Maddy asked.

The four-wheel-drive parked next to the convertible and Blair emerged, the revolver on his hip.

"As you can see," Jon said, "we need to be cautious."

Maddy had to admit she hadn't counted on a guard with a gun. She didn't intend to spend a weekend cooped up with Jon, though. "It can't take too long. I need to get home."

"Why? Got an appointment to bleach your hair?"

"This color is natural!" she retorted. "Are we parking here? Because I'm going to find a telephone and call a cab!"

As she started to open her door, Maddy felt Jon's hand clamp around her wrist. "Aren't you forgetting something, honey?" he murmured.

"What?"

"We vowed to save our marriage," he said. "And I think a massage-in would be just the place to do it."

Chapter Four

Jon didn't know what made him provoke Maddy this way. He had to admit, he enjoyed the fury that raged in her eyes when he teased, and the way her chest swelled with indignation. Yes, especially the way her chest swelled with indignation.

It was purely an objective interest, of course.

Besides, they could hardly march into the building and shanghai Gloria. Not with an armed guard at hand.

"Relax," he said, releasing Maddy's wrist. "We're here on business, not pleasure. But I do need you to stick around a bit longer. You said you wanted adventure, didn't you?"

She gave a little pout as he released her wrist, but whether she was expressing annoyance at his action or disappointment at his lack of follow-through, Jon couldn't tell.

"I guess so," Maddy conceded ungraciously. "What do we do next?"

"Our first task is to find out who Gloria is engaged to," he said. "Although why she and her fiancé should choose to attend a marriage renewal weekend—well, it seems a bit odd."

"Then we warn him, right?" Maddy asked.

The woman had about as much patience as a horse with a burr under its saddle, Jon reflected. "You mean so he can help Gloria give us the slip?"

"But why would he?" she protested as they got out of the motor home.

"Because he won't believe us," Jon said. "Besides, he's in no danger until they're married. Very few men are stupid enough to change their wills until they get the ring around her finger."

"That reminds me," Maddy said. "Aren't you going to wear your ring?"

Jon patted the small metallic circle in his pocket. "I guess that thing's going to come in handy, after all."

Before he could fish it out, a couple approached from the pickup truck. Jon decided not to do anything as obvious as putting on his ring in front of them.

They were both of medium height with dark straight hair. "Is this where we register?" asked the man.

"We just got here ourselves," Jon explained. "We're Jon and Maddy Everett."

"I'm Frank Ching and this is my wife, Lee," the man said.

They shook hands all around, then stood on the sidewalk feeling awkward.

Jon and Maddy Everett. The words had slipped out without Jon's thinking about them. He supposed they were going to have to maintain the pretense for as long as it took to corner Gloria.

He'd never had a partner before, and certainly wouldn't have chosen Maddy for that role. But it looked like he was stuck with her for the duration.

MADDY WAS BEGINNING to understand what Jon had meant about matters getting complicated. He wasn't a policeman; he couldn't simply march in and arrest Gloria. And they could hardly involve a bunch of innocent people in their quest for bounty.

Or rather, Jon's quest.

It wasn't Maddy's problem. She wasn't even going to stick around past tonight. Jon would have to act quickly if he wanted her help to catch Gloria.

Becoming a heroine and earning bragging rights among her friends might be fun, Maddy reflected, but she didn't intend to put herself at Jon's mercy any longer than necessary.

"Uh, aren't you forgetting something?" said Frank Ching.

"Excuse me?" Maddy followed his gaze to her sock-clad feet. "Oh. Sorry."

As she clambered back into the motor home, she heard Jon say, "My wife's kind of a flake. It's one of our problems."

"Are we allowed to talk about our problems already?" came Frank's voice. "I mean, without Larry present?"

Who, Maddy wondered, was Larry?

She skated back to join the others. Lee Ching regarded her footgear with surprise and amusement. The woman had an intelligent face but her shy manner made Maddy wonder if other people appreciated Lee. She wished she could learn more about the other woman, but there probably wouldn't be time.

The conference center had a few front steps. Maddy felt her cheeks redden, clomping up them and then skating inside, but she kept her head high.

She had to pretend that she'd chosen to enter this way. No one must know she'd come on the spur of the moment, with no shoes.

Not that it mattered. She'd be leaving before they found out.

Maddy expected to find a registration desk inside, or at least some kind of greeter wearing a name tag. Instead, they entered a lobby so filled with greenery and flowers that it might have been a hothouse.

Scented steam filled the air. Caged birds warbled, and it took a few seconds before Maddy realized they were realistic facsimiles and not actual birds.

Hearing water burbling as if from a waterfall, she suspected that the sound must be recorded until she spotted a low series of fountains against one wall. At least, Maddy assumed it was a wall; the trompe l'oeil painting of a rain forest made it hard to tell where the room ended.

In the haze, she could make out only blurry figures seated on low benches, half-obscured by the tropical foliage. It was impossible to see them all or guess how many there might be.

"What a bizarre setup," Jon muttered close to her ear. "This Larry person must be a weirdo."

Near them, Lee's delicate face trembled with uncertainty. "Frank," she said. "I don't think..."

"Come on." Impatiently, he tugged his wife forward. "You've got to stop being so fearful."

And you've got to stop being so bossy! Maddy wanted to reply, but the couple had already vanished into the foliage.

Peering through the mist, she tried without success to spot Gloria. She could see only a few people, and none of them had a mass of blond hair.

"I think we're supposed to sit down," Jon said.

"Aren't they going to give us directions?" Maddy didn't feel like sitting down; she felt like doing something brave and heroic and then going home. "What are we supposed to do, figure out the rules by ESP?"

"Put a lid on it, would you?" growled her escort, towing her along a narrow path through the greenery.

Maddy shrugged. "I suppose it's part of the experience."

"Excuse me?"

"The confusion," she said. "You know, helping us release control over our lives."

"And give it to who?" Jon grumbled.

"Some weirdo," Maddy agreed.

It might have been the mist obscuring their vision, or simply an unexpected downward slope in the path, but without warning Maddy careened forward, her skates rapidly gaining speed.

Jon broke into a downhill trot, hanging on to her arm to prevent a fall as she rolled toward an unseen destination. The skates accelerated until Maddy swore she could hear wind whistling past her ears.

"Gangway!" Jon shouted as they crashed through a fern. It was too late; amid screeches and gasps, they landed atop an older couple sitting on a bench. All four of them went sprawling in a tangle of arms, legs and skates.

It took Maddy a minute to regain her equilibrium. Then she pulled herself free and helped a sixtyish woman to her feet. "Are you all right?"

"Oh, dear, just a few thumps, nothing I'm not used to with seven grandchildren," said the woman. "Herb? Are you hurt?"

Her balding husband separated himself from Jon and stood up. "I knew this place was dangerous. Just kidding, folks! Everybody okay?"

"My idiot wife wore in-line skates." Jon removed his hat and poked out a dent.

"You shouldn't call names," said the woman. "Unless they're real names, of course. I'm Anne Stowe."

"Herb Stowe," said her husband.

Jon introduced himself and Maddy, and they went through the same handshaking ritual as with the Chings.

Suddenly a voice spoke from near Maddy's feet. "Is everyone comfortable?"

"Hidden speakers," advised Herb. "Better take a seat. I think there's an empty bench right over there." He indicated a leafy cove barely discernible through the mist.

With Jon's hand clamped around her arm, Maddy made it to the seat, which lay half-hidden behind a palm. Her hip ached from the collision, but she doubted Jon would be sympathetic.

"Hello, people," said the voice, now emerging from a palm tree. "I've chosen to begin our weekend in this unusual manner for a reason. I want you to leave your expectations behind. Forget how you usually act, the routines and ruts of your life. Together, for the next three days, we are going to work at breaking down those barriers."

Break down the barriers. The phrase rang familiar to Maddy. With a start, she realized who Larry must be.

"Jon!" she whispered.

"Put a lid on it!"

"But I know who Larry—"

"People can hear you!" And, indeed, she realized that their voices were echoing in the space, returning as a sibilant hum. Jon was right; they'd attracted too much attention already.

Maddy fell silent, but she couldn't help drumming her fingers restlessly on her knee. She hated inactivity, and she hated letting someone else take control. Even Larry Wicker.

The voice over the intercom resumed. "You must release your expectations and your preconceived ideas. Explore each other in new ways. To begin, ladies, please sit on your husband's lap."

Around them arose a rustle as, presumably, wives sat atop husbands. Maddy didn't move until Jon poked her.

"No!" she whispered angrily.

A powerful grip hauled her sideways until she found herself held tightly against him.

"Put me down!" Maddy hissed.

Close to her ear, he snarled, "Could you, just once, stop thinking about yourself and cooperate?"

About to snap back, Maddy caught herself. Did she really seem that self-involved to Jon? Her instincts cried out to move away, but she supposed that wasn't a good idea. Someone might notice.

She wondered if the armed guard punished intruders. Blair might take it personally that they'd lied to him and wormed their way inside.

No, Larry Wicker wasn't some mafioso. Actually, Larry Wicker was a man Maddy admired very much, and once she heard the phrase *break the barriers,* she'd realized this must be one of his personal enhancement seminars.

Larry Wicker, psychologist and marriage counselor, had risen to prominence five years ago with his best-selling book, *Barriers to Intimacy.*

He advocated learning to see through other people's eyes, turning one's world around and reexamining it from different perspectives. In subsequent books, he'd applied this theory to business, government and of course marriage.

Maddy admired him because, as far as she was concerned, Larry Wicker had rescued her father from himself.

After the death of Maddy's mother twelve years ago from cancer, Charles Armand had thrown himself into his work. Already wealthy, he'd seemed driven to double and triple his net worth—and to exhaust himself into an early grave in the process.

A former smoker, he'd taken up the habit again. Abandoning his exercise and diet program, Charles had gained thirty pounds. He'd worked seemingly endless days without a break for weekends or holidays, so obsessive that Maddy sometimes doubted he knew what he was doing.

She'd seen him self-destructing up close during the years she'd worked for Armand Inc. In many ways, Charles had seemed intent on destroying his relationship with his daughter along with everything else by his attempts to take over her life.

Then along came Lael, a charming divorcée whom Maddy liked instantly. She and Charles met when Lael joined Armand Inc. as the new head of accounting.

Four years ago, the couple had married, but within six months Charles's preoccupation with his work and with controlling everyone around him had led to a separation. Then someone recommended that he and Lael seek counseling with Larry Wicker.

Three months later, the couple reconciled. Since then, Charles had cut his business hours in half, stopped smoking, and resumed exercising. Not all of the weight had come off, but he was working on it.

Larry Wicker might be a bit egocentric, and something of a P.T. Barnum when it came to showmanship, but there was no questioning the fact that he'd saved Charles and Lael's marriage. He had also, in Maddy's opinion, saved her father's life.

At the thought, she allowed herself to relax in Jon's lap. If Larry Wicker thought this exercise was valuable, then it must be worth trying.

"Now, ladies," said the voice from the palm tree, "I want you to unbutton your husband's shirt. If there aren't any buttons, unhook his belt."

A few giggles bounced off the walls.

"Remember, no one is watching you. We've placed the benches for maximum privacy."

It occurred to Maddy that unbuttoning a man's shirt was about as much intimacy as Larry could expect couples to endure in a semipublic setting. Or was this just the beginning?

"Well?" murmured Jon.

Maddy caught a challenging gleam in his eye. For someone who'd been planning to drop her off at a call box, he'd certainly changed his tune. Or maybe he just wanted to embarrass her.

If Jon Everett wanted to play games, she'd show him who was the champ.

Slowly, she worked loose the top button of his blue work shirt, revealing a mat of fine dark hair. Then Maddy blew lightly across his skin.

Jon shuddered.

Undoing the second button, Maddy leaned over and touched her tongue lightly to his chest. Sitting on his lap, she could feel his quiver of response.

Carefully, she unworked the remaining buttons and smoothed his shirt away from his chest and stomach. He had a flat, hard build, unlike the office-bound boyfriends Maddy had known in the past.

She was contemplating what to do next when the voice of Larry Wicker spoke again.

"Having fun? I suggest you folks pursue this activity later when you're alone in your RVs. Let the woman be the aggressor. For most of you, that will be a change. Try something new. It just might change your perspective. Now I'll give you a moment to button up."

Reluctantly, Maddy moved back to the bench while Jon fastened his clothing. "Enjoy yourself?" she teased.

"I'm only human." He slanted her a challenging look. "As the man said, we can pursue this later."

"I'm going home later," Maddy reminded him.

"What about your great humanitarian concern?" he said. "And exactly how did you plan to get down the mountain?"

"I'll call a cab," said Maddy.

"All the way from here to Los Angeles?" He shook his head. "What a waste of money."

"It's my money and I'll waste it if I want to."

"Your money." His voice had a harsh rasp. "Yes, I suppose it is."

Maddy wondered what he meant. Jon had no idea she was an heiress, and even if he found out, why should he begrudge it to her?

The issue flew out of her mind as the speaker resumed. "We're going to turn the lights up now. I'd like you all to come onto the back patio, where I have an announcement to make."

Spotlights on the floor and ceiling began dissipating the haze. Maddy blinked in the sudden brightness.

As she stood up, Jon said, "You said you figured out who he was. Well?"

"Larry Wicker," she said. "Psychologist and author. He's a good man, really."

"Hokey," said Jon, adjusting his Stetson. "People don't need this kind of mumbo jumbo to save their marriages."

"My father did," Maddy remarked, relacing her boots. "It worked."

"How nice for him." Jon headed toward the back of the room.

Annoyed at being left, Maddy caught up to him with a few swift strokes of her skates. "Just because you didn't run across this seminar while branding your steers doesn't make it mumbo jumbo."

"Where I come from, people don't have time for this stuff," Jon answered tightly. "They have to struggle to survive."

"I'll bet if they came here, they might learn something," Maddy said.

"Yes, how to spend a lot of money and look like a fool."

Before she could think of a response, Anne Stowe emerged from the ferns. "I knew that was a shortcut! Look, Herb, it's our friend on roller skates!"

"And Cowboy Jon!" cried Herb, brushing some leaves from his gleaming pate. "Howdy!"

The couple's enthusiasm was so infectious that Jon took no offense at their teasing. "Howdy to you, too."

Maddy wondered why this gleeful pair had chosen to attend a marriage weekend. Maybe it was their form of entertainment.

But what was Gloria doing here, and where had she gone?

Outside, sunshine flooded the patio, which was actually a huge wooden deck designed as a series of platforms on varying levels.

Even inside, Maddy realized, the ramps and unusual angles had made it difficult to get a grip on the dimensions of the place. She supposed the multilevel design accorded with Larry's slogan of breaking down barriers.

Behind the patio, a wooded slope continued upward toward the mountaintop. The conference center sat on the last buildable land, judging by the steepness of the rise.

The magnificent natural setting provided stimulation of all sorts. Pine scents filtered across the patio, and hanging baskets of geraniums added a mint fragrance. Maddy could hear birds singing, real ones this time.

Couples gathered along the platforms, their attention focused on the highest one, where a microphone stood. Maddy counted twelve pairs, plus her and Jon. They were of all ages and assorted races, some in business suits and others in jeans. No one else wore in-line skates.

The chatter died as Blair made his way toward the platform, nodding to people with a touch of self-consciousness. The crisp cranberry-colored uniform flattered his dark skin, and Maddy wondered if he didn't tempt some of the less happy wives to desert their husbands.

Next to her, she felt Jon stiffen. "I wonder why he always wears that damn gun."

"Maybe it isn't loaded," she suggested.

"Rule Number One," he muttered. "Always assume a gun is loaded. Even if you emptied it yourself."

Maddy felt a twinge of fear. In their antics so far, it had been easy to forget they were putting themselves in real danger. Whatever Gloria might be doing here, she was still a cold-blooded killer. Maybe she was even in league with Blair.

A swell of applause drew her attention to someone advancing in the guard's wake. A chunky hand waved to the crowd, but with all the people pressed around, it was a minute before she could glimpse the short, rotund figure of Larry Wicker.

He wore a colorful open robe over slacks and a polo shirt, an odd combination that somehow looked natural. Maybe that was because Larry himself had a flamboyant air: a leonine head topped by a beret, large expressive eyes and a full beard trimmed just short enough to avoid comparisons to Santa Claus.

Despite his tempered smile, Maddy could see that he reveled in the crowd's adulation. And adulation it was: the applause swelled rather than diminished as he reached the top platform. It only muted when he raised his hands like a preacher.

"Thank you, thank you." Larry had a gravelly voice, midtenor range. "I'm so glad you all could make it. We have a very special weekend planned...."

As he showered them with generalizations, Maddy noticed that Jon was surveying the crowd intently. From his height of over six feet, he must be getting a better view than she was.

She tried to do what Larry would have advised: see through Jon's eyes. Maddy supposed he was checking for anything or anyone suspicious, but how could he tell in this lopsided world of patio platforms amid two dozen strangers?

"See those French doors?" Jon kept his voice low as his chin indicated a spot farther along the rear of the building. "That must be the entrance to Larry's private apartment."

He might be seeking escape routes, or alternate ways to break into the building. A mountain breeze raised goose bumps across Maddy's arms. The scene appeared so peaceful, but Jon's probing reminded her of their mission.

What on earth could be going on inside this building that would appeal to Gloria?

"Some of you may be wondering why we've got an armed guard." Larry gestured toward Blair. "This is the first time we've tried this. I'll tell you, in the three years since I bought this property, we've never had a problem here. But our last session, some people expressed apprehension about being so isolated. I'm sorry to say that our world has grown so dangerous that people have to worry even when they're in what must be the safest place in Southern California. So Blair is here to make sure nobody crashes the party or disrupts our solitude.''

He's lying.

Maddy didn't know where the thought came from, but it sprang into her mind without hesitation. For whatever reason Larry had hired Blair, it wasn't to reassure nervous guests.

She couldn't believe Larry Wicker would be involved with anything underhanded. Since the counseling sessions, her father and Lael had socialized with Larry on several occasions. Lael had praised him to her stepdaughter, urging Maddy to consult him if she ever had a problem.

In any case, if Blair had been hired to keep out gatecrashers, he was definitely a threat to her and Jon.

''There's someone else I'd like you to meet,'' Larry said, and called, ''Honey, come out here!''

Maddy heard a roaring in her ears as Gloria Hess emerged from the main building and strolled toward Larry. She wore a tailored three-piece suit and medium high heels, and moved with such easy confidence that she might have been a counselor herself coming to join a colleague.

''Ladies and gentlemen,'' Larry said, ''I'd like you to meet my fiancée, Gloria Granger.'' A murmur of appreciation arose from the watchers, along with a smattering of applause as Gloria reached her fiancé and he rested one arm around her waist.

''We've got a very special surprise in store for you,'' Larry went on. ''Don't we, honey?'' She smiled and gave a slight nod.

He couldn't possibly know the surprise that Gloria harbored, Maddy reflected.

Larry beamed at his audience. "This will be a first for one of our marriage weekends. On Sunday, Gloria and I will get married right here in the conference center, with you as our guests. What could be more appropriate than that?"

Amid the clapping and cheering, all Maddy could think was, *The man who saved my father's life is getting married. And then he's going to die.*

Chapter Five

The instant he felt Maddy tense at his side, Jon knew he had to stop her from blowing their cover.

He caught her shoulder so abruptly that she nearly fell on her in-line skates, and snarled into her ear, "Keep quiet!" Fortunately, the shouts of congratulations around them kept others from noticing her squawk.

"We have to warn him!"

"Don't do anything until we can talk alone," Jon growled, then realized the formal part of the welcome had ended.

Larry and Gloria stepped down from their platform into a sea of well-wishers. Taking advantage of the distraction, Jon pulled Maddy back into the room full of ferns and steam.

"We've got to do something!" she burst out. "The minute she steps away from Larry, let's grab her!"

"Now listen hard." Jon knew he didn't have much time to persuade her; Maddy was the most impatient woman he'd ever met. "What do you think Blair is for?"

"Set decoration?" she asked.

"It's obvious Gloria's told Larry some lie or other." Relieved that Maddy had stopped trying to pull away, Jon released his grip. "We don't know what he believes. Whatever it is, we might fit right into the scenario."

"I'm not sure I understand." Maddy watched him cautiously. The woman didn't take anything on his say-so, which, Jon had to admit, wasn't entirely a bad quality.

"He must believe she's in danger. Most likely she's told him that an ex-boyfriend is stalking her," Jon said. "But we can't be sure. She's an experienced liar, maybe pathologically so. She might have invented some story that could include a couple like us. Anything is possible."

"So if we say she's dangerous, he might think we're really the threat?" Maddy's mouth twisted ruefully. "Then how do we save him?"

"We've got all day tomorrow and part of Sunday," Jon said. "By then we should get a better idea of what's going on and come up with a plan. Or maybe by then we'll catch her alone and snatch her."

"I could invite Blair to join me in the spa," Maddy suggested. "You know, to keep him out of the way."

From the innocent sparkle in her face, Jon knew the woman had no idea what she was proposing. "You're going to get yourself in more trouble than you can handle. We don't know anything about Blair. He might be a longtime associate of Gloria's—he might render you very dead. Leave this to me, Maddy. You're just along to pose as my wife."

Her chin came up in a gesture of defiance that made Jon's fists clench. "First of all, I haven't promised to stay. And second, what makes you think you can do this alone? Don't forget, an hour ago you didn't think you needed me at all, but you'd never have gotten in if Blair hadn't thought we were a couple."

Jon hated to admit it, but she was right on that point. Not on the other one, though. "You can't help me. You're an amateur. You're cocky, and impulsive."

"*I'm* impulsive?" Maddy tapped one skate against the floor. "Who was it that shanghaied me into the motor home and nearly tore my clothes off?"

"Nobody tore anything!"

"And handcuffed me?" she pressed. "Without even checking my ID?"

The woman posed a definite threat to his sanity. Jon felt grateful that they were only posing as a couple. Otherwise he had a feeling their problems would have been well beyond Larry Wicker's powers to cure.

"Just pipe down," he said. "We've got some immediate problems to deal with."

"Such as?" Maddy challenged.

"Such as, turn around and look who's coming our way," he said.

Her expressive face registered dismay as she spotted Blair marching sternly toward them. Jon wondered if Maddy realized how thoroughly she revealed her emotions to anyone who cared to observe her.

He hoped she would keep quiet while he tried to stall Blair, who had undoubtedly discovered their lack of registration. Jon's mind flicked over the possibilities: delayed mail, a flaky wife who forgot to stamp the envelope....

"We didn't register!" Maddy announced as Blair reached them. Jon could have strangled her.

"So I've discovered," he said. "What's going on here?"

The man's frank manner didn't accord with the notion that he was an associate of Gloria's, Jon reflected. But it would be unwise to trust him. Even the most upright people could, in Jon's experience, turn against you if enough money was involved.

"We got married last week," Maddy said. "And we've done nothing but fight. I want an annulment, but my husband insisted we give it one more try. We came up here hoping there would still be an opening."

"Mr. Wicker likes to have an even dozen couples," Blair said. "That's what he's planned for."

"It wouldn't kill him to make an exception for once." Jon's annoyance was directed more at Maddy than at Blair, and he recognized at once that it wasn't a very diplomatic way to press their case.

Maddy seized on his tactlessness. "I told you our marriage couldn't be saved! You see, Blair? The man's uncouth and crass." She mimicked Jon's tone. "'It wouldn't kill him to make an exception.' Is that any way to talk about Larry Wicker?"

"You're blowing this out of proportion!" Jon wasn't sure he wanted to argue with Maddy, but he didn't miss the rueful understanding in Blair's expression. Maybe a spat would work to their advantage. "Like you always do! And while we're on the subject, would you please put something on your feet besides those skates?"

"Why should I?" she snipped. "You don't even take off that cowboy hat when we make love!"

Other couples, wandering in from the patio, paused to regard them in astonishment.

"I don't think we should debate this in front of these people," Jon muttered.

"We don't have to debate it at all!" Maddy cried. "I want a divorce! Or an annulment! Whichever is quicker!"

"That's so typical of you." Jon felt himself getting into the swing of things now. "Always taking the easy way out!"

"Whoa, there!" Here came Larry Wicker through the crowd, Gloria smooth and assured at his side. Jon felt a tremor of alarm at finding himself so close to his prey. She couldn't help remembering his face in the future.

He forced himself to believe that it didn't matter. As long as he nabbed her this weekend, he'd have no reason to run across her again.

"Now, what's going on here?" Larry wore a reassuring expression that Jon had seen on the faces of experienced horse trainers about to introduce a colt to the bit. The master was enjoying the chance to demonstrate his skills for everyone.

"These folks didn't preregister," Blair explained. "They just got married and they're already having problems."

"Oh, that's such a shame!" Anne Stowe pressed into view among the onlookers. "They're really lovely. Herb, it's that sweet pair, you know, the one on roller skates."

"I don't see why we couldn't bend the rules and accept one additional couple this time," Larry boomed jovially.

Mistrust flickered across Gloria's face. "Thirteen's an unlucky number."

"We're not thirteen couples, we're fourteen," Jon pointed out. "Including the two of you."

Larry patted his fiancée's shoulder. "That's right. I think this young couple are exactly the kind of people we want to help. I've planned this weekend as a catharsis, an experience to change our lives. By the time Gloria and I walk down the aisle, it will be as if all of you are walking with us, renewing your vows. Let's share with our new friends here, Mr. and Mrs.—?"

"Everett," said Jon.

"Have them fill out the papers at their convenience," Larry told Blair, and shook Jon's hand. "Welcome aboard."

"Thanks," he said. Beside him, Maddy affected a pout.

That had been a close call. And much as Jon hated to admit it, he couldn't have done it alone.

Maybe Maddy did have more inside her head than the roots of her hair. That didn't mean he had to spend any more time than necessary with her, however, Jon reflected as they headed toward the motor home.

"What's our next step?" she asked as he slid the vehicle into gear and headed for an open camping space.

Jon nodded toward a yellow sheet of paper he'd clipped to the dashboard. "Luau tonight, I think."

Maddy grimaced. "Not that! I mean, what's our next step to catch Gloria?"

Jon didn't answer immediately. The campgrounds consisted of about two dozen turnouts, each semiprivate, and he eased the camper into an empty one. It took several minutes to get it lined up with the sewer, water and power hookups.

"Do you want me to make friends with Blair and try to find out when she might be alone?" Maddy persisted.

Killing the motor, Jon turned to confront her. "Listen carefully. *You* are not to do anything. I am the expert here. All I want from you is to go on pretending that we're newlyweds who don't get along. Understood?"

He could have sworn her hair bristled around the roots, but maybe she was just shaking her head. "I'm not an idiot, Jon. I've already been useful, haven't I?"

"Beginner's luck," he growled. "Maddy, keep out of this. This woman is dangerous, and we don't know the extent of her game plan."

She regarded him with a superior air. "I'll bide my time, all right. But don't count me out. Now, do you have a phone in here or do I have to hike back to the conference building?"

About to go hook up the utilities, Jon paused in disbelief. "Who exactly were you planning to call? Your psychiatrist?"

Maddy planted hands on hips defiantly. "You don't expect me to go through the entire weekend dressed like this, do you? That *would* arouse suspicion."

"All right," Jon conceded. "There's a cellular phone right here." He lifted it from beneath the dash. "Call whoever you want, but it's expensive, so keep it short."

"I'll pay you back." Maddy grabbed the phone as if it were a lifeline, which was what it probably felt like to her.

Jon jumped out and went about setting up camp with practiced efficiency. Larry Wicker had done an excellent job of choosing his appointments; very few professional campgrounds were as well laid out and maintained as this one, he noted as he attached the water and electricity.

Through the trees, Jon could hear other campers setting up patio chairs and awnings. He noticed that many of the voices sounded strained, some artificially polite and others cracking with irritation.

After seeing how his family had suffered from poverty and misfortune on their ranch, he'd never had much sympathy for well-to-do folks who whined about their difficult lives. And it stood to reason that anyone who could afford one of these weekends was at least middle class.

On the other hand, the Chings and the Stowes had seemed like nice people. Jon remembered the old cliché that money couldn't buy happiness. He hoped these guys found the help they needed, although so far he hadn't been impressed with Larry Wicker.

At least the location's natural setting fit with Jon's tastes. He inhaled the clear air and listened to the cracklings and rustlings in the underbrush. After dark, the woods would come alive with foxes and possums, skunks and coyotes, maybe even a mountain lion. Jon resolved not to tell Maddy about these possibilities or she'd probably never set foot outside the camper again.

Finishing his tasks a few minutes later, Jon paused in the late afternoon shadows and mulled the question Maddy had raised earlier. What exactly *was* their next step?

His preference would be to isolate Gloria, stuff her into the camper and depart. The obstacles were obvious: Blair, the large number of people around, Larry himself, and of course the fact that the police would be notified if anyone saw Jon taking Gloria.

In fact, since she had apparently told her fiancé that she was in danger, he suspected the police would be notified the moment she turned up missing. And the absent motor home with its late-arriving occupants would be the obvious suspect.

They might not even make it down the mountain. Of course, there was a warrant for Gloria's arrest in Texas, but she would fight extradition. With Larry to post bail, she would flee, leaving Jon with nothing.

One hundred thousand dollars. It wasn't a fortune, not by Maddy Armand's standards, but it had the power to change Jon's life. Still, to his surprise, he didn't exactly look forward to the moment when he bid farewell to his temporary wife and went to claim his reward.

Jon wished Maddy wasn't so darned pretty. He wished her face didn't reflect every sentiment that rippled across her soul. He wished he wasn't beginning to suspect that, beneath her playgirl appearance, she was smart as a whip.

Most of all, he wished she wasn't Charles Armand's daughter.

Jon straightened his shoulders, reminding himself that he had a job to do. A pampered city girl no place in his rough-hewn life. Just trying to picture Maddy on a ranch in Texas, in-line skating through the cactus and running over a rattlesnake, was enough to knock sense into a man.

As for Gloria, he would manage to come up with a plan before she married Larry. No doubt by tomorrow an idea would suggest itself.

He just had to make sure Maddy didn't come up with one first. Anything she proposed would likely involve putting herself into dangerous situations with no thought of the consequences.

The prospect of harm coming to Maddy disturbed Jon. Since he'd shanghaied her, she was in a way his responsibility. Besides, he would never want anyone to think he was so petty as to take revenge on Charles Armand by injuring an innocent woman.

Dusting off his hands, Jon climbed into the motor home.

Maddy, as he'd feared, was still chatting on the telephone. She sprawled in the passenger seat, legs plopped onto the driver's chair. Jon had to step over one of the skates, which lay scattered across the floor, to avoid stumbling.

Heading back toward the bathroom to take a much-needed shower, he couldn't help overhearing Maddy's half of the conversation.

"Honest, I think a helicopter would attract too much attention."

He stopped in midstride. *A helicopter? For what?*

"Bitsy, you can't charter a plane just to make a luggage drop. You're being melodramatic."

Who was Bitsy? And what kind of maniac would even consider chartering a helicopter or an airplane to deliver a suitcase?

Maddy listened for a moment, then went on. "I really need the stuff tonight. It's going to be awkward enough wearing this same outfit to the luau . . . My nails? Oh, Plentiful Pink, I think, but it's getting chipped. Okay, pack some Fabulous Firehouse Red. And you know, a selection of stuff. Swimsuit, definitely. Something fancy, and a sundress. One of everything. Shoes to match, don't forget the accessories . . ."

For two days?

"Hold on." Maddy put her hand over the receiver. "Jon, is something the matter?"

"I heard the part about the helicopter," he said.

"The helicopter's out." She shrugged as if it were perfectly natural to consider delivering a suitcase by air. "Bitsy's going to bring everything herself."

"Does she know where we are?"

Maddy's foot tapped the yellow sheet clipped to the dash. "There's an address right there."

"One more thing," said Jon, trying not to worry about the enormous cellular phone tab she was ringing up. His bills went to his parents' home and were paid out of the dwindling funds he'd left on account. "Who's Bitsy?"

"My housek . . ." Maddy stopped with a fake cough. "I mean, my roommate."

Jon didn't challenge her, but it seemed odd that her housekeeper would worry about the state of her nail polish. Or that a roommate would, either, for that matter.

A different world, that's what she lives in, Jon reflected, and headed for the shower.

He washed quickly, surprised to find sand in his hair when he shampooed it. The breeze at the beach must have blown it there.

The stall was tiny, with barely room for Jon's large frame to maneuver, and he didn't linger. A few minutes later, he switched off the water, opened the glass door and reached for his towel.

Maddy handed it to him.

"Hey!" Torn between a desire to slam the glass door for privacy and an instinctive refusal to retreat, Jon wrapped the towel around his waist. "What are you doing in here?"

"We need to talk," Maddy said. "Lay down some ground rules."

"The number one ground rule is for you to stay out of the bathroom when I'm taking a shower," he grumbled.

"My back is turned. See?" Through the rippled glass, he watched her blurry figure pivot.

"Great. Now you're facing the mirror."

"It's all steamed up. Besides, what are you so modest about?" There was nothing indistinct about Maddy's voice. "We're married."

"Don't get carried away." Cursing the awkwardness of moving in the tight space, Jon hurriedly dried his torso and toweled his hair. He had half a mind to step out buck naked and give Maddy the shock she deserved. Or maybe she wouldn't be shocked at all.

"You should be grateful," Maddy said. "I've decided to stay."

On the verge of making a sarcastic remark, Jon reconsidered. She had a point. If Maddy stormed out of here, he'd have no excuse for remaining. "Mind if I ask why?"

"Larry Wicker helped my father and stepmother save their marriage. I figure I owe him." Maddy splashed water on her face from the sink, then scrutinized herself in the foggy mirror. "Do you think I'm getting a sunburn? I told Bitsy to pick up my car but I forgot to ask for sunscreen. I knew there was something I left out!"

"You'll survive." Jon couldn't stand here in the stall forever, so he stepped out. In the cramped space, his damp body loomed over Maddy.

"Cozy in here." She made no move to leave.

"Excuse me, but I can't reach my clothes," he pointed out. The work shirt and jeans hung from a peg behind Maddy.

"You aren't going to wear those to the luau, are you?" she demanded.

"No, I thought I'd go like this." Impatiently, Jon reached past her and grabbed his pants. The woman didn't even duck. "Actually, since you'll be wearing the same clothes, I might as well, too."

"You know," she said, "you really do have a terrific build. I'll bet you could be a male model if you wanted to."

"I wouldn't waste my time," Jon snarled, trying to figure out how to wedge himself in a position to don the pants without leaning against her.

"It pays very well," Maddy returned. "And it can lead to an acting career."

"Every cowboy's dream." Jon didn't know where the sarcasm came from; it wasn't his usual style. Maddy brought out the worst in him.

"You're hopeless. I almost think you like living like this." She gave a yawn and stretched like a cat, her body sleek and tawny and popping half out of her halter top.

Jon's brain clicked into gear, informing him that there was no way to get dressed in this room with her present. He would have to leave, since obviously she wouldn't. Of course, he supposed he could follow his masculine instincts and corner her against the sink, loosen her straps and . . .

Nope. Absolutely not.

Then something clinked on the floor of the bathroom.

"You dropped it!" Maddy cried, swooping down to retrieve the gold ring in the shape of a dove. "Be careful! Besides, weren't you going to wear it?"

"Yes, I was. Since we're 'married.'" Jon plucked it from her fingers and popped the ring into place. It went on so smoothly it might have been designed expressly for him.

A tingling sensation ran up his arm, directly into his brain. He supposed it came from the close room and the steam.

Then he took another look at Maddy.

He must have been crazy, keeping her at bay. The life force thrummed through her with an elemental exuberance that stripped away Jon's inhibitions.

He'd never met a woman who so clearly embodied nature's wholesomeness, who was so perfectly shaped to fit against him. It would be a crime not to yield to the desire rushing through him.

From the widening of her pupils, he could tell Maddy felt the same way.

Chapter Six

With a mischievous smile, Maddy untied the back of her halter. It seemed only natural, as Jon had just dropped his towel.

He was magnificent. She allowed herself a moment to admire his muscular body in its shower-fresh purity, and realized his gaze was caressing her breasts with equal enthusiasm.

A moment ago, she'd been feeling a touch of annoyance with this man. He didn't seem able to relax and trust his instincts, and he kept trying to relegate her to the boring role of do-nothing assistant.

Now she couldn't remember why she'd found him so hard to deal with. Being married to him, at least temporarily, had obvious advantages.

Very obvious, Maddy reflected, as his hands stroked upward from her waist and his thumbs teased her nipples. She leaned against the sink and let her eyelids flutter shut, sliding into pure sensation.

A moment later Jon's mouth brushed across hers. There was nothing tentative about the gesture; he was simply taking his time. She hoped he would take more, a whole lot more.

Her arms wrapped around him, reaching upward to encompass broad shoulders. Everything about him felt unfamiliar and yet destined for her, virtually a part of her.

Somewhere deep in Maddy's brain stirred the troubling thought that this attraction had come upon them both suddenly, and might leave again just as quickly. But she didn't care.

Not when his mouth was claiming hers with wolflike ferocity, and his hips were pressed into hers, delivering an unmistakable announcement of his readiness for action.

Maddy and Jon staggered together out of the bathroom. Somewhere nearby must lie the folding couch, but they couldn't separate long enough to look for it. Instead, they stumbled against a chair and then a shelf, lost in the wondrous sensation of skin against skin, tongue against tongue, inflamed body against inflamed body.

They had finally located the couch and were tumbling across it when a sharp knock came at the door.

"Go away!" Maddy called, and felt Jon's hand close over her mouth.

"Shh!" He held still, listening.

She had assumed it must be Bitsy, then realized her housekeeper couldn't possibly have arrived that fast, even if she *had* hired a helicopter.

"Jon and Maddy?" called a hearty male voice. "It's Herb Stowe! Everybody's heading for the luau!"

Anne's voice added, "We didn't know if you had the schedule. Wouldn't want to miss that delicious food!"

Oh, yes, we would. Vaguely, Maddy recalled that she and Jon had a mission to accomplish, but it seemed less than urgent. Food could wait, Gloria could wait, everything could wait except—

Jon wrenched himself away with a groan. "We have to go. It would look strange."

"You're impossible!"

"Don't tempt me." His gaze lingered on her bare torso.

"Let's go late." Maddy couldn't believe anyone possessed this much self-control. "Nobody cares, anyway, right?"

"That's what you think." A shake of his head ruffled Jon's shaggy hair. "Everybody would know what we'd been up to. Doesn't fit with a couple on the verge of an annulment, does it?" Louder, he called. "Give us a few minutes, okay?"

"Sure thing!" came Herb's voice, and Maddy could hear the older couple moving away.

Jon sat on the edge of the couch. "I've got to get a grip on myself."

Maddy didn't want him to get a grip on anything but her, and she wasn't used to being frustrated. Only the memory of Larry Wicker standing beside the murderous Gloria earlier today helped calm her. She had made a commitment to save him, hadn't she?

Whatever she and Jon felt for each other could wait. It was so basic, so much a part of life, that Maddy couldn't imagine it would ever fade.

As Jon headed for the bathroom, she sat up and put her mind to the most pressing problem of the moment: what to wear to the luau.

JON STEADIED HIMSELF on the edge of the sink. Maybe it was the humidity and closeness in here, but he didn't quite feel like himself.

Was there some disease he'd never heard of that made a man fall passionately in love with the first woman he encountered? Maybe it was something you picked up at the beach, like sand in your hair.

He finished getting dressed in an uncomfortable cloud of longing. It was important to tear his thoughts away from Maddy and what they would do later tonight, after the luau. He had to focus on Gloria. He had to remain alert, in case he got a chance to snatch her tonight.

Tucking in his shirt, Jon regarded himself in the mirror. Flushed and sweaty; not the right appearance for the occasion, was it?

He started to wash his hands, remembered the ring and removed it. Then he proceeded to clean up.

By the time he'd finished, he felt normal again. With a start, he realized that his wild desire for Maddy had vanished.

About to slip the ring back into place, Jon paused.

He didn't believe in magic, but he had read about aphrodisiacs. Back in high school, he'd had a football teammate who was always sending away to mail-order houses for some powder or other guaranteed to turn girls into lusty playmates. None of those had worked, and he doubted one existed that could turn him into the obsessed lover he'd been a few moments ago.

And yet, Maddy had said something about the rings possessing special powers. Jon had dismissed the idea, yet the first time he'd worn the ring, he'd swooped down on Maddy with a runaway lust that exceeded anything he'd felt even at the height of adolescence. Since taking it off, he hadn't felt the same until after his shower, when he put it on again.

It might be his imagination, but Jon didn't intend to take chances. He stuck the ring into his shirt pocket and went out.

There was no sign of Maddy. "Hello?" he called. It wasn't easy to hide in a motor home.

Her flushed face poked out of his closet. "I'm in here."

"In the closet?" It was so small, he didn't see how she could fit.

"I didn't want anyone to see me. At least, not until I got a second opinion."

Maddy emerged, bare-shouldered and bare-legged. In between, a Hawaiian-print beach towel draped suggestively around her body, held in place with a couple of safety pins.

"You're kidding," said Jon.

Maddy tugged at the wrapping. "Well, it's kind of the right style for a luau. Besides, people are going to wonder if I show up in those shorts again."

"People are going to wonder even more when you turn up in a towel," Jon stated. "Especially if you appear tomorrow in a designer wardrobe with matching accessories and—what was that nail polish color? Flaming Firehouse Red?"

Still, the way the blond hair flowed over her tanned body was downright appealing, even without the effect of the ring. It wouldn't take magic to make the two of them passionate. Yet Maddy wasn't throwing herself into his arms; her reaction had died as quickly as his.

The whole business puzzled Jon, and he decided not to mention it. He didn't want to sound like a fool. Besides, he might want to have that experience of passion again, before he said *sayonara* and hit the open road. He would keep the ring handy, just in case.

Maddy ventured in search of a full-length mirror, which was nowhere to be found in the RV. That discovery aroused cries of disappointment and derision from the vicinity of the bathroom. "I can't believe it! How do you tell what you look like?"

"What's to tell?" Jon ambled toward her. "I always look the same."

"Don't you have a Hawaiian print shirt?" she demanded. "We look like the odd couple."

"I thought that was the idea. We're supposed to be incompatible."

"Oh, all right." Maddy opened the motor home's side door. "Let's go. I'm hungry."

Jon couldn't believe what a scatterbrain she was. "Aren't you forgetting something? Like your skates?"

"I can't wear skates with this." Maddy hopped down onto the grass. "I'm going native."

Jon hoped they wouldn't be expected to dance. He could imagine the outcry if his cowboy boots stomped on Maddy's bare toes.

But it was her choice. By now, he'd learned better than to argue over details.

MADDY HAD NEVER shied from wearing her pajamas to a costume party or a bare-midriff ensemble to a formal ball, but she felt a little odd about the towel.

For one thing, she wasn't here as Maddy Armand, madcap heiress, whom everyone expected to act crazy. She was supposed to be the bride of Jon Everett, presumably a normal woman.

For another thing, bare feet might have sex appeal in a fashion photograph, but walking on them was something else. Maybe real islanders had tough soles from a lifetime of shoelessness, but Maddy's feet winced at every poke of gravel and twig.

As they ambled toward the conference center along with a few other stragglers, she noticed an attractive Hispanic couple in their late thirties. They walked stiffly, not touching.

The woman wore a flowered pink sundress that showed off her tan. The man was immaculate in slacks and a designer polo shirt.

Maddy wasn't used to feeling frumpy, but she knew she and Jon didn't present an impressive appearance. Usually people admired and envied Maddy Armand. Sometimes they resented her; that went with the territory. But she was universally noticed, talked about and copied.

It was hard to get used to being Maddy Everett, whom nobody knew anything about. Surely it wasn't that big a deal, being nobody special, Maddy told herself, or even being regarded as just some oddball in a towel. She would get used to it.

Jon strolled along without any hint of self-consciousness, although he still wore his dusty clothes from earlier. She doubted the man gave much thought to what he threw on his back. He probably didn't even own a tuxedo.

The evening air felt cool against her bare chest and legs. She resisted the impulse to move closer to her "husband," even though they'd been snuggling hot and heavy a few minutes ago. Something about his erect posture and distant gaze warned that he didn't feel cuddly.

What *had* happened to them in the bathroom? One minute she and Jon had been quarreling, and the next they'd been tearing each other's clothes off. It didn't make sense.

Most of the time he acted as if he wouldn't care if she disappeared from the face of the earth. The heat of the shower and his own unclad state must have aroused him.

Men were like that, Maddy supposed. They went off like firecrackers one minute and fizzled the next.

She was glad now that they'd been interrupted. She didn't want to make love with this rough character. Her admiration for his powerful frame and teasing grin didn't mean she had to do something about it. A woman could appreciate a man's appeal without losing control of herself.

The vast lobby of the conference center, with its foliage and secluded benches, had been transformed into a tropical paradise tonight, she discovered as they arrived.

Japanese lanterns cast a merry glow from an arrangement of overhead lines. Inside the front door, a long table groaned beneath platters of fresh fruit, salads and yams. A large plate of salmon presided in the center.

When they stepped inside, Gloria handed Maddy an orchid for her hair. "Welcome to the luau." The woman gave them a crisp smile and turned to the Hispanic couple.

As Jon led her away, Maddy assessed Gloria's clothes. She wore an off-the-shoulder, toga-style white gown trimmed with gold braid, slit at midthigh to reveal slender legs and golden sandals. Maddy remembered seeing the dress in a shop window at the beach.

It cost a lot of money, money that had come from a dead man. At least, Maddy reflected, she'd come by her towel honestly.

Blair had changed into a khaki uniform with short pants, the kind an English officer might have worn in India. The gun remained strapped to his hip.

"What, no roller skates?" teased Anne Stowe as the older couple sauntered over to them. "My dear, what a clever outfit."

"We weren't expecting a luau," Maddy explained.

"You won't even have to change for the massage-in tomorrow," announced Herb.

"Oh, that's right. I forgot about the massage-in," Jon murmured. "Just what every marriage needs."

"Your sarcasm is uncalled for," Maddy told him. To the Stowes, she said, "He's such a grouch."

Jon glared at her, playing the role of irritable newly-wed—or so she assumed. "I'm sorry I don't run around barefoot in a towel. It isn't my style. And I hate to tell you, but it isn't yours, either."

Maddy didn't know where Larry Wicker came from, but suddenly he was there, standing behind and almost between them. "Now, Mr. Everett, if there's one thing we discourage, it's putting down our spouses."

"Can't a man speak the truth?" Jon muttered.

"The truth is in the eye of the beholder," said Larry.

"Easy for you to say. Your fiancée isn't wearing your linen closet."

Everyone laughed except Maddy. She suspected Jon wasn't entirely joking. What did he expect her to wear, under the circumstances?

Maybe she should have borrowed something. In fact, that wasn't a bad idea at all.

"Excuse me," she said, and slipped away.

She found Gloria adjusting a flower arrangement on a side table. Velvet orchids, pristine calla lilies and an aristocratic bird of paradise sprayed in front of the woman, flopping in the vase.

Her slender hands moved among the flowers, tweaking them into position, which wasn't easy considering the astronomical length of her bloodred, perfectly shaped nails. A mane of blond hair, caught at the crown by a diamond-studded comb, framed a face with doll-like features rimmed in makeup a touch too dark and too hard.

And the expression on her face was one of cold contempt as she glanced across the room at the man she was to marry.

The viciousness of that look stopped Maddy in her tracks. She had never seen such naked evil on anyone's face before.

There was no time to retreat, however. Gloria's attention shifted to Maddy, and the features rearranged themselves into polite scrutiny.

Gloria's first words were, "People have been saying we look like twins."

The unspoken words that followed would have been *and I don't like it.*

We're both accustomed to being unique, Maddy thought. "That's because they don't know us," she said.

"Your husband, that Texan..." Gloria began. She hadn't missed a thing, Maddy realized, including their license plates. "Is he rich?"

"Not exactly." Maddy hadn't expected to be questioned, and she was relieved when Gloria didn't pursue the matter.

Instead, the other woman said, "Well, he's handsome, anyway. I suppose the two of you have fun in bed."

"Sometimes." Maddy had been planning to ask Gloria for the loan of a shawl, but that didn't seem like such a good idea anymore. Her skin crawled at the idea of wearing something that had decorated Gloria, as if pure poison oozed from her pores. "So...you must be excited about the wedding."

"A wedding is a wedding." Gloria shrugged, as if it took too much energy to pretend enthusiasm in front of someone who didn't matter. She must be saving it all for Larry.

"Are you going to have bridesmaids?" Maddy asked.

"I hadn't thought about it." Long thin fingers poked at the flowers again, so hard a petal tore on one of the callas. "Honestly, weddings are kind of a bore, don't you think? I mean, they're simply a means to an end. To being married, of course."

"Well, if there's anything I can do, please let me know," Maddy said in a spurt of inspiration. "You'll need someone to help with your hair and everything."

And if nothing else, it would give her a chance to be alone with Gloria. Maddy didn't think she could slap handcuffs on the woman by herself; Gloria was slightly taller and had the intensity of a coiled cobra. Still, Maddy might be able to help Jon catch his prey.

"That's not a bad idea," Gloria said. "You'd have to find something more suitable to wear, though."

"I've got lots of stuff!" Maddy exclaimed, with a silent prayer that her flaky housekeeper would indeed find her way up the mountain. "I just wore this to annoy my husband."

Gloria's expression softened. "Now there's an attitude I can appreciate. Not with Larry, you understand, but most men deserve that sort of thing."

"Especially Jon." Maddy feigned a conspiratorial look. "He's such a chauvinist."

"I think the two of us could get along nicely," Gloria murmured. "People keep saying we must be sisters, and brides always have their sisters in the wedding party. In fact, you might set me off nicely. But you'll have to pull your hair back. I'm wearing mine loose."

"Oh, sure," Maddy said. Under other circumstances, she would have felt flattered. Now she felt vaguely unclean.

But it would be worth it. Gloria's bridesmaid. It was the perfect opportunity.

"So TELL ME, how did you two meet?" Larry asked after Maddy disappeared behind a potted fern.

Suppressing a spurt of anger at being abandoned to field these questions alone, Jon recalled that he didn't need Maddy or anyone else to run interference for him. Just because she had a glib tongue and an easy manner with people didn't mean he couldn't handle himself just fine. "At the beach," he said.

"You don't know any people in common?" the psychologist pursued. "Mutual friends? Business acquaintances?"

Jon shrugged. "No. Does it matter?"

"It can help bring people together." The rotund man smiled. "But it can also tear them apart."

"Maybe she's right. Maybe it was a mistake." He might as well play the role to the hilt. Besides, Jon couldn't help wondering what their bearded host would make of all this. "We're like night and day."

"The important thing," said Larry Wicker, "is to break down the barriers."

Great, Jon reflected sarcastically. That's what a troubled couple needed, clichés.

But Larry wasn't finished. "You have to see yourself as partners. A team. That doesn't mean you have to be identical. In fact, it's an advantage to have different strengths and weaknesses, as long as you complement each other. But there must be mutual respect."

Frank and Lee Ching had wandered over and stood listening attentively. "But you can have the traditional relationship, can't you?" Lee asked. "Where the husband works and the wife stays home?"

"That's fine," Larry said. "But remember, on a team, both partners have to be satisfied with the arrangement."

"Our sons will be in college soon and my wife doesn't want to go back to work," Frank said. "We need the money."

"I have a degree in fashion design but my experience was years ago," objected his wife. "I couldn't get a job in my field. I'd be lucky to get a clerk's position in a department store, and I'm too shy to deal with the public."

"She's too hooked on her soap operas and her garden club," objected Frank.

Larry stopped the discussion with an upraised hand. "We'll go into this in more depth in our group sessions tomorrow."

Jon peered over the shorter man, trying to spot Maddy. There she was, by the flower arrangement, in deep conversation with Gloria.

His instincts urged him to stride over there and yank her away before she spoiled everything. But that would only arouse suspicion.

Besides, in a way, Larry Wicker was right. Their strengths and weaknesses complemented each other. Maddy might actually be able to extract some information.

The Hispanic couple he'd seen earlier joined the expanding group around Larry, introducing themselves as Bo and Sarita Mendez. "How is the Magical Marital Weekend different from Marriage Encounter?" Bo asked. "We heard about that through our church but there wasn't one scheduled for several months."

"They complement each other but they're quite different," Larry said. "Marriage Encounter takes a more serious approach, with a strong religious element. They work on couple communication, examining the roles and expectations we fall into during the course of a marriage. It's an excellent program and I recommend it. I plan my weekends more as an escape, a time to relax and lower our guard, to become more playful with each other."

Sarita nodded. ''That's what attracted me. We both need a break.''

From the obvious expense of their clothes and their well-groomed appearance, Jon wondered what they needed a break from. He pictured his father, skin leathered by the Texas sun, dragging sheep into a pen for shearing, and his mother hoeing her vegetable garden while sweat trickled down her neck.

Then he thought about Charles Armand taking the ranch away from them, and gritted his teeth. The man owed them big-time; their modest retirement home and Social Security stipend weren't nearly enough.

''So tomorrow,'' Larry was saying, ''we'll start with an 8:00 a.m. workout in the gym for those who want it. The massage-in follows, and then we'll have small therapy groups. After that, it's nature walks, followed by private exercises in your trailers. Hopefully some folks will be inspired to rediscover each other sexually.''

The man didn't leave any thought unexpressed, Jon reflected dourly. He couldn't let them use their imaginations as to what people might do in their trailers; he had to spell it out. As far as Jon was concerned, a married couple's interaction was a private matter.

But he would play along, of course. For Larry Wicker's sake, although the guy might not appreciate it.

''We're sure looking forward to the wedding on Sunday,'' Anne Stowe piped up. ''What a marvelous touch!''

''I'm a lucky man.'' Larry beamed. ''Isn't she beautiful?''

''Pretty is as pretty does,'' Jon muttered, then caught everyone staring at him as if he'd just said something rude, which he supposed he had. ''I was referring to my own wife, you understand.''

''Now, now,'' said the psychologist. ''She's a lovely girl. Something attracted you to each other in the first place. Don't discount that.''

Jon remembered the ring, so light he could barely detect it in his pocket. *Something attracted us to each other in the first place.* Yes, but what?

Sternly, he replayed Larry's list of activities for the following day to figure out what might offer the best chance of nabbing Gloria. The nature walk sounded promising. He wondered if they would head toward the road. If so, maybe he could arrange for Maddy to drive the motor home down for a quick getaway.

Right. As if he really wanted to have *her* driving the escape vehicle. They'd wind up wrapped around a tree or upside down in a gully. Or maybe, he mused, Maddy would end up sympathizing with Gloria and springing her.

Partners, indeed. To be partners, they had to be able to trust each other. And he didn't see how that was possible.

He snapped out of his thoughts as Maddy slipped her arm through his. "Having a good time?" she asked brightly.

He gave a slight nod. The conversation had turned to Larry's latest book and its ascent of the bestseller charts. The participants were lavish in their praise.

Jon didn't get it. If there wasn't one hundred thousand dollars at stake, he never would have come near this place, or Larry Wicker either. As far as he was concerned, this "break down the barriers" stuff was a lot of double-talk.

A slight pressure on his arm notified Jon that Maddy wanted them to move away, and he was more than happy to oblige. Maybe these other folk didn't care about food, but he had a cowboy-size appetite.

However, Maddy halted him on their way to the food table, standing where no one would overhear. "I think Gloria's starting to like me. I mean, as much as she likes anybody."

"Congratulations." Jon reined in his irony, though, as he realized that she might have accomplished something worthwhile. "Learn anything useful?"

"Well, sort of." Maddy flashed a smile at him so delightful that Jon momentarily forgot his skepticism. "She wants me to be her bridesmaid! I'll be helping with the wedding, hanging around with her, that kind of thing. Can you beat that?"

"Terrific." And he meant it. "I take back everything I said. I'm glad you came along."

She beamed. The woman really did light up a room when she was happy. "And she hates Larry, no surprise. The poor man. I mean, all that intelligence and all that success, and he picks a woman who wants to kill him."

She barely suppressed a skip as they made their way to the buffet. Jon had to grin at her enthusiasm, and at something even better that had just occurred to him.

Maddy's participation in the wedding had given him the germ of an idea. A very good idea, indeed.

Chapter Seven

Jon awoke in darkness to the sound of the phone ringing.

He lay in stunned immobility for a moment. No one had this phone number except his parents, and they wouldn't call at this hour of the night except in an emergency.

An attempt to roll over and check the bedside clock landed him nose-first in a dust bunny, and he remembered he was lying on the floor in his sleeping bag, wedged between the folded-down kitchen table and the stove.

Cursing, Jon staggered to his feet, battling his disorientation, and lunged for the phone next to the driver's seat. He fumbled the receiver, caught it inches from the floor and jammed it to his ear. "Yes?"

"Is Maddy there?" asked a quavery female voice.

"What time is it?" Jon snapped.

"I don't know. About 2:00 a.m., I guess."

Some dingbat was calling Maddy at 2:00 a.m.? "I'll get her," he growled.

Faint moonlight didn't prove much help as Jon trudged back toward the couch, now opened into a bed. He missed its comfort compared to the floor, but he didn't want to get soft. He'd spent plenty of nights in sleeping bags on hard ground, traveling the country in a jalopy and a tent before he scraped up the money for a used RV.

Besides, he supposed he might as well act like a gentleman as long as it didn't cost anything.

Maddy lay on her side, blond hair fluffed across the worn quilt. In sleep, her face took on a sweet innocence that would have touched Jon if it hadn't been for the circumstances.

He shook her by the shoulder. "Hey! Telephone for you, princess!"

No response.

"Wake up! I'm paying for the damn call!" It had always irritated him that, with cellular phones, you paid whether you were the caller or the receiver. "Move it!"

Maddy's eyes flew open. "Don't make such a fuss... What time is it?"

From here, he could see the digital clock. "It's 2:17 a.m. That's Pacific Daylight Time, in case you were wondering."

"I wasn't." She sat up, rubbing her eyes. Maddy wore one of Jon's oldest shirts, a threadbare plaid item, and he had to admit it had never looked better. The front was unbuttoned halfway down, revealing the tantalizing valley between her breasts, and the shirttails left her slender legs invitingly bare.

She took her time examining Jon in the moonlight, which reminded him that he'd worn nothing but his underpants to bed. "Nice physique."

"I could say the same for you." He felt the stirrings of desire, not the hyped-up variety he'd experienced in the bathroom but something slower to build and yet more profound.

"You said something about a phone call?" she asked sleepily.

"Oh, yeah. For you."

Maddy swung bare feet to the floor and padded toward the front of the motor home. Jon had to admit that she didn't seem as confused as he had been by the rude awakening. Maybe she was accustomed to chitchatting at all hours. Not a problem when you could sleep until noon, he supposed.

"Yes?" she said into the phone, and then, "Where are you?" and, "What do you mean, in a ditch?"

Without waiting to hear more, Jon pulled on his jeans and shirt. The caller must be her housekeeper, who had obviously gotten herself into some kind of trouble.

"Well?" he asked as Maddy hung up.

"It's Bitsy," she said. "She parked about a mile away and tried to sneak in, and she's got her ankle caught in some branches in a ditch."

"Sneak in?" Jon repeated as Maddy found her shorts and yanked them on over the plaid shirt. "Why didn't she just deliver your stuff to the front gate?"

"I told her to be discreet," Maddy said. "I meant that she should make up some plausible excuse. I should have known better than to leave Bitsy any leeway."

"You're not coming with me," Jon said.

"I'm not?"

"No shoes," he pointed out.

"I am so coming," Maddy said. "You've got extra shoes, haven't you? I'll borrow a couple of pairs of socks to make my feet fit."

"You'll look like Bozo the Clown."

"Who cares?" She slid open a couple of drawers without asking permission, found his socks, and stuffed her feet into three pair. Jon sighed, knowing that was all the socks he owned. Well, he'd worn dirty socks often enough in the past, and he could do so this weekend.

Then she dug through the closet and found his one pair of shoes, which he reserved for times when the boots were being reheeled. The woman was determined, and Jon decided not to argue further.

It might be useful having Maddy along. At least she was on the same wavelength as Ditsy Bitsy, which might help them find her.

Jon had to admire Maddy's courage and her housekeeper's loyalty. Too bad the pair didn't have enough sense between them to come in out of a hurricane.

"Wait a minute," Jon said. "If your friend is stuck in a ditch, where's she calling from?"

"Her flip phone." From Maddy's tone, one would assume everybody carried a telephone while sneaking into an encampment in the dead of night.

It was a good thing she'd brought it, though, Jon reflected. Otherwise Blair would undoubtedly have found the woman the next morning and made them all look like fools.

He led the way out of the RV, trying not to laugh as Maddy clumped after him in the oversize shoes. "How long has your, uh, roommate lived with you?"

"About six months."

"Came highly recommended, did she?"

"Not exactly," said Maddy. "She was my manicurist. She got fired for painting people's nails weird colors, and she needed a place to live, so I gave her one. Well, wouldn't you?"

Jon didn't answer. There was no appropriate response, except maybe, "You hired your manicurist as a housekeeper? Are you crazy?" which he doubted Maddy would appreciate. Besides, he was supposed to think Bitsy was her roommate.

He grabbed a flashlight and went outside.

The campground lay silent at this hour. Only the distant hoot of an owl and a few rustlings disturbed the stillness. Overhead loomed an almost-full moon, casting an orange glow.

In his years of pickup work as a detective, bodyguard and bounty hunter, Jon had spent plenty of time roving the night. He knew its hazards, the errors in depth perception,

the way noise carried to unexpected reaches, even the unpredictable awakenings and meanderings of people themselves. He knew how to step to minimize the noise, and
paused frequently to listen for suspicious noises.

Maddy was obviously doing her best to follow his lead,
moving stealthily across the landscape, but she couldn't
control her movements in those clodhoppers. To Jon's sensitive ears, she thumped down the path like an elephant in
ballet slippers. The sooner they got away from the other
RVs, the better.

Earlier, he'd noticed a hiking trail leading into the brush.
It traveled roughly in the direction of the front gate, and he
headed for it now.

They had just reached the shelter of the trees when Jon
heard a noise from somewhere near the conference center.
He lifted his hand, bringing Maddy to a halt.

He heard the sound again, this time clearly revealed as
footsteps on gravel.

Maddy heard it, too. "Oh, great. An insomniac."

No; the steps were too purposeful and measured, almost
military in their precision.

"It's Blair," Jon whispered.

"He can't work all day and all night, too," Maddy
pointed out.

"Well, something must have woken him up." While Jon
debated what to do next, Maddy made the decision for him
by stomping past and proceeding down the trail.

He kept the flashlight low, aiming it past her in hopes of
preventing a stumble. Fortunately, Maddy didn't try to go
fast, and, after receiving a couple of branch whacks across
her bare legs, she kept to the center of the trail.

The path led downward, stopping at the edge of a ravine
and continuing along the rim to their right. Playing his
flashlight in the gully, Jon saw only brambles.

"She must be in there somewhere," Maddy said dubiously.

Jon wished he'd brought two flashlights, but then, their use of the light already risked attracting Blair's attention. Assuming, of course, that he would head along the path rather than merely checking the campgrounds.

Jon wished he knew more about the camp's security devices, as well as Blair's schedule. Normally, had he planned an operation like this, he would have made a point of scoping those details out in advance.

Tonight he would have to wing it. Worse, he was working with an amateur.

"You head that way," he told Maddy, pointing to his right along the path. "Stay on the trail. I'm going into the ravine in the opposite direction. If I don't find her, I'll come back."

"What if I run into Blair?" Maddy whispered.

"Think of an excuse," he said.

She hesitated in the moonlight, a funny, brave little figure in her oversize shoes, three pairs of socks, raggedy shorts and gigantic shirt. The woman might be a pampered heiress but, Jon admitted silently, she had guts.

Moonlight turned her skin to ivory and her eyes to giant pools, with the faintest glimmer of blue. She'd thrown herself into this adventure, and she hadn't backed down.

He thought about Blair, the great unknown factor, and felt a wave of concern for Maddy. If Blair was in league with Gloria, he wouldn't stop at murder.

"I'll tell you what," Jon murmured. "You sit down just below the rim of the ravine here, where no one can see you. I've got the flashlight, so I'll do the searching."

Maddy shook her head.

"Why not?"

"Bitsy's depending on me," she said. "I know she must be scared."

"I'll find her," Jon promised.

"We can work faster if we both look." Maddy started along the path. "Go on. I'll be fine. There's plenty of moonlight."

He watched her for a minute, wondering when he had started to care what happened to this woman from another universe, this daughter of his enemy.

She didn't need Jon to protect her; she had money, and influence and a father with the ruthlessness of Attila the Hun. But right now she appeared small and fragile as she paced close to the gully, peering into its tangled depths for some sign of her friend.

The sooner he left, the sooner he'd be back, Jon told himself, and edged off the trail into the cleft.

This time of year, there was no water running through here, although in early spring the channel probably ran full to the brim. The banks were about seven feet high, and the ravine no more than eight feet in width, clogged with branches and debris.

Jon wondered what the intrepid Bitsy had worn, and suspected she hadn't dressed with much foresight. He was grateful for his boots and heavy jeans as he lowered himself past jutting rocks and thistles.

Animals must live in this gully, burrowing into its earthen sides. He hoped Bitsy wouldn't give herself away by screaming.

Jon hadn't wanted to alarm Maddy any more than necessary, but Blair's nocturnal patrol made him suspect that a sensor had been tripped. That meant either that Larry was paranoid about his property or that Gloria had spun a credible tale replete with threats upon her life. Installing this type of equipment cost a bundle, and Larry wouldn't have done it because of idle fears.

Jon especially wished he knew more about Blair. The man was the wild card in the game, he mused as he poked along the gully, occasionally calling Bitsy's name in a low voice.

In his experience, men who chose freelance security work tended to have checkered pasts. Some were ex-convicts, employable only by the shady, the desperate or the naive. Others had a background in the military and had never been able to adjust to civilian life.

A few, like Jon, were men of action who found themselves thrust outside the life they knew and rejected the prospect of getting trapped inside four walls. Jon had done a brief stint on a small-town police force, but found he didn't enjoy the chain of command. He preferred to be his own man.

Maybe someday he would find a job that paid decently and let him call the shots. But for that you needed money or connections, and he had neither.

At least, not yet.

He waded through the branches and brambles, heading toward a bridge that spanned the ravine between the front gate and the conference center. Bitsy must have entered somewhere nearby.

Jon's pulse sped as he heard a soft cry behind him. Catching hold of a root to keep his balance, he swung around, and the call came again.

He recognized the sound of his name. And Maddy sounded upset.

SHE FOUND BITSY with her ankle wedged between a rock and a log, tears streaking her dirty face. Even by moonlight, the housekeeper made a pathetic sight.

"Oh, Bits!" After calling Jon as loudly as she dared, Maddy clambered down to her. "Did you break something?"

"Two nails!" The former manicurist made a disgusted pout. "Can you believe that? Two nails! It took me ages to get them this long!"

"I meant your ankle." Then Maddy caught sight of the luggage: a large backpack still in place on Bitsy's shoulders, a lumpy duffel bag draped over the log and a king-size suitcase that had slid to the bottom of the ravine. "You didn't have to bring everything I own."

"It hardly made a dent!" Bitsy protested, brushing aside a strand of Daring Russet-dyed hair so bright its color penetrated even the darkness. Something sparkled, and Maddy spotted a design of tiny rhinestones glued atop Bitsy's nail polish.

"I'm sorry about your nails." Maddy yielded to a twinge of guilt, knowing she was at fault. She'd taken off heedlessly on this venture, and commanded Bitsy to assist her without considering the possible ramifications.

Even when people worked for you, that didn't make them any less important than you were, Maddy knew. She hadn't meant to risk Bitsy's safety; she simply hadn't given the matter any thought.

Then she noticed what her housekeeper was wearing: a trench coat, with a dark scarf wrapped around her throat. The only thing missing was sunglasses, but even Bitsy wouldn't wear shades in the middle of the night.

"What are you dressed for, a spy caper?" Maddy asked.

"You said to be discreet."

"I meant low-key," Maddy said. "Never mind. I should have spelled it out."

"The problem is, how do I get back to the car?" Bitsy whined. "I think I can still drive, but I'm not so sure I can walk. Oh, I didn't have time to go to the beach so I had my cousin pick up your sports car. He said it did zero to ninety in a flash."

Maddy winced. Bitsy's cousin was a borderline juvenile delinquent majoring in rock music appreciation at a community college. "As long as he got it home safely."

"It's fine."

To her relief, she heard steps approaching on the path. A flashlight touched them, and then Jon leaned over the edge of the gully, reassuringly solid in this moon-dappled wilderness. "How is she?"

"Bruised but not bowed," said Maddy. "She says she can drive home okay."

Jon assessed the situation with a sweep of the light. "You stay with the suitcases. I'll help Bitsy back to the car."

About to protest, Maddy realized he made sense. No point in them both thrashing around, creating a maximum disturbance. Besides, the triple layer of socks didn't make the shoes fit well enough for her to walk with any confidence. "I guess so."

Jon dropped down beside them. "Hi, I'm Jon."

"Wow." Bitsy's eyes widened beneath their thick lashes—Just Like Nature's, guaranteed waterproof. "You're a hunk. Gee, Maddy, no wonder you took off."

"We're on the trail of a murderess," Maddy couldn't resist confiding. "But don't tell anybody."

"Especially your father," Bitsy said. "He wouldn't like it. By the way, he called. You forgot your stepmother's birthday."

"Oops." Maddy had penciled the date on her calendar, but she never looked at her calendar. "Send flowers."

"I already did," Bitsy replied. "And a necklace made of camel's teeth by some refugee children at a mission school. The kind of thing you would have sent."

"Great," said Maddy, who had been surprised to find that her stepmother actually wore her gifts, at least when Maddy was visiting.

"One of the teeth had this neat cavity," Bitsy added. "It was kind of split in the middle and fanned out."

"Excuse me," Jon interjected. "If you two could tear yourselves away, I think we should get this over with."

"We're being followed," Maddy whispered. "By a man with a gun." She didn't know why she'd felt compelled to add that, except perhaps to keep Bitsy's voice from rising any more decibels. Or perhaps to make a better story for her friends when she got back.

"Really?" Bitsy hugged herself nervously.

"Hold still." Jon, who had been rocking the log gently, pulled Bitsy's ankle free. "Now, try to flex it."

Bitsy wiggled her foot. "It kind of hurts."

"Probably a sprain," Jon said. "After you get home, apply ice and keep it elevated. Use an elastic bandage if you have one, and stay off your feet for a few days."

"What about my Jazzercise class?" asked Bitsy.

"Oh, for heaven's sake, you heard what he said!" Maddy wondered if she ever sounded as foolish as her friend. She didn't see how that was possible, but judging from Jon's reactions since they'd met, he probably thought so.

Maybe she was starting to see things differently, living away from her protective cocoon. It was hard to admit that she'd been self-indulgent and frivolous, but Maddy supposed there might be some truth to that idea.

As she waited with the suitcases, hearing the crunching sounds that marked Jon and Bitsy's journey, she reflected that her father would probably like Jon.

The man has backbone. He knows how to strike out for himself. I like a man who hasn't gone soft. She could hear her father's voice so clearly, she almost believed he'd actually said the words.

Charles Armand certainly hadn't liked any of the young men Maddy had brought home over the years. She hadn't been all that enamored of them herself, at least not for long.

Her father had accused her of selecting boyfriends for their dashing looks, their expensive clothes and their ability to sense the latest trends. But the truth was that the men had selected Maddy, not the other way around.

Was that the kind of lightweight male she appealed to? Then where, Maddy wondered, did Jon fit in?

Because she could tell she attracted him. Why, he'd practically ravished her the first time they met. Still, the way he blew hot and cold, it was hard to tell what the man was thinking.

Mostly, he seemed to care about catching Gloria and raking in the money. Maddy wondered what Jon would do if he knew how much she'd inherited from her mother, and stood to inherit from her father.

That probably wouldn't influence him, she thought. Jon wasn't the kind of man to romance a woman for her money; too many strings attached. He was the kind of guy who insisted on being in control of his own life and, she felt certain, his own money.

Maddy smiled. She'd never dated a man like him before. Maybe she ought to try hiding her identity more often.

In the distance, a car started. The motor purred low and steady; Bitsy had brought the Lexus.

A few minutes later, Jon returned with surprising stealth. "I didn't even hear you," she whispered.

"Your friend is fine," he said. "Nice car."

"Usually I drive the . . ." Maddy stopped herself on the point of explaining that she preferred her sports car for everyday use. "I mean, it's her father's car."

"I see," Jon murmured.

Shouldering the backpack, Maddy let him carry the suitcase and the duffel as they clambered onto the trail. Now, she realized, came the most difficult part; getting back to the RV without being observed.

She wished her housekeeper hadn't taken her so literally about being discreet. She would have to remember to be more specific to Bitsy in the future.

The path felt steep going back, partly because they were walking uphill but also because of the weight of the luggage. Feeling the pack dig into her shoulders, Maddy wondered exactly what Bitsy had packed. From the heft of it, there must be more than clothes.

Shoes, she supposed. Bottles of nail polish. Makeup. Her hair dryer, of course. An electric razor. Shampoo and mousse and conditioner.

She'd never realized they weighed so much.

For a moment, Maddy wondered what it would be like to travel without so many accessories, just to take off with one change of clothing and a toothbrush. Okay, a hairbrush too.

It might be fun. But it sure would get inconvenient after a while.

She glanced ahead at Jon, who carted her cases with ease. He kept sweeping the flashlight from side to side, and tilting his head as if it helped him to listen better.

What kind of woman did he usually get involved with? Jon didn't strike Maddy as the flirtatious type, but with his rugged good looks, he wouldn't have to search for female companionship.

Maddy realized that what she really wanted to know was how she compared to the other women in his life. They must be more self-sufficient; that wouldn't be difficult. She formed a mental image of a tall brunette, a cowgirl or truck stop owner who took no guff from anybody and could deck most men in a fair fight.

None of them had managed to hold on to Jon, she reminded herself with a wave of relief. But she didn't expect to, either. Didn't want to. Shouldn't want to. Would forget about him the minute he drove off into the sunset.

Ahead of her, Jon halted abruptly. Wrenching around, he hissed, "Hide! Here, take these!" and shoved the duffel and the suitcase at her.

Maddy grabbed them and dove behind a bush. She sank into an uncomfortable heap and lay there, not daring to move.

From the direction of the campground came Blair's voice, commanding Jon to halt in his tracks.

Chapter Eight

From where she huddled, Maddy heard the rumble of masculine voices. They were far enough away to make it hard to follow the conversation, but she gathered that someone had tripped a sensor and that Jon was explaining he couldn't sleep and had gone for a walk.

Blair said something about Gloria and precautions, and Jon responded in a conciliatory tone that he'd done security work himself and understood the demands.

The two men walked away together. Blair didn't seem to be threatening Jon, but then, of course, he hadn't seen Maddy crouched here with the suitcases.

The grass felt damp against her legs, and the cool night air pricked at Maddy's cheeks. Stifling a yawn, she wrapped her arms around herself and waited.

She was beginning to nod off when she decided Jon wasn't coming back any time soon. He must have deliberately led Blair in the opposite direction and kept him occupied so she could return to the motor home.

Now she had to figure out how to get the suitcases there. If Bitsy had managed to drag them as far as the ravine, Maddy was determined she could carry them the rest of the way.

Easier said than done, she discovered as she strapped on the backpack and picked up the other two pieces. Her arms felt as if they were pulling loose at the sockets.

She had to give Bitsy credit for brawn if not brains. Stifling a groan, Maddy wrenched her way forward.

The biggest obstacle turned out to be her shoes, or, rather, Jon's shoes. They fell off at the slightest pretext, and she didn't want to risk stopping and opening the luggage. Searching around for shoes in the dark was a good way to get caught, and besides, with Bitsy's taste, she'd probably packed nothing but high heels.

A knot of tension across Maddy's back had transformed itself into a series of high-strung wires by the time she reached the RV. With a noise halfway between a moan and a sob, she tugged open the door and dragged up the duffel, then the suitcase.

Inside, there was no sign of Jon, and given his dimensions relative to the smallness of the vehicle, she couldn't have missed him. Maddy wondered what two men found to talk about at such length; probably baseball statistics.

Too keyed up to go to bed, she flicked on a light and opened the suitcase. Its contents had jumbled mercilessly, and unless they were hung at once, Maddy could see they'd be useless all weekend. The odds of Jon's possessing an iron she put at about ninety-nine thousand to one.

The RV's only closet, as she'd discovered earlier, was barely large enough to squeeze into. A few pairs of Jon's jeans and work shirts filled it completely.

They would simply have to go.

Poking around, Maddy found some empty storage space in the cooking area, not surprising since Jon's collection of cookwear consisted of a small saucepan and a medium frying pan. She folded his clothes and set them on the shelves beneath the sink.

It was odd how, even through the scent of laundry soap, she could detect an aroma that reminded her of Jon. She could picture these jeans molded to his thighs and these shirts sculpted across his chest.

Remembering their near-tryst in the bathroom, Maddy felt desire twist in her throat and seep through her body. This was different from what she'd felt then—more subtle, more tentative—and yet she had the sense that it belonged more truly to her.

She wished Jon would come home now. If he was as wide awake as she was, maybe they could explore each other a little more. Or a lot more.

For some reason, the prospect scared Maddy. She'd imagined herself in love several times, but always deep inside she'd known her heart was only on loan. With Jon, there could be no limits, no way of controlling her reaction. Anything might happen.

It was a good thing he hadn't come back yet, Maddy told herself. A good thing she hadn't had a chance to act on her impulses, and a good thing he couldn't see how she was rearranging his personal space.

In the closet she hung several dresses and a jumpsuit of silver Mylar. By the time she'd finished tucking her blouses and pants, underwear and shoes into nooks and corners, and arraying her jewelry and gear in the bathroom, the RV could have passed for an overstuffed boutique.

The luggage itself posed the final problem. The duffel could be crammed into a storage compartment; the suitcase and the backpack would have to go into an outside storage bin. Maddy left them near the driver's seat for Jon to stow tomorrow.

She pulled off her shorts and Jon's shirt, instantly missing its snuggly softness. Changing into her cotton nightgown hand-embellished with teddy bears, Maddy got back into bed.

The last thing she remembered thinking before she fell asleep was that Jon certainly must be hitting it off with Blair.

A LIGHT TAP at the side door awakened her. Maddy's eyes flew open, registering the fact that only a thin wash of daylight had arrived, before she checked the clock and saw it was 6:00 a.m.

Outrageously early.

The sound of heavy breathing drew her attention to the stuffed sleeping bag rising and falling on the floor toward the front of the RV. Jon had returned.

Not wanting to wake him, she hurried to the side door and cracked it open.

Gloria stood there brushing a strand of blond hair from her face. She wore jogging shorts and a tank top that displayed her spectacular figure to advantage.

"Jon's still asleep," Maddy whispered.

Gloria made a face. "Listen, I thought we should go through your wardrobe and pick out a bridesmaid's dress."

Maddy breathed a silent prayer of thanks to Bitsy for bringing everything so promptly. It would have been hard to explain why she didn't own a change of clothes.

"Are you wearing a white gown?" She already knew the answer, but she didn't want Gloria to pick up on that fact. Receiving an affirmative, Maddy said, "Well, let me bring some things out here. Just a sec."

She selected a hand-dyed peach-to-lavender shaded silk dress, and an off-the-shoulder jungle print rayon sheath with a coordinated soft jacket. Thank goodness Bitsy had included things no sensible person would bring to a weekend like this.

Standing in the doorway, Maddy held each up in turn so Gloria could get the full effect.

The other woman's mouth formed the word *Wow*. "You have an incredible wardrobe," she said. "Your husband must be richer than I thought."

"No, I just spend money like it was water," Maddy said. "I guess I'm going to have to stop now that we're married."

"Marriage is such a drag, isn't it?" Gloria gave a self-conscious laugh, catching herself. "I mean, usually. Larry's different."

"He can buy you nice clothes," Maddy prompted.

"And how!" Gloria grinned conspiratorially. "Well, let's go with that pinkish one. It looks more suitable for a bridesmaid."

"Definitely." Maddy tiptoed inside and replaced them in the closet. Gloria showed no sign of leaving, so she peered back outside.

"Want to get some exercise?" Gloria asked. "This is a good time. The gym's empty."

"Sure. I'll change right away."

Splashing water on her face and making rapid use of her toothbrush, Maddy slipped off the nightgown and dug out a midnight blue, star-spangled leotard with a matching cape. Putting on her dyed-to-match running shoes, she jotted a quick note to Jon and went out.

Gloria was jogging in place on the grass. In the morning sunlight, the woman's face showed the strain of nearly forty years of hard living, but the body was trim and toned.

Gloria would be a tough opponent in a fight. She was also a good two to three inches taller than Maddy and had longer, deadlier nails. If anyone was going to get handcuffs on her, it would have to be Jon.

"You really are a clotheshorse," Gloria commented as they trotted toward the conference center. "I'm lucky you didn't meet Larry first."

"He's not my type," Maddy said.

"Why not?" Gloria's response made it clear that sexual response played no role in her selection of a man. "He'd keep you in better style than that cowboy of yours."

"There are compensations," Maddy said.

"I thought you wanted an annulment."

Oh, that's right. "I keep changing my mind," she improvised.

They trotted through the lobby, its collection of jungle plants a good deal less mysterious in the morning light, and down a hallway. At the end, Gloria pushed open a heavy door to reveal a gym roughly the size of Maddy's living room. But then, Maddy's living room was larger than some people's houses.

A weight machine, several treadmills and a large mat comprised the equipment. Gloria went directly to a VCR and put on an aerobics video.

Soon the two of them were warming up on the mat, side by side, their manes of blond hair flying. From a distance, they really would look like twins, Maddy supposed.

JON COULD HARDLY MOVE through the motor home for all the junk festooning its hooks and shelves. Why did women need so much paraphernalia, anyway?

He appreciated the way Maddy had slipped out without awakening him. He appreciated even more that she'd left him a note.

So she was exercising with Gloria. By now, Jon felt more or less confident that Maddy wouldn't reveal too much. The friendlier the two women got, the better.

He'd had a remarkably productive conversation with Blair. The man clearly wasn't hooked up with Gloria; he lived in the nearest town, a wide place in the road called Mountain View. Larry had hired him several times before for weekend duty, and not too long ago he'd served in the Marines.

The alarm system was new, Blair had explained; Larry had installed it only last week. After hearing Gloria's claim that an ex-boyfriend was stalking her, Larry had even contemplated hiring round-the-clock guards, but decided it might make his guests uncomfortable.

Blair was an easygoing guy with an eye for a fast buck, like Jon. Not that it would pay to get too friendly, but it felt good to have taken the man's measure.

And Jon's idea was ripening just as he'd hoped. Later today, he would work out the details with Maddy.

There was nothing like a wedding to bring people together, he supposed. Or tear them apart.

He decided to try the exercise equipment himself. Not that he felt any need to spy on Maddy, but staying in shape wasn't easy on the road. Even a daily run didn't keep his muscles tip-top.

Donning shorts and a T-shirt, Jon headed for the conference center.

He spotted a few people stirring on the way over, and the smell of pancakes and sausage filled the air. He figured he'd rustle up some grub after working out.

A few loping strides later, Jon went through the lobby and found the gym. He paused in the doorway to watch the two women leap and bounce along with an instructor on the video, who called out encouragement to her unseen class.

Gloria moved with grim determination, working every part of her body as if fighting a daily battle against encroaching age. Her jaw was tightly set and her forehead lined with concentration.

By contrast, Maddy seemed buoyed by inner enthusiasm, eyes half-closed so she could better enjoy the music as she danced. She had an energy and spring that Gloria lacked, a natural suppleness that made Jon ache to catch her waist with his hands and pull her against him.

That spangled leotard didn't hide a single line of her slim body, although the cape bouncing up and down added a comical effect. The contrast between the two women helped clarify Jon's impression of Maddy: unaffected, spontaneous, naive despite the gloss of sophistication.

For a moment, he wondered if he was taking too much of a risk by involving Maddy in his plot. There was always a chance she might get hurt. A twinge in the vicinity of where his heart used to be warned that he didn't want that to happen. But he'd abandoned his heart long ago, along with his ranch and his family's dreams.

The music changed, and the two women began leaping into the air, kicking higher and higher. Maddy hit the floor and bounced upward as if she had steel coils in her ankles. He shouldn't underestimate the woman; she was tougher than she looked. Jon had a feeling Maddy would quickly recover from any setback.

Feeling reassured, he headed toward the weight machine and set to work.

"I SEE WHAT YOU MEAN," Gloria murmured as the video changed pace and the two women settled into a pattern of toning and stretching to cool down their muscles.

Maddy followed her gaze to where Jon was dominating the machine with a series of rapid pulls and pushes. He worked quickly but methodically, creating a rhythm so strong he didn't need musical accompaniment.

"About what?" she asked.

"About marriage to a poor guy having its compensations," Gloria explained in a low voice. "At least, a poor guy who's built like that."

The T-shirt plastered to his chest revealed every torque of Jon's muscles. Sweat beaded on the bronze skin of his face and arms, giving him a golden sheen.

Those arms could have picked Maddy up without strain, carried her back to the motor home and tossed her lightly across the couch. She could just imagine those broad shoulders looming over her, those narrow hips pinning her to the mattress as Jon lowered his shaggy head over her....

Maddy felt her stretches speeding up and her heart beginning to pound. This wasn't the effect you were supposed to get in a cooldown, she reflected.

"I don't suppose you'd share him?" Gloria teased. "Kind of a bridal gift?" She wore a knowing smile, the smile of a woman who can and will take off with another woman's man.

Unexpectedly, a flame of jealousy seared Maddy's throat. Despite her hardness, Gloria was still a beautiful woman, and most men would respond to her instinctively. A guy like Jon, used to a rough-and-ready life, wouldn't hesitate to enjoy himself if he got the chance.

But, Maddy told herself sternly, she wasn't being fair. First of all, Jon hadn't done anything to indicate he was an alley cat. Second, if he did find himself alone with Gloria, his response would be to lock her up and take her to Texas, not make love to her.

Which meant Gloria's suggestion might not be such a bad idea, after all.

"You're kidding, right?" Maddy said.

Pale eyes lined in harsh black blinked at her in surprise. "You'd actually consider it?"

"There's plenty to go around," she temporized, waiting for the other woman to say more. She sensed that unless the impetus came entirely from Gloria, the other woman would become suspicious.

The older woman's expression softened. "You're pretty damn generous, Maddy. But forget it."

"Not your type, huh?" Maddy teased, reluctant to abandon the idea. Getting Gloria and Jon alone together would be a real coup, even if the prospect did set her teeth on edge.

"It's not that." Gloria stopped stretching and hugged her knees on the mat. "Sooner or later, you'd regret your offer. And I'd rather keep you on my side."

"Thanks. But you know how men are—if he wasn't sleeping with you, it would be somebody else."

Gloria shrugged. "Maybe. I'll give it some thought. He *is* a tempting chunk of change."

Drop it, Maddy told herself. *She'll go for the bait on her own time, or not at all.* "You don't have to tell me!"

As they headed for the showers, she digested what Gloria had said about keeping Maddy on her side. Apparently the other woman regarded her as a potential ally, maybe even an accomplice.

A dangerous possibility, but maybe a useful one, too.

AFTER SHOWERING and changing into pin-striped shorts and a coordinated T-shirt with a pin-striped tie, Maddy grabbed a Danish and coffee from a buffet set up in the lobby. She'd contemplated wearing something dressier, but this felt more appropriate for the next activity on the day's schedule: the massage-in.

By the time Jon joined her, the rest of the couples were wandering in. Herb and Anne Stowe, as always, greeted them with cheerful enthusiasm. The Chings seemed reserved, but also glad to see them.

The other couple they'd met yesterday, Bo and Sarita Mendez, stood apart, not speaking to each other or anyone else. They held themselves ramrod straight, Bo consuming a bear claw and Sarita restricting herself to a cup of coffee.

Maddy wondered if the woman maintained her trim figure by skipping breakfast. That would make anybody crabby, she supposed, but she doubted that was the extent of the couple's problems. They didn't seem to like each other, or themselves very much, either.

Well, look at you. Dr. Freud in person.

Maddy had always thought she would enjoy being a therapist because she loved giving advice and meddling in other people's affairs. But she knew she didn't have the discipline for all those years of study, not to mention the life experience to understand people who were different from her.

In a way, this weekend was proving to be a growing experience, Maddy realized. She'd left behind her queen-of-the-roost status and was learning how other people reacted to her without the patina of money or fame.

Gloria's interest surprised her a little. Not that Maddy would normally choose to hang out with a murderess, but it was nice to be liked for herself.

Or for how easily Gloria believes you can be manipulated, if she ever needs to.

Gloria herself had gone to her quarters to change. Now she returned in black slacks, a bare-midriff blouse tied below the bust, and the usual heavy makeup, at almost the same moment that Larry made his appearance from his office.

He appeared well-rested and confident; Maddy supposed he must be enjoying his fiancée's lovemaking with gusto. Although approaching fifty, Larry strode into the room with a hint of a swagger, more like a young man than a mature one, and greeted them with a broad grin that got even broader when he spotted Gloria.

Maddy remembered reading that Larry had been divorced twice, once when he was in college and then later, after several years of marriage. She wondered whether he'd been inspired to learn more about relationships because of his own sad experiences, or whether it was simply a case of an expert who can solve everyone's problems except his own.

Based on Larry's poor judgment in selecting Gloria as his bride, she suspected the latter possibility was the right one. The man glowed with happiness as his fiancée wiggled up to him and slipped her arm through his.

Sneaking a sideways glance at Jon, Maddy caught the narrowing of his eyes as he stared at Gloria. He'd hardly given Maddy a glance when she finished exercising. All the man wanted was to get his hands on that reward.

Maybe she shouldn't blame him, since she'd always had more money than she needed, but it bothered her that he was so fixated on money. Maddy realized that, without verbalizing it, she'd been assuming that Jon, like her, was primarily motivated by a spirit of adventure.

Now she reminded herself that whatever she might get out of this weekend, she couldn't expect her relationship with Jon to outlast it. She had to force her optimistic spirit to bend to what her mind knew to be true. *We come from different worlds, and we'll be heading back to them on Monday.*

It was with relief that she heard Larry announce the massage-in. She needed a break from her thoughts. Then it occurred to Maddy that a mutual massage session was hardly conducive to distancing herself from Jon, but she couldn't figure out any way to avoid it.

During breakfast, a discreet crew of assistants had set up massage tables throughout the indoor jungle. Shades were lowered on the room's front windows, reducing the light to a mellow amber.

"Pick up some of our massage lotion and choose a table with your partner. I want the men to lie down first. We're working on breaking those barriers," Larry announced into a microphone. "For most of us, that means switching the roles in which the man is always the aggressor."

Collecting a bottle of lotion and following Jon, Maddy reflected that she liked it when Jon was the aggressor. Most men found Maddy intimidating because of her wealth. Of course, that didn't mean she intended to let Jon run the show, aggressive or not.

There is no show to run, you idiot. She had to stop thinking of the way he'd looked flexing his muscles on the weight machine. Or how he'd attacked her in the RV yesterday.

Yet here he was, pulling off his T-shirt and lying on the table, looking so large and powerful she wondered how the thing could hold him without collapsing.

"Begin by warming the lotion in your hands...." Larry's voice droned hypnotically. With a grimace, Maddy obeyed.

As soon as she began to knead Jon's back, she discovered that the scented oil had an aphrodisiac quality. It felt silky and sensuous beneath her hands, and the aroma reminded her of musk and candlelight. Dinner for two in a secluded grove, and Jon's body laid out for her enjoyment.

It surprised her to find that Larry Wicker was right: when the man lay passive and the woman took control, the dynamics became stimulating almost to the snapping point. The more she rubbed him, the more Maddy wanted to find out how far she could go in molding Jon to her will.

If they hadn't been in a semipublic place, she might have rolled him over . . . Well, not literally; he would have landed on the floor with a splat.

The whole idea beginning to give her a headache, she concentrated on probing the tension in Jon's back. As his muscles relaxed, so did Maddy. She didn't have to prove anything, or do anything. They were simply enjoying the moment.

When it came time to switch positions, she flopped down on her stomach, her arms pillowing her cheek. After the morning's exercise, a nice rub would probably put her to sleep.

Jon, however, had other ideas. As his fingers danced across her skin, he murmured, "Learn anything from Gloria?"

"She thinks you're cute," Maddy whispered. "I tried to set her up with you, kind of a last fling before the wedding, but she backed out."

"You did what?" His voice came out in a low growl.

"To get you two alone together, what do you think?" she said.

Jon rubbed silently for a few minutes, his hands reaching beneath her shirt to the bare skin. Maddy wished she could observe his face. "I see," he said at last. "Well, I've got a better idea."

"Shoot," Maddy muttered, annoyed that he didn't appreciate her initiative in trying to set him up with Gloria.

"Actually, I've got two ideas," he said. "But I'm not sure I want to tell you about them yet."

Maddy lifted her head to glare. "Why not?"

"I'm used to doing things my own way." A large hand pressed her head down into her cradling arms. Then he assaulted her shoulders and back with such intensity that Maddy nearly cried out. "I'll let you know what you need to know, when you need to know it."

"But—"

"You're too impulsive. Smarter than I thought at first, but not a seasoned pro, either. Now be quiet before Larry comes over here and scolds us."

Reluctantly, Maddy yielded to Jon's control. She didn't like letting him touch her any way he wished, without being able to respond. Every instinct urged her to argue, negotiate, take charge of the way he was handling her.

That was precisely the point of the exercise, she supposed; to break down the barriers. Except that she and Jon weren't really married and she didn't *want* to break down any barriers.

Especially when his strokes became gentler, unsnapping her bra and exploring the exposed edges of her breasts, then down to her hips. How dare Jon run his hands beneath her shorts and across her derriere?

"Hey—" she protested.

"Can it," he muttered unromantically.

Maddy fell silent, not wanting to attract notice. Okay, so Jon was in charge, but she could control her response. She didn't have to notice the way he eased her legs apart and probed her inner thighs, right up to the sensitive core.

He paused to warm more oil on his hands, then raised his hands to her shoulders again. With a sigh, Maddy yielded. She didn't try to resist as his hands slid over her shoulder blades and around beneath her, to the softness of her breasts. In another moment, he would catch the tips and find them already erect....

"Great, folks!" boomed Larry's voice. "Coming along, are we? Well, I hate to tell you, but it's time to take a break! We're going to have our small group sessions now, and then lunch. But don't worry! Right after the nature walk, I've got a series of exercises planned for you to do alone in your trailers. That will give you a chance to finish what you started here!"

Finish what they started? Annoyed, Maddy straightened her clothing and sat up, wishing her breasts didn't feel so full. She had no intention of finishing anything, no matter what her body might indicate.

Jon's amused grin as he observed her did nothing to soften Maddy's temper. Whatever might happen when they were alone in the RV, it wouldn't involve him teasing her and getting away with it the way he just had.

In fact, she reflected, two could play at this game. If he didn't watch out, Jon Everett was going to find himself panting for his new bride and having nothing but a cold, hard bounty and an empty road to show for it.

Chapter Nine

The plan had been to divide the participants into four groups of three couples each for counseling sessions. The addition of Maddy and Jon might have thrown the numbers out of whack, but at the last minute one of the other couples came down with severe allergy attacks and retreated to their trailer.

"That's an unfortunate side effect of these beautiful mountains," Larry told the group over the loudspeaker. "But don't worry—I'll meet with them privately while you folks are enjoying your nature walks after lunch."

He then called out names and split them up, sending one group to the patio, another to the gym and a third to his expansive office, with the fourth to remain in the lobby.

"I'll circulate among you to help get discussions started," Larry said. "I want you all to begin, one person at a time, by explaining why you decided to come on this weekend."

Maddy had lost track of which group they were in, as she tried to keep Gloria in her sights. The blond woman cruised through the crowd, murmuring compliments and asking if anyone needed anything, then excused herself to confer with the staff about wedding preparations.

"I hope she'll be around for the nature walk," Jon muttered as he led Maddy toward the patio.

"Is that one of your ideas for catching her?" It made sense; they would be in an isolated setting, although in the middle of the day with lots of other people walking around.

"I thought maybe we could work something out. Especially since you two have become such great friends." Jon didn't meet Maddy's gaze as he steered her out the back door, and there was no hint of sensuality in his grip on her elbow. He seemed to have forgotten their massage the instant it ended.

The man had nerves of steel and a heart of lead, Maddy reflected in annoyance.

As they took seats in a semicircle, she noticed that the other two couples were the Chings and the Mendezes. She breathed a silent prayer of thanks not to be cooped up with the ever-hearty Stowes. It was going to be hard enough to pretend to bare her soul without having a cheering section sound off at every other word.

Larry had started with another group, and for a while the six of them sat staring at each other in silence. Maddy became aware of the call of birds from the woods, while a cool breeze played across her bare arms and legs.

Above them towered the mountain peak, dwarfing the conference center and its inhabitants. Did everyone else feel as out of place as she did?

As if to answer in the affirmative, Sarita Mendez said, "I don't see why we're doing this. It's a waste of time."

"Maybe you should go first," Maddy said.

"Excuse me?"

"We're supposed to explain why we came on this weekend," she reminded the dark-haired woman, who sat on the edge of her seat as if afraid she might wrinkle her white linen suit.

Sarita crossed her legs in a protective gesture. "I came because my husband insisted on it."

"He must have a reason." Maddy didn't know why she was taking the moderator's role, except that nobody else seemed willing to.

"Yes, I do," Bo said. "Maybe this wasn't the best idea, but we've got a lot of barriers between us. I liked Larry's slogan of breaking them down."

"Barriers!" sniffed his wife. "What we have are two busy careers—we're both attorneys. Plus two small children, in-laws who don't approve of my working and want me to stay home with an apron, and a husband who never helps with the housework."

"My wife is omitting the fact that we have a full-time housekeeper," Bo said.

"I don't see how we can deal with these kinds of problems without Larry," Frank Ching observed. "I certainly can't offer advice, because we've got the opposite problem. My wife has always stayed home but now our kids are ready for college and she needs to get a job and help with the finances."

"And I think he's being unfair," Lee said. "That's the reason *we* came."

Then everyone focused on Maddy and Jon. "What about you?" asked Sarita.

"We just got married and we hate each other," Maddy said, and was surprised when everyone laughed.

"Well, not hate," Jon muttered.

"Despise," she said. "Look at him." She gestured at the Stetson, which Jon had put on when he changed into his usual jeans and work shirt after exercising. "The guy thinks he's riding the range. Well, I'm not the range."

Again, people chuckled.

"At least you have a sense of humor," Lee said.

"It's not so bad, coming from different backgrounds," Sarita offered. "Bo and I are too much alike. Or maybe we thought we were, and now we're discovering that there are subtle differences we didn't count on."

"Lee and I agreed on everything for years," Frank said.

"That's what he thinks," said his wife.

Frank Ching paused with his mouth open, as if he'd just received a revelation. "You mean we didn't?"

"I wanted to be a fashion designer, remember?" said his wife. "You didn't approve, so I stayed home. Now you want me to work, but what can I do? Sell clothes in a department store? You know I'm not good at meeting people."

"You might be better than you think," Maddy suggested.

"I'm too shy."

"Nobody likes a pushy saleslady. I'll bet you'd be terrific at some upscale store."

"Really?" said Lee.

"I suppose we should have talked about this more," admitted her husband.

"Bo and I used to talk," said Sarita, "but all we did was argue."

"That's the best way to reach a verdict," said her mate. "Present all the arguments and then choose the best one."

"Spoken like a lawyer!" said Maddy. "Do you allow objections and continuances? And who reaches the verdict?"

"You've got a point," Bo said. "Maybe we ought to stop acting like lawyers in our private life."

Everyone fell silent, absorbed in their thoughts for a moment before Jon said, "That's my wife. She can solve everyone's problems but her own."

Maddy knew he was picking a fight for the sake of their cover. But right now she didn't feel like squabbling; she was too touched by what had just happened.

She hadn't exactly solved anyone's problems, but she *had* helped loosen people up so they could solve their own. Too often in the past, she'd been so much a target for people's admiration, envy, resentment or status-seeking that she hadn't had a chance to simply interact with others.

She liked blending in with the crowd. She'd never felt this free before, with no need to prove anything, nor this accepted.

With a start, Maddy saw that she'd spent her life rebelling against her father's control. But in the process of trying to break free, she had allowed her rebellion to define who and what she was.

I don't even know myself, she thought. *Maybe I have strengths I never suspected. Maybe I could do a lot of things more useful than skating at the beach all day.*

Then she realized the other couples were responding to Jon's remark.

"You shouldn't put down your wife," Lee Ching said. "Someday she may meet a man who tells her she's wonderful, and Pfft! She'll be gone."

Jon shrugged. "A woman who won't stand by her man isn't worth having."

"What about a man who stands by his woman?" challenged Sarita.

"You've got the ladies angry now," warned Frank with amusement. "You are in great danger, Mr. Everett."

"He thinks I'm a steer he lassoed on the ranch," Maddy grumbled.

"Not a steer," Jon said. "A cow."

The women hooted. Even Jon laughed. "Okay, that wasn't very flattering. And I didn't lasso her."

"Actually, you sort of did." Maddy was picturing the handcuffs when she realized she couldn't mention them.

"How *did* you two meet?" Larry slipped into an extra chair, joining the conversation midstream. He managed it artfully, Maddy had to admit to himself.

"At the beach," Jon said.

"He thought he knew me," Maddy explained. "I guess I looked like someone else."

"The only other person you look like is Gloria," Bo said.

It took all Maddy's self-control not to exchange startled glances with Jon. The man hadn't meant anything serious by the remark; he didn't realize Jon really had been searching for Gloria. "Well, thank you."

Larry beamed.

"It was a whirlwind romance," Jon said. "And a big mistake."

"Don't you love each other?" Larry asked.

Maddy didn't know how to answer, but Jon saved her the trouble. "How do you define love?"

"How do *you* define it?" the counselor shot back.

"I have no idea," said Jon.

"Then why did you marry her?"

"Because she's gorgeous," Jon said. "Why are you marrying Gloria?"

Larry hesitated; he obviously hadn't expected for his own relationship to be dragged into the discussion. "She's the most charming, intelligent woman I've ever met."

"Have you known her long?" Maddy prodded.

"A short time," the therapist said. "You could say it was a whirlwind romance, too."

"Then how do you know it will last?" Jon asked.

"I'll admit, I don't have the world's best track record when it comes to marriage." Larry leaned back in his chair, the sun glinting off his balding head. He had a satisfied, well-fed air about him. "I dated my first wife all through high school, and we got along fine until we tied the knot. Then we fought like cats and dogs. My second wife and I worked together for over a year before we married, and it was a terrible mistake."

"So this time, you thought a quickie relationship couldn't hurt?" Jon said.

"Don't you think you're being kind of hard on him?" asked Frank.

"Marry in haste, repent at leisure," Jon replied.

Larry chuckled. "I don't think I'm going to regret anything."

No, because if they couldn't stop this marriage, he'd be dead. Maddy wondered what would happen if they told Larry the truth right now. *Your fiancée murdered her last three husbands, and Jon and I are here to drag her back to Texas to face trial.*

Then she caught sight of Blair, the first time she'd glimpsed him all morning. Apparently he'd caught up with his sleep after last night's patrol, because the man had a cocky edge to his stride as he circled the conference center watchfully.

The gun on his hip appeared bigger than ever.

Instinct told her that confessing the truth to Larry wouldn't change anything, even if he was willing to consider what Maddy and Jon said. As a therapist, he would be accustomed to mulling things over, discussing them, speculating about them and only taking action when the correct course became crystal clear.

That meant he would marry Gloria on schedule, probably giving the two of them the heave-ho first with plenty of help from Blair. By the time Larry got around to checking out his wife, it would be too late.

Maddy bit her lip and kept quiet.

Larry spent a few more minutes with the six of them, then moved on to another group. Maddy wondered if her parents' sessions had been this brief and superficial.

Judging by what her father was able to pay, she suspected they'd received more in-depth treatment. Besides, Larry hadn't been distracted at the time by his own imminent wedding.

After another half hour, they adjourned for lunch. The staff had prepared sacks of sandwiches and potato salad, which the guests ate at picnic tables on the patio. Gloria came to sit with Maddy, Jon and the Chings, but only nibbled at a small salad.

The woman had to keep her figure perfect, Maddy reflected. Gloria's appearance was her stock-in-trade; she couldn't afford to let it go. And a spectacular appearance it was. The morning's exercise had given a glow to her cheeks, and the bare-midriff blouse revealed a fabulously nipped-in waist.

Maddy had a hard time accepting that this woman could be so cold-blooded as to select and marry a wealthy man with the intention of killing him. It violated everything she believed about humanity and decency.

Gloria didn't act like a monster. She said "please" and "thank you" when she asked Lee to pass the salt; she laughed at Frank's jokes; when a strand of hair blew into her mouth, she commented wryly about eating split-end soup.

Everything about her seemed normal. No wonder Larry and that man in Texas had been caught off guard. Who would suspect such an attractive person of such ugly intentions?

Remembering Jon's suggestion from earlier, Maddy said, "Would you like to take a nature hike with us, Gloria?" Too late, she realized she would have to include the Chings, too, so she did.

Fortunately, the other couple declined, saying they wanted to continue their discussion about Lee going to work. Gloria mulled the prospect of a walk without much enthusiasm.

"I'm not big on nature," she said.

"Then maybe we should rehearse for the wedding." Better to spend time in each other's company, Maddy decided. "So you can show me what exactly you want me to do."

"Oh, we can do that tomorrow morning," Gloria said. "The wedding isn't until two o'clock. Besides, you probably already know the basic idea—you've been in weddings before, haven't you?"

"Tons." Half a dozen, at least, including her own father's. "I've got that take a step, pause, take a step routine down pat."

"Perfect." Gloria stretched. "I suppose a walk isn't a bad idea. Of course I'll have to take Blair with us. Larry's going to be tied up, and I'm not supposed to wander away alone."

The last thing they needed was Blair underfoot. "You wouldn't be alone—you'd be with us," Maddy said. "I don't see why you need—"

"Oh, Larry would have a fit." Gloria tossed her plastic salad bowl into a trash can. "Don't worry. Blair just blends into the background."

They'd have to do their best, Maddy reflected. But she didn't see how they were going to snatch Gloria under the circumstances, and it didn't take a genius to see that time was running out.

ONE OF THE STAFF MEMBERS handed out printed sheets as the guests finished eating.

Standing on his small platform, Larry explained over the microphone, "I know some of you are heading back to your trailers now, and others will do so after your nature walks. These are guidelines for breaking down your most intimate barriers. I'd like you to experiment with them."

Jon glanced impatiently at the sheet. Item Number One was to undress each other. Item Number Two was to apply lotion to each other. Item Number Three was to tell each other what you liked best about each other.

What a bunch of hogwash. A man and a woman didn't need that claptrap to connect sexually. All they had to do was follow their instincts.

Besides, if things went the way he planned, he and Maddy wouldn't be stripping each other or playing any of these games. They wouldn't be following their instincts either, unfortunately. They'd be hightailing it out of here with the camper, and he'd be on his way to becoming a whole lot richer than he'd ever imagined.

Jon allowed himself to experience a moment of regret at what he'd be giving up. He hadn't expected to like anything about his stay at this camp or his enforced closeness to Maddy, but surprisingly, he'd enjoyed himself more than he had in years.

Since losing the ranch five years before, he'd become an outcast by choice. He'd avoided staying in one place very long or forming any close friendships, and he hadn't realized he missed them.

Maddy, by contrast, had a knack for getting close to people. He could see how the others responded instinctively to her friendliness. Even that witch Gloria had been taken in by her.

Without his being aware of it, Maddy had become a point of reference. When he dressed, Jon found himself wondering what odd getup she would be wearing today. When he got hungry, he automatically looked for her to join him. When he had a cynical observation about their surroundings, he voiced it to Maddy.

This emotional dependency could be dangerous. It could threaten everything that mattered in his life. Trying to ignore the wrenching sensation in his gut, Jon told himself it was a good thing they'd be parting soon.

Having Blair along on the walk wasn't what he'd planned, but it might not be such a bad thing. At least he didn't have to worry about where Blair might be lurking. With a little luck, Jon could pull off his plans just as well this afternoon as he'd expected to do during tomorrow's wedding.

Maybe better.

As Maddy cleared their table and the Chings rose to go, Jon became aware of something else. Gloria was regarding him with a veiled hint of allure.

Was it possible she found him attractive? What irony! Jon had to admit, he liked flashy blondes, but not women with poison running through their veins. Besides, despite the superficial resemblance, Gloria could never hold a candle to Maddy.

On the other hand, her lustfulness might give him just the chance he needed to grab her.

"Let's head out," Jon announced as Blair, summoned by Gloria's discreet wave, joined them in front of the conference center. "I've been curious about the woods above here. Let's explore that way."

Blair shook his head. "Sorry, but the alarm system runs just behind the center. We have to stay inside that."

"Well, where can we go?" Maddy asked.

"Most of the people want to see the botanical garden." Gloria gestured toward an area on the far side of the conference center from the campgrounds. "It's full of native plants." She pronounced the words with distaste.

"Aren't the woods full of native plants?" Jon said.

"Exactly." Gloria slipped her arm through his. "Let's check out the real thing."

Her boldness reaffirmed Jon's impression of why the woman had agreed to join them. She must have decided to accept Maddy's earlier offer about sharing Jon's favors.

That certainly did present interesting possibilities. She might even walk into the motor home of her own free will.

"There's the path down by the ravine," Blair said. "Where you were walking this morning, Jon."

"It would give us a little privacy, at least." Gloria shot him a smile full of double meanings. "Away from all these busybodies."

As they stood talking, the other guests had dispersed, most toward the botanical gardens and a few toward their trailers. Jon doubted any of the others even suspected the existence of the ravine trail.

Larry himself was strolling toward the ailing couple's RV, as he'd promised. That ought to keep him tied up for a while.

With Gloria's hand on his arm, Jon led the way toward the woods. Blair and Maddy lagged behind; he could hear them exchange occasional desultory comments, but mostly they seemed absorbed in their own thoughts.

Jon's heartbeat sped up. The next half hour would be a tricky one, with a lot riding on it. And a lot of things that could go wrong.

He'd never worried much about messing up before; he wasn't a man given to excessive introspection. But there was a lot at stake here.

How would Maddy feel when it was over? She'd said that she wanted adventure, and she'd amazed him so far with her flexibility and daring. But she might not have bargained for quite as much adventure as she was likely to get.

Blair, of course, was the unknown quantity and the greatest risk. Split-second timing would be vital.

Gloria's hand ran lightly up Jon's arm as they left the pavement and stepped onto the earthen path. She probed his muscles as if checking a prize stallion.

"Your little bride is sweet," Gloria said. "And willing to share, you know."

Jon switched into the role of not-so-bright stud. "She'd better be. I don't let my wife call the shots."

"I guess not," murmured Gloria. "Any chance we could lose them?"

"You tell me," he said. "Blair's your pal, not mine."

Gloria peered over her shoulder. "They're walking slow. If we speed up, we could get ahead in no time. Do you have any idea where this trail comes out?"

"It loops back higher up," he said, glad he'd had a chance to check out the territory last night.

"Then we could make it to the motor home all by our lonesome," whispered Gloria.

"You don't think your fiancé might object?" Jon asked. He needed to be sure of Gloria's intentions. If he'd misunderstood, the result could be a nasty blowup.

"Oh, what's life without a little danger?" she teased. "It's my last day as a free woman, after all. But do you think your wife will barge in on us?"

Jon shrugged. "She's the one who set it up, isn't she? I think she'll get the picture. Maybe she and Blair can get a thing going."

Gloria whistled. "You *are* a tough hombre."

"The toughest," Jon said.

Under normal circumstances, he wouldn't have minded a tryst with a pretty woman, even a deadly one, so long as her vicious intentions weren't riveted on him. Today, however, Jon found Gloria completely unappealing.

He couldn't help contrasting her callousness to Maddy's concern for everyone she ran across. And the snakelike coldness of Gloria's eyes kept being replaced in his mind by the warm flash of Maddy's expression, honest and richly alive.

He wondered if he would ever meet anyone like Maddy again. Unlikely, since he doubted there *was* anyone else like her. But surely he'd meet some suitable woman, once he established himself back in Texas in his own business, ready to settle down at last with a comfortable bank account.

Gloria's leg kept bumping his as they walked, a suggestive movement that did nothing to soften Jon's dislike. Couldn't she sense his distaste? The woman noticed nothing but her own wants.

He realized that he'd been expecting the same kind of behavior from Maddy, to act spoiled and selfish, but that hadn't been what he'd seen. Sure, she had fancy clothes and a housekeeper and expensive cars, but none of that had affected the person she was at heart.

Okay, so you like her, Jon told himself grimly. *Now get over it.*

They'd increased their lead over Maddy and Blair to the point where he could no longer hear the other couple's voices. Silently, he thanked Maddy for playing along.

He forced himself to smile at Gloria and stroke her hair back from her temple. It felt dry and brittle, not silky like Maddy's. "Let's get a move on. The motor home's just beyond the head of the trail—"

Before he could finish, a scream ripped through the air behind them. Maddy's scream.

Adrenaline pumping through his body, Jon spun around and charged down the trail.

Chapter Ten

Maddy had deliberately lagged behind Jon and Gloria, hoping Blair wouldn't be alarmed. And, to her surprise, he'd matched her slow pace without complaint. Apparently he didn't believe Gloria was in any real danger.

She felt a twinge of guilt at deceiving the man. He might get fired as a result of this business. If so, she decided, she would send him some money later, maybe help find him a new job.

"Do you live here at the conference center, or is this just a temporary post?" she asked.

They were strolling toward the ravine, not yet at the point where the trail turned to run alongside it. "I live in Mountain View." Blair spoke with a soft voice when he wasn't barking orders. "That's a town about five miles from here."

"You work for Larry full-time?"

His gaze swept the woods, ever alert. "Nope, just when he needs me. One weekend a month, usually."

"What do you do in between?" Maddy asked.

Blair smiled. "I help out at the veterinary clinic where my fiancée works. I'm good with animals, and I sure do like being around my lady. She's a veterinarian herself."

"In Mountain View?" Maddy was making mental notes in case she later needed to play benefactor.

Blair nodded. "The owner's leaving, and we're trying to work out a deal to buy the clinic. I think we'll be able to swing it soon."

"Good for you." Apparently her help wouldn't be needed, after all.

They rounded the bend and walked alongside the gully. In daylight, Maddy could see broken branches and a muddy footprint marking the point a short distance ahead at which they'd descended to rescue Bitsy.

She wondered how far Jon and Gloria had gotten. It didn't seem possible that things could work out so easily. Gloria obviously had decided to accept Maddy's earlier suggestion of a rendezvous with Jon, and was cooperating in her own capture.

As for Blair, he showed not the slightest sign of anxiety that his charge was out of sight. But then, why should he? She was under Jon's protection.

Then Maddy sighted something that sent her heart skittering in her chest. Something black and yellow lay snagged on a branch where Bitsy had gotten stuck the night before.

Maddy recognized those colors. Its shape and size told her what it must be, because she'd seen Bitsy wearing it before.

It was a baseball cap. No harm in that, except that across the front was printed the legend: Armand Inc. 30th Anniversary.

Only a handful had been made. Thrilled at attending the party with Maddy last year, Bitsy had kept her hat as a souvenir. She sometimes tucked her hair under it when she didn't have time to fix her coiffure.

Last night in the dark, no one had noticed it, and Bitsy must have forgotten it in her distress. How like that nitwit to think acting discreet involved wearing a trench coat, tucking her hair into a cap—a black-and-yellow one at that—and sneaking through the brush carrying tons of luggage.

If Blair spotted it, he couldn't miss the fact that the cap was too clean to have been hanging there long. Having spotted Jon walking near here this morning, Blair would realize at once that something odd must be going on.

The Armand Inc. slogan would likely result in a phone call to her father and—well, things could get out of control quickly. Maddy had to distract Blair before he noticed the cap. Never mind that she might spoil Jon's opportunity with Gloria; he'd said he had another plan in reserve. At least this way they would survive to try again tomorrow.

Without giving it any more thought, Maddy screamed and ran forward.

Pounding footsteps proved that Blair had fallen for the trick. He raced after her, calling, "What is it?" They were past the cap before Maddy answered.

"A bee!" She shrieked again and waved one hand choppily as if fighting something off. "A huge one! Where is it? I'm allergic! I can die from those things!"

"Well, let's get out of here, then." Blair propelled her forward with a hand to the small of her back. "There's probably a hive around here somewhere."

"Is it a killer bee?" Maddy gasped. "Have they reached this far north yet?"

From farther along the trail, Jon pelted into sight with Gloria trailing behind. "What—?" He stopped abruptly. "Are you all right?"

"She was attacked by a killer bee," Blair said dryly.

"It scared me." Maddy hugged herself. "I'm allergic."

Three people were glaring as if she'd behaved like a child, and a bratty one at that. Maddy wished she could sink into the ravine and never return.

But no one had noticed the cap.

JON DIDN'T SPEAK to her until they had parted from Gloria and Blair. He walked slightly ahead of Maddy, not meeting her gaze, his back stiff with anger as he strode toward the motor home.

She thought of a dozen ways to explain what had happened, to argue her case and to point out the disaster that she'd averted, but they all left Maddy feeling at a disadvantage.

Why should she apologize? Why did he assume she was a scatterbrain who had panicked at the sight of a bee? Couldn't the man give her credit for some sense?

When they were inside the RV and Maddy had latched the door, Jon finally spoke. "This may be a game to you, Miss Beach Blanket, but you just cost me a bundle."

"I didn't cost you anything!" Maddy snapped. "You said you had another plan!"

"Much more difficult, and dangerous." He pulled off his boots and tossed them to the floor with a pair of angry thumps. "Today was perfect. Every detail. I almost had her."

"That's what *you* think." Maddy waited for his reaction. She didn't intend to plead; she wanted to throw at least a little doubt into his pompous self-assurance before explaining.

Jon ignored the comment. "Five more minutes, that's all I needed. She was coming here of her own choice."

"Thanks to the way I set things up," Maddy pointed out. "It was *my* idea for her to have an affair with you."

"You don't get it, do you?" Jon's eyes narrowed as he regarded her. "This isn't a game and nobody gets points for effort. The only thing that counts is results."

"And the only results you would have gotten is to have Blair shoot you in the back!" Maddy snapped.

For the first time, uncertainty clouded Jon's expression. Uncertainty, and something darker that she couldn't read. "What do you mean, he would have shot me in the back?"

"Well, I don't know that for sure." Maddy was glad she'd finally gotten the man's attention, but she hated having to backtrack.

"What exactly did Blair do?" She'd never seen Jon this taut before, his eyes narrow, jaw tense, skin tight across his forehead.

"Nothing." Before he could blow up again, Maddy lifted her hands in a conciliatory gesture. "Bitsy left a clue, a rather large one. Her hat. It's got Armand Inc. printed on it, and it's bright yellow and black. If Blair had seen it, he'd have known you were up to something last night."

Jon regarded her as if she were a light bulb burning rather dimly. "How's that?"

Maddy couldn't believe she had to point out the obvious. "I figured he would put two and two together. You wandering around in the predawn hours, now me distracting him while you hurry ahead with Gloria. He'd have connected it to her being in danger. At least I think he would."

Understanding spread across Jon's face, but he didn't look pleased. "So you screamed to protect me?"

She nodded.

He blew out an exasperated breath. "Maddy, don't ever protect me."

"But we're partners, aren't we?" Seeing his slow burn, she added, "I don't mean the money."

"I know you didn't." When his gaze met hers, she read frustration but something else—regret, maybe. Was he sorry he'd joined forces with her? But then he wouldn't even have made it this far.

"I had to make a split-second decision," she said.

The hard lines around his eyes softened. "I guess you meant well." He pulled Maddy down beside him. "Listen, I don't need your protection. Don't ever do anything like that again."

Sitting there so close they were almost touching, Maddy realized how little she knew Jon. This was the first time since they met that she'd seen him in action, and he'd become someone different from the man she knew—harder, meaner, less civilized.

She was used to guys who could be tamed at a snap of her fingers. Jon was made of something wilder and more primitive. Could he ever belong to a woman?

She could swear she'd seen flashes of tenderness in the way he gazed at her sometimes, but apparently that didn't mean much in a pinch. Or maybe she simply was the wrong woman.

Maddy wished that thought didn't hurt so much. She didn't want to fall in love with Jon. They had nothing in common; he certainly wouldn't fit into her life, and she had no intention of fitting into his.

Yet she wished she could tame him, just once.

She remembered the exercise sheet they'd been given, but Jon must have thrown it away. Besides, she no longer had the illusion that the vulnerable act of making love would mean anywhere near as much to Jon as it would to her.

You're always taking on impossible challenges, her father would have said. *Then you leave other people to pick up the pieces.*

In this case, Maddy reflected, the only person who would be picking up the pieces was her.

"What's your alternate plan?" she asked.

Jon leaned back wearily, tipping his hat onto his forehead. "Let's discuss this later. I didn't get much sleep last night, in case you'd forgotten, and I could use a rest."

Maddy felt the hairs rising on her neck. "You don't trust me, do you? You think I'm going to mess up again."

"I think the less anybody knows about my business, the better."

"You have a hard time with sharing, don't you?" Maddy bristled. "This is *our* business. If something goes wrong, don't I get in trouble, too?"

"You'll charm your way out of it, I have no doubt," Jon muttered. "Now why don't you go see if they've got a damn beauty salon or something around here. Get your nails done."

"My nails?" Maddy hadn't even noticed them today, she'd been so busy. Now that she looked, they *were* chipped and they *did* need a manicure, but she had no intention of letting Jon know that. He'd meant the remark as an insult. "If you want to take a nap, go ahead. Bitsy packed a couple of books, so I'll read."

"You'll talk," Jon said.

"Not to you!"

"You're talking now," he pointed out. "I want to sleep."

"So sleep!"

"I can't lie down. You're sitting on half the couch."

She was trying to frame a suitable reply when someone knocked at the door. Jon stifled a groan as Maddy went to answer.

It was Larry Wicker. "I heard something I thought I should check out," he said.

Maddy felt her heart freeze, and tiny ice crystals ping in sequence down her aorta. Blair must have seen the hat after all. Or Gloria had grown suspicious. Or...

"Come in," Jon said from behind her.

IN A WAY, Jon was glad for the interruption. Now that his initial frustration had ebbed, he was left with a host of mixed and unwelcome feelings about this afternoon's fiasco.

And about Maddy.

He kept wanting to finger her hair, slip an arm around her, touch her in some way. He knew that all he had to do was lie down and put his hat over his face, and she would go away, but he hated to shut out the sight of her rapidly changing expressions.

After tomorrow, he would never see her again. If it hadn't been for her overreaction to that cap, he and Maddy would be taking their last drive together right now.

He supposed he couldn't blame her. By Maddy's lights, she'd not only been right in what she'd done but resourceful, to boot.

It was almost a shame to give her up after they captured Gloria. Maddy could have been a useful partner, if she hadn't been Charles Armand's daughter and too rich to settle for life in a motor home.

He certainly had no intention of marrying her for her money. As far as Jon was concerned, that kind of action meant selling yourself into slavery. He had no illusions about the fact that, given too much power, Maddy Armand could turn into a tyrant.

So could he, Jon supposed. He needed a wife who stood up to him. A Texas woman, the kind with sensible clothes and short fingernails. Maybe long blond hair and bright blue eyes and a funny crinkle at the corners of her smile, though...

Nope, he couldn't ask for that. And he didn't intend to.

Still, he wasn't thrilled to see Larry Wicker prowling into their motor home. How much had the guy heard of their conversation? Silently, Jon cursed himself for not thinking about the fact that voices might carry.

"It sounded like you two were quarreling." Larry took a seat on a chair. "I'm afraid I've been somewhat neglectful this weekend. Scheduling my wedding during the event sounded like a terrific plan at the time, but maybe I've shortchanged my guests."

"We weren't quarreling about anything serious," Jon said.

"Quarrels are always serious." The short man scratched his beard and stretched out his legs. Jon half envied the fellow's ability to find adequate legroom in a motor home.

"We just don't love each other," Maddy said, to Jon's annoyance. He didn't want to get involved in a pseudointellectual discussion about feelings and relationships. "Isn't it possible, Larry, that some marriages just can't be saved?"

The counselor gave a wry laugh. "I'm the living proof, aren't I? Sometimes I wonder why I always pick the wrong women. Until now, anyway. We bring our own weaknesses as well as our strengths into marriage. The important thing is to be willing to work on ourselves."

Jon couldn't hide his skepticism any longer. "As far as I'm concerned, most people have more important things to work on than how to communicate with their wife. Like making a living."

"Well, I make a pretty good living, but I've never been happy alone." In this one-on-one setting, Larry had lost the pomposity that always irked Jon. "What's life really about, anyway? In the final analysis, it's about the people you love."

"You didn't answer my question," Maddy prompted. "Maybe our marriage can't be saved. Maybe we just need to move on."

"What makes you think the grass will be greener anywhere else?" responded Larry. "My point is that it's important to start where you are. Whatever you learn now will stand you in good stead later, even if you do decide to go ahead with an annulment."

Jon had to give that notion some thought. Maybe this craziness, being shut up in a motor home with Maddy, wasn't all a waste. Maybe dealing with her would help prepare him for the marriage he'd always expected to make someday. Except he was having a harder and harder time picturing himself walking down the aisle with some other woman.

That would change as soon as they parted company, he decided. Tomorrow at the latest.

"At least you folks don't have the problem I do, although I suppose most people wouldn't consider it a problem," Larry went on.

"What's that?" Maddy asked.

"Money."

"Money?" Jon had the impression the guy was a best-selling author with buckets of dinero. "You're hard up?"

Larry laughed. "No, I mean too much money. It attracts women for the wrong reason."

"But not Gloria?" Maddy probed.

Larry shook his head. "She didn't even know who I was. She was working as a hostess in Las Vegas. I'd come into town for a convention. Three other psychologists and I went out for dinner, and she seated us. The other guys were younger and handsomer, I don't mind admitting, but I'm the one she flirted with."

That wasn't hard to figure out, Jon thought. Larry had probably been speaking at the convention, and Gloria would have seen his name and accomplishments advertised. If he hadn't come into the restaurant, she might have found some other way to approach him, or else she'd have kept studying the market until some other millionaire wandered within grasp.

"Well, good luck tomorrow," Jon said. "You're taking a big step."

A glimmer of uncertainty showed on Larry's broad face. "Don't I know it. A guy in my position, I'm easy game for gold diggers. My alimony is already approaching the national debt. But I don't think Gloria's that type of gal."

No. She's a lot deadlier.

Jon was surprised to find he sympathized with Larry. Usually, he didn't have much patience with rich people. Maybe it was because the guy had actually begun to act like a human being this afternoon, or perhaps because he knew how close Larry was to getting himself murdered.

Or maybe just the fact that Larry had earned his money by his own honest effort, without ripping off anybody else.

They talked for a while longer about marriage, and the difficulty of predicting how people would react to changing circumstances, and the monkey wrenches that life throws into people's lives.

By the time Larry left, Jon was glad he'd come here to get Gloria. Not just for Larry's sake, but for that of the future patsies she would have offed before the law caught up with her.

He was even glad that he'd talked to Larry about marriage. Until now, Jon had imagined getting married as being like signing a contract. Once you drew up the terms, you knew where you stood, and you had only to do your part to succeed. Now he could see it was more like running a ranch. Sometimes you both had to deal with circumstances you hadn't foreseen.

After showing Larry out, Maddy hovered in the doorway as if expecting Jon to say something. But he hadn't been kidding; he *was* tired. And he needed his reflexes in tip-top shape for tomorrow.

"See you at dinner," he said and, stretching out, plopped his hat over his face.

THERE WAS NO beauty parlor at the conference center. Maddy found an empty picnic table near the motor home and sat down with a bottle of Fabulous Firehouse Red polish. Bitsy had also packed two shades of pink and one of olive green, ever hopeful of steering her employer into the outer reaches of fashion. This afternoon, Maddy was definitely in the mood for red.

The scent of nail polish remover overpowered pine as she set to work. She had to admit that Bitsy had spoiled her; what was a manicure without a soak, and a cuticle trim, and nail moisturizer? Well, she could rough it as well as the next woman.

Maddy quirked an inward smile. She didn't suppose Jon would consider this roughing it, sitting at a picnic table applying nail polish. But then, what did a man know about things like that, anyway?

After tomorrow, he would go his way and she'd go hers. She supposed this weekend would change a lot of things, for both of them. Jon would get a hundred thousand dollars, which ought to let him make a down payment on a ranch, if that was what he wanted.

As for herself, Maddy recalled her realization this morning that, until now, she had let her rebellion against being Daddy's little girl define her life. She could do anything she wished: go back into public relations, find an animal rescue center that *didn't* regard her as a meal ticket, even finish getting the college degree she'd valued so little that she quit halfway through senior year.

Then a new thought occurred to her, something that tilted her world on its axis. She didn't want to work in an office or on a schedule. She wanted to share her love of life and her caring directly with others.

This was the scary part: even if she could bring herself to get a degree in psychology, she didn't want to counsel somebody and then go home and eat a frozen dinner. She wanted little bodies to cuddle, sleepy voices calling her name, small souls growing up under her guidance.

Good heavens, she wanted to be a mother!

Maddy knocked over the bottle of polish and had to grab it to keep more than a few drops from spilling onto the table. A mother? But that more or less required a father, didn't it? She supposed women these days didn't always go by the rules, but Maddy felt instinctively that she needed a partner to take care of boring details like discipline.

Of course, she wouldn't want to get tied down for the rest of her life with laundry and housework. But when you were an heiress, the laundry and the housework didn't have to be part of the bargain.

Maddy was mulling this revelation about herself when two people emerged from the luxury trailer parked off to her right. From their swimsuits, it was a safe guess they were headed for the spa.

Surprised, Maddy recognized the pair as Bo and Sarita Mendez. Gone were the ramrod-stiff spines and cold distances. Bo had his arm wrapped around his wife's waist, and she bumped against him teasingly as they walked.

They waved to Maddy and she waved back, which also had the helpful effect of drying her nails. One more coat and she'd be finished.

Bo and Sarita must have followed Larry's exercise list, she realized as she smoothed on more polish with long, quick strokes. Getting away from their daily pressures and short-circuiting the lawyerly debates had obviously restored their pleasure in being together.

With a sigh, Maddy wondered what it would be like to meet a man who would love her for herself. Someone tall and strong, like Jon, but not so grumpy. Independent, to a degree, and self-reliant. Also sophisticated, but not so rigid that he couldn't wear jeans once in a while.

For the first time, she felt a surge of excitement at what the future might bring. As soon as she and Jon parted ways tomorrow, she was going to start looking for Mr. Right.

Chapter Eleven

Jon awoke to a twilight rich with the scent of hickory coals and barbecuing burgers. It was exactly the smell to which a man wanted to awaken when he had a Texas-size appetite.

Prodding the Stetson off his face, he picked up the small noises of Maddy moving around in the bathroom. Well, "moving around" might be an exaggeration; in that tiny space, about all a person could do was twitch vigorously. But she was definitely in there, probably fixing a face that undoubtedly had no need of fixing.

If not for Maddy's unnecessary attempt to protect him, Jon reflected, he would now be roaring along the Interstate, hell-bent for Arizona, with Gloria cussing him out from the rear of the motor home. Maddy would be safely home with Batsy Bitsy and a houseful of designer clothes.

He didn't believe things always worked out for the best. He wasn't even sure they sometimes worked out for the best. But Jon had to admit he was looking forward to a hearty dinner instead of a sandwich on the lam.

He was rinsing his face in the kitchen sink when Maddy emerged in a blare of silver and scarlet. She wore some kind of pants outfit that resembled a moon suit except it didn't cover her face. As Jon finished drying his face on a towel, he observed that the shiny silver fabric clung to her waist, and the scooped neck revealed the tantalizingly round tops of her breasts.

Bright red fingernails and lipstick, and a tawny mane rioting across her shoulders completed the image of a femme fatale, only not quite as fatale as Gloria.

Involuntarily, Jon whistled.

"I don't believe it!" Maddy planted her hands on her hips. "You actually approve?"

Jon finger-combed his hair and set his hat in place. "I'm not dead yet, honey."

A smile lit up her face. "Well, cowboy, care to have dinner?"

"I thought you'd never ask." He reached past her and opened the door, holding it for her. She had to brush against him to pass, a fact that didn't go unnoticed by one single inch of Jon's physique.

He caught a whiff of lily of the valley as she went by, an old-fashioned fragrance that reminded Jon of turn-of-the-century carriages and ladies in long dresses. Ladies who leaned out the windows above the saloon, and showed a man about the same amount of chest as he was observing now, with a promise of more to come.

There would be no more to come in this case, however. Jon didn't waste time on what other people might consider scruples, but he knew better than to risk his future on a little indulgence. Or a major indulgence.

They found the party already in full swing, with couples spilling through the lobby and onto the patio. Even the recorded country music and the scent of charcoal grilling couldn't account for the suddenly relaxed air with which the people danced and sauntered arm-in-arm.

Jon supposed Larry's sensual exercises must have worked. He didn't put much store in love-by-numbers, but any time a man and a woman took their clothes off, or better yet took each others' clothes off, something was likely to happen.

Even the graying Herb and Anne Stowe were waltzing with gusto. The fact that their dance bore no resemblance to the two-four beat hardly mattered.

With his hand on her waist, Jon steered Maddy to the buffet table set up on the patio. He was surprised that they would serve food outside, and even more surprised to find there weren't any flies buzzing around. Chalk one up for the dry California climate, he supposed.

He'd take those monstrous Texas horseflies any time. Maybe not with his food, though.

Jon and Maddy wolfed down their hamburgers with equally hearty appetites. He tried not to pay much attention to her, but that was impossible, the way the silver Mylar kept picking up bits of lantern light and twinkling at him.

Gone was yesterday's stubborn girl in in-line skates, and the clown stumbling around last night in shoes five sizes too large. Tonight Maddy had become a sophisticated lady, aglow from her golden hair down to a pair of glittery high-heeled sandals.

She's the most beautiful woman I've ever seen.

Jon caught himself. *Beautiful and rich. Don't forget that. Charles Armand's daughter. Look but don't touch.*

Beyond her, he glimpsed Larry dancing with Gloria on an elevated level of the patio. The therapist radiated happiness.

In contrast to her fiancé's subdued gray suit, Gloria's outfit smacked you in the eye. Her black net gown revealed a gold bikini underneath, or at least, that's what it resembled to Jon. The peekaboo effect seemed more cheesy than sexy to him, but it obviously appealed to Larry.

He had to admit that, by contrast, Maddy had good taste. A silver jumpsuit might not be what Grace Kelly would have worn in one of her movies, but it combined a space-age effect with pure classical elegance.

Since when had he become a fashion critic? Jon wondered. The moonlight must be affecting him, or maybe it was the physical satisfaction of a much-needed nap followed by a man-style dinner. Surely it couldn't be Maddy herself, that crazy, spoiled, unpredictable female who might yet land him in the poorhouse, or jail.

"Care to dance?" he asked.

"You dance?" Maddy lifted an eyebrow.

Where did she think he'd been raised, in a barn? "People dance in Texas," Jon said. "Believe it or not."

"But you're a cowboy," she said.

"Try me."

"I intend to."

They stood up, only to discover a line dance was next on the playlist. Other guests pulled them apart and in a moment Jon could barely see Maddy as the lines whirled and marched in step.

He knew the moves; he'd learned everything from ballroom steps to square dancing at the community center in Vaughan's Gap. Back then, he'd preferred the less-intimate numbers because they meant he didn't have to snuggle up to a girl who had something even more intimate in mind. After which, Jon knew, her Daddy was likely to come after him with a shotgun.

He hadn't been the marrying kind then and he wasn't now. At least not until he'd made his small fortune and could find the right kind of woman.

But tonight, he didn't want the right kind of woman. He wanted to dance with Maddy.

It was a relief when the music changed into something slower and more sultry. Maddy appeared before him, mysterious in the moonlight, and Jon drew her away from the others onto a corner of the patio.

"Having fun?" she murmured.

"I am now." He slipped one arm around her waist and cupped her hand. Next to him, she felt small and warm, and she smelled wonderful.

He had expected a battle for the lead, but Maddy molded herself against him, her cheek to his chest, and followed his steps as if they were joined at the hip. Which, more and more, they were.

The woman possessed an instinctive sensuality, emphasized by starlight and silver. She felt like a natural extension of Jon as they curved a path through the semidarkness.

The other people faded away; he didn't know if they'd left, or were dancing somewhere else, or had fallen into some alternate reality. Or maybe it was he and Maddy who had entered another realm.

It was a realm in which they understood each other without speaking; in which, the moment he wanted it, she reached up and wrapped her arms around his neck; in which he knew that he could catch her hips and he would feel the life force bursting through her, and into him.

Jon hesitated, his breath coming ragged. "What's wrong?" Maddy asked.

"Too much," he said.

She let out a long sigh. "I guess we're tempting fate, aren't we?"

"Fate and a whole lot of other things," he said.

They separated, cool air rushing between them. Jon felt a wave of longing so intense he nearly grabbed Maddy and pulled her back against him. He could not afford to make love to this woman. It went against every instinct for self-preservation, every shred of good judgment.

Staff members provided a welcome diversion. From a side door, two helpers emerged with a huge wedding cake. "We thought we'd give you a little preview of tomorrow!" Larry called out. "You might call it having our cake and eating it too!"

Candles glimmered in the twilight. Jon caught Maddy's hand and led her toward the others.

Close call, he thought. Years of practicing self-restraint in every aspect of his life had come to the rescue.

But what about Maddy? Where had she found the strength to resist?

He glanced at her face, but in the dimness could tell nothing. She was staring wistfully at the cake, like a child peering into a lighted window at Christmas.

Was it possible there might be something that even an heiress wanted but couldn't have? Jon shrugged off the thought. If so, it was none of his business.

MADDY DIDN'T KNOW what had come over her tonight. It wasn't like that mad lustfulness she'd felt the first time she met Jon, or again in the trailer.

This was deeper and far more threatening to her emotional health. Jon wasn't the kind of man you could count on. Tomorrow he would go his own way; or, if matters got delayed somehow, then in another day or week or month.

He wouldn't stay. And for the first time in her life, Maddy was ready for something beyond fun and games.

Maybe it had to do with her discovery that she wanted children. Maybe it was some primal instinct honed zillions of years ago as women stomped berries into wine with their bare feet and waited for their men to come home dragging mastodon chops. She wanted a partner, someone she could count on.

Definitely not a cowboy who would be driving off into the sunset any minute now.

A wave of envy swept over Maddy for the happy couples around them, laughing like newlyweds as they shared cake and a renewed sense of togetherness. They'd made their commitment; most had homes and children already. She had never coveted anyone else's life before, but she did now.

How would Jon react if he found out who Maddy really was? He wanted money, enough to risk his life for it, but he also valued his independence. Either way, it wouldn't help; he'd either marry her because she was rich, which would never work, or he'd reject her because her wealth threatened him.

You can't pretend the money doesn't exist, her father had lectured once. *It's a fact, Maddy. You are who you are because of it, whether you admit it or not. And how other people see you is shaped by it.*

But not this weekend. For once, she'd arrived simply as herself. Maddy released a small sigh, wishing it could last. The other couples actually liked her for herself. And Jon, that arrogant man with the soul of a mule, had taken her in his arms and nearly made love to her while dancing.

Maybe things could work out between them; she allowed herself a shred of hope. Once Jon delivered Gloria to Texas, he and Maddy could stay in touch. Things might develop, if she was willing to be flexible.

She supposed marrying Jon would mean living on a dusty ranch that smelled of cow poop and echoed with chickens clucking. She'd have to wear jeans and leather boots, bounce around on a horse and figure out how to cook hamburgers.

Well, as long as Jon didn't expect her to pluck the chickens, she supposed she could manage.

Maddy brought herself up with a start as Jon handed her a plastic glass full of champagne and the bubbles began fizzing up her nose. Ah, champagne. Ah, cake with icing, and fancy clothes and people socializing. Ah, civilization.

Life as a cowgirl might be fun for a while, but they'd need their own airplane so she could pop into Dallas to shop and get her hair done. And a chef, because she was going to get tired of hamburgers awfully fast. And maybe Bitsy to do her nails.

It wouldn't work. The whole idea was insane. Tomorrow, Maddy knew, she had better be prepared to say "adios, Jon Everett," and mean it.

When everyone had been served champagne, the toasts began. To Larry and Gloria. To the Magical Marital Weekend. To all of us. To Blair, standing self-consciously at one side, for protecting us. To our children, our friends, our jobs, the future.

By this time, people were getting tipsy and Herb Stowe had begun toasting every member of his Elks Lodge by name. Jon caught Maddy's hand and, barely giving her time to deposit her glass on a table, pulled her away.

"We need our sleep," he growled, rattling a sheet of paper as they exited the lobby. "Here's the agenda for tomorrow."

Maddy squinted at it with the help of a spotlight in front of the conference center. Brunch would be followed by a spiritual renewal ceremony. Free time was scheduled while members of the wedding party rehearsed; then came the wedding itself, and then a reception-farewell party.

"You haven't told me your plan," Maddy said.

"It can wait until morning." Jon released her arm, leaving her to trot alongside as he strode toward the motor home.

"Why?"

"I haven't finalized the details yet."

"You still don't trust me."

He swung around to face her so abruptly that Maddy nearly collided with him. "Let's not forget one thing. This is my project. I'm the one responsible for capturing Gloria. I'm also the one with the experience. It's time you trusted *me* a little, Maddy."

"How were you planning to get me home afterward?" she demanded. "You haven't even told me that."

From the exasperation on Jon's face, she could see that her transportation wasn't among his highest priorities. "I'll leave you in a safe place. You can call your roommate from there."

"Gee, thanks," Maddy muttered. "What a delightful ending to a fabulous weekend."

"You chose to stay of your own free will." Jon resumed his march toward the RV. After a moment's hesitation, Maddy hurried after him, wobbling along on her high heels.

She wanted to argue, but couldn't. She *had* wanted to stay, because she needed adventure. She just hadn't thought much about what that adventure might lead to.

As they filed into the motor home, Maddy wondered what it would be like to make love to Jon, even just once. The thought scared her and thrilled her at the same time.

Determined not to let herself dwell on the impossible, she snatched her teddy bear nightgown from the closet and headed for the bathroom.

"Why do you wear that?" Jon asked.

"What, this?" Maddy brandished the garment. "You mean as opposed to wearing nothing, or as opposed to some slinky black number?"

"Either." Jon tossed his hat onto a hook and began unbuttoning his shirt.

"Because I like it," Maddy said. "Why? What do you think I should wear?"

"Something that makes you look like a woman instead of a little girl," Jon remarked. He'd undone three buttons, revealing a broad chest matted with light brown hair.

"Why should you care?" Maddy felt vaguely affronted, but she wasn't sure if it was because he had criticized her sleep shirt or because he was undressing right in front of her, as if she didn't matter.

"Just a tip for the future," he said. "One of these days you're going to meet a man you can't twist around your little finger, Maddy."

"Like you?" Defiantly, she unhooked the belt of her jumpsuit. No reason to squirm around in that tiny bathroom. If he felt safe enough to undress before her eyes, she could do the same to him.

"Goes without saying." He unbuttoned his cuffs and pulled the shirttails out of his jeans.

"Maybe I don't care." Maddy tossed the belt aside and kicked off her high-heeled sandals. "I like doing things my own way."

"Then the only man you'll end up with is some wimp who doesn't mind getting bossed around." Pulling off the shirt, he tossed it into a corner. The only source of light, a small lamp by the couch, played gently across his glistening skin.

"Or a guy who isn't threatened by my independence." With only a moment's hesitation, Maddy unzipped the front of her jumpsuit.

"Threatened?" Jon cocked a knowing smile at her. "We'll see who's threatened." He removed his belt and tossed it in the direction of the shirt.

Maddy unhooked the front of her bra and then gave in to the instinct to yawn. She'd only meant to give Jon a peeka-boo effect, but the bra had a mind of its own, flopping open and letting the cool air play across her breasts. "Oops."

A bemused expression crossed Jon's face. Maddy had the impression they were playing a grown-up version of First One Who Blinks Loses. "I intimidate you, don't I?"

"You?" Maddy resisted the urge to yank her jumpsuit shut. "Not at all."

"Not even when I do this?" Jeans riding low on his hips, Jon stepped across the small space and ran the palms of his hands across her nipples.

Heat poured into Maddy's core and seared all the way up to her cheeks. "Doesn't bother me." The words weren't enough, she could see as Jon lifted his hands away with a grin, so she leaned forward and brushed her breasts across his bare torso. "How's that?"

"Higher," said Jon.

"What?"

"Like this." He scooped her into his arms, mouth coming down hard on hers, his chest crushing hers. Maddy tried to push herself away, but her body refused to obey.

She wanted to experience, just for a moment, the pleasure of yielding to his onslaught. No one had ever claimed her this way before, tilting her head to make their mouths fit better, then reaching down and catching her back and bringing her against him until she could feel his full arousal.

Maddy didn't want to give in to Jon. She didn't want to be dominated, or manipulated, or taken in this primitive masculine way. She didn't want to relinquish control.

But she had to, not because of Jon, but because of herself. She chose to give away her independence, just this once. She chose to cling tightly as he carried her to the couch, and chose to be lowered beneath him as his tongue plundered the recesses of her mouth.

When he pulled off her jumpsuit and tossed it into a heap, Maddy's heart cheered. She was already peeling down his jeans, contrary to reason and good judgment, opening herself to even more of his totally unacceptable actions.

Any minute now, she would come up with an irrefutable objection, and he would give an exasperated sigh and pull away.

"What are you doing?" she asked, realizing he had indeed pulled away and was retrieving something from behind the couch.

"Putting on my battle gear," he murmured, disposing of the foil packet the same way he had discarded her jumpsuit.

"You won't be needing that," Maddy said, watching in fascination as he slipped on the condom.

"Call it a whim," he said, and leaned over her again. "Where were we?"

"You win," she said.

"Excuse me?"

"This game." Maddy knew she wasn't making sense, but the reality of him made her breath catch in her throat. He was huge, all muscles and tawny power and white teeth flashing with laughter. "You can quit now."

"I'm not quite done," he said, and drew his tongue over her breasts.

Maddy gasped, and arched toward him. Jon explored lower, raising strokes of fire along her skin. Maddy's hands fluttered along his back and buttocks as she finally accepted that they had passed the point of no return.

Their mouths joined as he drove into her, a double assault on her senses that threw Maddy onto a plane of sheer ecstasy. She couldn't hold back, couldn't regulate herself, could only match his eager thrusts with her own and cry out helplessly as wave after wave of pure joy washed over her.

But Jon still wasn't finished. Not until he'd shifted her into a half-sitting position and enjoyed her that way, and pulled her on top of him and stimulated her to move along his shaft with increasing rapidity.

The peak of intensity caught Maddy by surprise. She wanted more, she didn't want this to end, and it didn't end, it went on and on as he flipped her and united them over and over, like a wild beast. A caveman. A creature beyond anything she had known, or ever would again.

Only as they lay together afterward, their breathing gradually subsiding, did Maddy become aware of the sheen of perspiration covering their bodies. Oddly, she had no interest in showering, or putting on her teddy bear nightgown, or doing any of the other little acts that would announce she was retreating into herself.

She snuggled against Jon, and wished the night would never end.

HE DIDN'T KNOW what had come over him. That maddening woman had provoked him too far, and he hadn't been able to think about scruples or self-preservation or anything else.

Oh, hell, Jon didn't give a damn about scruples. But he didn't understand this surge of protectiveness he felt, and he didn't like it.

What he and Maddy had shared went beyond anything that had happened to Jon before. He knew it was more than physical. He cared about her, and wanted her to belong to him, and wanted to prove to her and to himself that he didn't really care at all.

He had come to believe over the years that life teaches cruel lessons, and those who don't learn them suffer the most. The first lesson he had learned was that he and people like Maddy had nothing in common.

They might make each other happy for a short time, but the breakup would be even more devastating when it came. And it surely would come.

The most sensible thing would be to go on as they'd planned—capture Gloria, and say goodbye. Maddy was expecting it. And there was more at stake than a little disappointment on her part: his future, his past, everything he believed in. Jon couldn't afford to change the game plan now.

And yet...

"It's simple," he forced himself to say, before he could change his mind.

"What?"

"The plan for tomorrow." He could feel her stirring beside him, curiosity rousing her from sleepiness. "You're going to take Gloria's place."

"What?"

He told her the rest. She would join Gloria in her dressing room before the wedding, as early as possible.

"Then you persuade her to come back to the motor home," Jon said. "Use your judgment."

Maddy blinked, not fully awake. "Why should she come back to the motor home?"

"That's the tricky part," Jon admitted. "You'll have to size up the situation. Either persuade her to come with you, on the pretext of looking at something, or pretend to injure yourself and send her to fetch something for you, or talk her into wanting one last fling with your virile husband before she ties the knot. Whatever works."

Maddy groaned. "I'm terrible at lying."

"I have faith in you."

"That's a change."

"Lots of things have changed," he said, and hated himself for implying more than he meant to deliver.

"I'll try," she said hesitantly. "Then what?"

"I grab Gloria," he said. "If you're here with her, we take off. Otherwise, you put on her dress and walk down the aisle in her place. Let's hope she's wearing a veil."

Maddy propped herself on one elbow. "And when Larry discovers I'm not his fiancée?"

"You tell him Gloria thought it was a great joke, because the two of you look like sisters. Promise to go swap clothes with her. Instead, change into your street clothes and hightail it for the motor home."

"What about Blair?" She didn't miss much, Jon had to concede.

"With luck, he won't get suspicious until it's too late," he said. "Otherwise, bring him along and I'll tell him the truth about Gloria and offer to share the reward. I have a feeling he'd go for it."

She nodded sleepily. "You're probably right."

Her head drifted down until her cheek rested against Jon's shoulder. He could feel her breathing grow softer and more regular.

He knew he'd better enjoy the sight now. After tomorrow, he would never see her again.

Chapter Twelve

Maddy found it hard to eat brunch the next morning, even though the staff had fixed a banquet of sausage and eggs, fresh fruit and muffins.

How could Jon sit so calmly beside her, chatting with the other couples and scarcely appearing to notice her? This morning, he'd been cheery but distant, not like any man she'd known before.

Maddy didn't jump into bed with men lightly, but she'd taken her share of lovers in thirty years. Her first serious boyfriend, she'd discovered, was attracted by her looks and her money, and couldn't have cared less about what lay behind the blond hair and fat wallet.

Getting over her hurt, she'd purposely chosen as her next romance a more sophisticated man who had plenty of money and plenty of women. He also had plenty of ego, she'd discovered in short order.

Then had come Bobby, a man she'd nearly married except that he always said yes to her father and got a pained expression whenever Maddy did something impulsive. Her next boyfriend had agreed to everything she wanted, and bored the spirits out of her.

She'd never met anyone like Jon before. He was the kind of man that a woman dreamed about, the tough guy from another world whom she couldn't keep but never forgot.

Maddy didn't want to lose a man she would never forget. She either wanted to keep him, or to forget him.

Well, there wasn't much she could do about it. She'd agreed to the plan, and after the way she'd insisted he could trust her, she could hardly back out now.

Glancing at the head of the table, where Gloria sat picking at her breakfast beside Larry, Maddy experienced a pang of uncertainty. What if Jon was wrong? What if Gloria hadn't killed her husband, and now Larry's wedding day would be wrongfully destroyed?

You're just making excuses. In your heart, you know she did it.

Putting together Gloria's comments about men and marriage, Maddy knew this was no delirious bride marrying the man of her dreams. This was a calculating fiend in feminine disguise.

Maddy owed Larry something, for her parents' sake. And she owed Jon something because she'd promised it. And he didn't owe her anything; they both agreed on that.

Maddy hated being fair. She would soldier through today as planned, but that didn't mean she had to stay out of Jon's way forever. She might just turn up under his nose sometime when he least expected it.

And drive him utterly crazy. Biting back a smile at the thought, Maddy told herself she would make Jon regret ever planning to leave her. Then they'd share a good laugh about it.

As for that ranch in Texas, with enough money, it could be made livable. A Jacuzzi and a home entertainment center would work wonders.

Larry's announcement that the Spiritual Enhancement Service was about to begin broke into Maddy's thoughts. She arose with the others and went onto the patio.

A glorious summer day was breaking over the mountains, arriving late due to the long shadows of the peaks. From their twitters, the birds were only now awakening, and tiny stirrings in the underbrush indicated that chipmunks and squirrels hadn't yet finished their nocturnal foraging.

Maddy's sense of oneness with nature was disturbed by the sight of Gloria and Larry donning white robes and ascending the highest platform. Surely they hadn't decided to get married now and skip the formal wedding? That would foul up everything.

Even when they began quoting from an inspirational essay, and she realized this was no marriage ceremony, Maddy's pulse didn't entirely return to normal.

Until now, she hadn't allowed herself to dwell on the things that could go wrong with their plan. It wasn't in Maddy's personality to worry.

But what Jon had proposed was both audacious and contrary to everything Maddy had been taught. Despite her small rebellions over the years, she'd never deliberately offended people or hurt anyone. Kidnapping a bride moments before her wedding and humiliating the groom at the altar might be considered more than a minor breach of etiquette.

You aren't being rude, you're saving Larry's life.

She knew what her father would say. He would tell her to call the police and let them handle the matter. Never mind that Gloria might skip bail, and would certainly fight extradition, and that Jon might never collect his bounty. Never mind whether the police ignored the warning altogether, or arrived too late for Larry's survival. It wasn't her problem, Daddy would say.

But it was. Hers and Jon's. She owed him this much. As for what he owed her, Maddy told herself he didn't owe her anything that wasn't in his heart. She would have given odds, however, that there was more in his heart than he was willing to admit.

She would just take today one step at a time, and somehow get through it.

"O SPIRIT OF THE mountains, fill us with your nobility. Lift us from the valley of our self-indulgence, up to the peak of human sharing."

Jon had a notion Larry must have written this service himself. It had a 1970's feel-good tone to it that struck him as contrived.

Jon didn't need fancy phrases to experience the grandeur of nature. There was more sense of connectedness in grooming a horse or milking a cow than in all the grandiose gestures, white robes and spiritual enhancement ceremonies ever conducted.

It was particularly ironic to see Gloria pretending an enlightenment that she couldn't even conceive of. The woman gave new dimension to the word *phony*.

And what about him, Jon Everett, Mr. Every Man For Himself?

He hadn't missed the flicker of disappointment on Maddy's face this morning when he greeted her with impersonal courtesy instead of tenderness. She deserved better.

And she would get better. From some fellow of her own background, not from Jon.

His main concern now had to be whether he could trust her, and whether the elements of his plan would come together. This business was more complicated than Maddy imagined, and she had to perform her part to perfection.

Nothing ever goes the way it's supposed to.

That was one thing he'd learned on the range, when a simple morning ride might turn into a battle to save a lamb from a coiled rattlesnake before it could strike.

Always bring your gun.

It waited in the glove compartment of the motor home, loaded and ready. He hoped he would never have to use it on a human being. He hadn't even liked having to shoot the rattlesnake.

Never look back.

That was going to be the tricky part. Even now, Jon knew he was looking back with regret to his parents' lost ranch and broken dreams. Would he feel the same way about Maddy in years to come?

The ceremony ended at last. Jon and Maddy joined a handful of people who lingered as the other guests returned to their motor homes.

The efficient staff had cleared away breakfast and turned the lobby into a churchlike sanctuary. With some heavy rearranging, the potted plants formed a backdrop to rows of seats and a broad center aisle.

A man Jon hadn't seen before joined Larry and Gloria. Thin and middle-aged, the fellow wore glasses and a dark suit and carried a Bible. Apparently they'd lassoed a minister from the nearest town.

What an unholy service this would be, uniting victim and would-be murderess, Jon reflected. He remembered the grief on the faces of Sid Owens's children after their father's death. There was more than one score to settle today.

Maddy paused beside him, her expression vacillating between eagerness and anxiety. "Let's just tell him," she said.

"What?" The word came out as a growl.

"Larry's a grown man. He can protect himself if we tell the truth," she said.

"You're backing out?" He couldn't believe she would do this.

"No. It's just an idea." Maddy's worried gaze met Jon's angry one. "Somebody could get hurt. Why go through with it? Just for the money?"

"For a lot of reasons." He kept his voice low, watching as the figures before them conferred with the minister. Blair waited near them, a half smile playing about his mouth.

"I've been thinking," Maddy admitted. "I promised to do this, and I will. But we don't have to. If you need money, I know where you can get a good job. Security work or whatever you want. I have some friends who could arrange it.''

Jon felt his jaw tighten. He would work in the mines or dig ditches before he would accept a favor, even indirectly, from Charles Armand. ''No, thanks.''

''That's your problem—you're too proud!'' Maddy snapped. ''If you could rein in your ego enough to get along with people, you could have made plenty of money by now!''

''Is that so?'' He fought against the instinct to storm at her, or stalk away. They had to avoid attracting attention at all costs.

''My father says that people who make the right choices get ahead,'' Maddy went on. ''If you don't, then you have no one to blame but yourself.''

''Are you with me today, or against me?'' He didn't have to struggle to keep the words low-keyed this time; they came out that way. Quiet and deadly.

Maddy released a long breath. ''I just thought—I'm only trying to—oh, Jon...''

Before she could continue, Gloria waved at them. ''We're ready to start!''

''Here goes nothing,'' muttered Maddy, and headed for the bridal party.

She wouldn't back out, Jon felt certain. Almost certain.

He, at least, no longer had any doubts. *People who make the right choices get ahead. If you don't, you have no one to blame but yourself.*

There was Charles Armand's philosophy in a nutshell, and his daughter believed it, too.

With an unexpected sense of relief about the choices that he, too, was making, Jon retreated to sit in the back row and watch the rehearsal.

He couldn't relax, however. The first thing that struck him was the realization that Blair had been asked to serve as best man.

Why didn't a famous man like Larry Wicker have a friend to serve in that capacity? Not that Jon cared about the state of Larry's social life. What bothered him was that he hadn't counted on Blair being part of the ceremony, and he hated change, even one that might prove beneficial. It reminded him of how many things could go awry.

On the other hand, tied up with the wedding, Blair would be unable to patrol the grounds, which meant Maddy and Gloria could move around unobserved. It was perfect. Or was it?

Restlessly, he swung from his seat and slipped outside. The most frightening possibility was that Larry might have added a new guard to take Blair's place.

No one stirred in front of the building. Apparently the guests had retreated to change into more formal clothing, and Jon didn't see any guard. He also didn't spot any unfamiliar vehicles, which was a good sign, because a new guard would have had to drive here in something.

Either Larry had dismissed his concerns about the threat to Gloria's safety, or figured even a pesky ex-boyfriend wouldn't crash a wedding ceremony. And, of course, Blair would be standing right by the altar in case of need.

Slightly reassured, Jon ducked into the building again. He checked his watch. It was half past eleven, with the wedding scheduled to start at one. An hour and a half to go.

Back in the lobby, the wedding party had begun the rehearsal. Lingering in the obscurity of a potted palm, Jon observed without being seen.

Larry and Blair stood by the altar, the groom grinning foolishly. The man actually believed Gloria had fallen in love with him and that they would lead a happy life together. How could he be so blind? Even Jon caught subtle clues in her body language, more in what she *didn't* do than in what she did. She never spontaneously touched her fiancé; never gazed at him admiringly when no one was noticing, never praised him to others, never radiated joy as he was doing now.

The smile that stretched across her face as she waited at the head of the aisle had a studied hardness to it. But she *was* beautiful. No, not quite beautiful but striking, Jon reflected. Kind of like that rattlesnake he'd shot.

A staff member flipped a switch on a tape deck, and a familiar march poured out. At a quirk of the minister's eyebrow, Maddy stepped from beside Gloria, where she'd been shielded from Jon's view. Clutching a mock bouquet of ruffled napkins, she moved with stately slowness toward the waiting men.

For a moment her miniskirt and light pink blouse faded and he saw her gowned in white, as she would be in another hour and a half. Tiny spurts of energy kept her figure animated even as she paced herself, and about halfway down she made a subtly self-deprecatory shrug as if to say, "Don't anybody laugh, I'm doing my best."

He wondered how he had imagined anyone could mistake her for Gloria, even beneath a veil. She'd be spotted the minute she appeared.

Or was he simply so attuned to her that he, and he alone, would notice the substitution? But, of course, he wouldn't be here.

Maddy had almost reached the altar. Staring at her back, Jon continued to visualize her in white. She would make a beautiful bride, wouldn't she?

Someone else's bride. Some day Maddy would indeed get married, and it wouldn't be to Jon. What would the man be like? Some patsy picked out by her father? A renegade with long hair and in-line skates?

By then, maybe Jon would be married himself, to that Texas woman he'd been vaguely imagining. A sturdy lady with a practical nature. But he couldn't quite see her. For some reason, the only face he could imagine beneath a white veil was Maddy's.

Now it was Gloria's turn to march. How could anyone miss the arrogance in her step? She was an actress playing a part mastered long ago. One that she would, if no one stopped her, probably play again.

With a grimace, Jon headed back to the RV. There were a few things he needed to get ready.

Now, HOW AM I going to pull this off?

As soon as the rehearsal ended, it dawned on Maddy that the burden had fallen onto her shoulders. Between now and two o'clock, she had to lure Gloria to the motor home, but she couldn't be too obvious about it.

"Are you in a hurry to get dressed?" she asked the bride. "Maybe we should look over my clothes first and make sure you still like the same outfit."

Gloria shook her head. Today, the woman held herself a little straighter, like a marathon runner with the finish line in view. Or a hunter with her prey fixed in her sights.

"No, I've got to make sure the flowers arrive," Gloria said. "They should be here by now. There are supposed to be free-standing displays, and our bouquets, and a circlet for my hair."

"You aren't wearing a veil?" Maddy asked.

The other woman pursed her lips. "I bought one with the gown. But that seems awfully old-fashioned, don't you think?"

Maddy tried to assess the situation quickly. It didn't matter what Gloria intended to wear, only that a veil would be available. No one would know that the bride hadn't changed her mind at the last minute.

"It's up to you," she said. "Maybe you could try them both on and we'll see."

"Go get your dress." Gloria dismissed her with a gesture. "We'll have lots of time to try different things. Oh, and the photographer. Now, where is he?"

Maddy had forgotten there would be a photographer. That posed yet another complication. Would he be hanging around the dressing room? Wouldn't he of all people twig on the fact that the bride had been replaced by a substitute?

With a sigh, she hurried out. She would have to do her best. Maybe things wouldn't work out. Was that so terrible?

It would be to Jon. He'd never forgive her. And she knew that if she did anything less than her best, she'd be betraying his trust.

If they were ever to have a future together, she had to merit his respect today.

At the motor home, she found Jon stretched on the couch, wearing his regulation jeans and blue shirt. "Aren't you going to change?" she asked.

"For what?" he said. "I won't be attending the wedding."

"Oh. I forgot."

They ought to have more to say to each other after last night, Maddy reflected, but Jon had already tipped his hat over his face. Was he really taking a nap or just avoiding conversation?

"This is getting more complicated than I thought," she said. "There's going to be a photographer. He'll probably follow us around like a lapdog."

"Tell him to get some shots of Larry," Jon muttered from beneath the Stetson. "He's the celebrity, after all. The guy could probably sell them to a tabloid and make some money on the side."

"It might work." Feeling reluctant to leave, Maddy retrieved her dress from the closet and hung it on a freestanding hook for inspection. "This is kind of wrinkled."

"Get the staff to iron it," Jon mumbled.

"I'm not sure which shoes I should wear."

"How about your in-line skates?"

She picked up a sandal and threw it at him. It struck Jon in the middle of the chest, provoking an "umph!" and the removal of the hat. "That was uncalled for," he said.

"You're rude, crude and uncivilized!" Maddy snapped. "I don't know why I bother with you!"

"I don't, either," he agreed rather mildly, considering he'd just been hit with a shoe.

"You're not even nervous about what's going to happen, but then, why should you be?" she burst out. "I'm the one most likely to be left holding the bag!"

"Don't worry, *I'll* be holding the bag, but I don't know that I'd refer to Gloria that way," Jon said. "Although after a few years in prison, it might fit."

"This is a game to you, isn't it?" Maddy couldn't understand why she felt so emotional. Tears pricked at her eyes and her throat had gone raw. She wasn't in love with Jon, and she didn't care whether he drove off into the sunset and she never saw him again. She was sorry now she'd gotten herself mixed up with this adventure. Why couldn't she have stayed at the beach, finished in-line skating and gone to a movie?

"Everything's a game," Jon said. "Sometimes you win, sometimes you lose."

He was deliberately annoying her, but Maddy didn't bite this time because thinking about the beach had reminded her of something. "Where's the ring?"

"Excuse me?"

"The ring!" she repeated. "The one that was stolen from the little shop."

"Oh, that one." Jon fished it from his shirt pocket. "I've been carrying it around in case anyone questioned whether we were married."

"How come you haven't worn it?" she asked.

Jon inspected it in the sunlight flowing through a window. Even from where she stood, Maddy couldn't miss the exquisite workmanship, the dove so detailed it almost appeared to be alive. "It gives me an odd feeling," he said.

She glanced at the ring on her own hand. After wearing it for two days, she'd almost forgotten it was there except for an occasional tingling. "Why?"

"Both times I put it on, I..." Jon broke off. "Never mind."

"You what?"

"Wanted to make love to you."

Maddy made a face. "Oh, it takes some kind of magic to motivate that, does it? Well, you weren't wearing the ring last night." Honesty made her add, "At least, I don't think you were."

"Maybe I've been carrying it around too long." Jon tossed the ring into the air, and Maddy grabbed for it. She could almost have sworn the dove's wings fluttered as it landed back in Jon's hand.

"It doesn't want to leave," he said.

"It doesn't know you very well." Maddy shook her head. "You haven't got an ounce of tenderness to your name. If that thing was magic, it would be wasted on you."

Jon's fist clenched over the ring. "Let's get one thing straight, Maddy. I haven't led the kind of pampered and privileged life you have. I can't afford the luxury of sentimentality. I do what has to be done, and that's the end of it."

A lump caught in her throat. Her vague notion of reconnecting with Jon later had been childish, Maddy realized. The man was incapable of true love, or bonding, or building a future.

"Whatever you make of your life, I hope it brings you happiness," she said. "But somehow I don't think it will."

With as much dignity as she could muster, she grabbed the dress and hurried out of the motor home.

Chapter Thirteen

As she walked back to the conference center, Maddy noticed several new vehicles in the driveway. One bore the name of a florist's shop, and the other of a photographic studio. Things were definitely getting more complicated.

She tried to ignore the ache in her chest. You couldn't get blood from a turnip or love from a ruffian like Jon, she supposed.

Maddy had half a mind to ruin his plan out of spite, but her conscience wouldn't let her. Whatever he might think of her, he wouldn't be able to say she had wimped out.

Turning her thoughts to the task ahead, she tried to figure out how to lure Gloria to the motor home. Perhaps they could go there to take a picture, but that would mean dragging along the photographer, and he would raise the alarm in a hurry.

Somehow she had to accomplish the switch at the last minute, or nearly the last minute. But how?

Her nerves made her jump when she opened the lobby door and saw Blair standing nearby. He was watching the florist's helpers bustle about installing stands of flowers, however, and didn't appear to notice her.

She headed down a hallway toward Gloria's private chambers. Larry came out just as she approached, and waved Maddy inside. "She's been looking for you. They want to take pictures."

Inside, the private apartment had a spacious living room with the kind of impersonal but artfully arranged furnishings that bespeak a decorator. One of the staff members finished arranging a bowl of fruit on the coffee table and went out, with a faint smile at Maddy.

She found Gloria in the bedroom, which was littered with wedding paraphernalia—bouquets, the veil, the wedding dress, white shoes, wads of tissue paper and lacy stockings. Light flooded the room through the translucent curtains over a pair of French doors that opened onto a private patio.

Gloria stood by a low mirrored table wearing an embroidered kimono, one foot elevated on a stool to display the blue garter around her thigh as a dark-haired young woman snapped her picture.

Maddy's heart sank. A female photographer made things even trickier, because she wouldn't have to leave while they were dressing.

"There you are!" Gloria gestured to Maddy. "My maid of honor," she told the photographer. "Maddy, this is Juanita."

"Benita," corrected the woman, thrusting out a hand and shaking Maddy's firmly.

For the next fifteen minutes, they posed: Maddy fixing Gloria's hair, Gloria stepping into her gown, Maddy trying on Gloria's veil. She couldn't imagine what Gloria would do with these pictures. The groom would probably be dead before they got the proofs back.

Unless, of course, Jon succeeded in his task, but getting the bride to the RV was looking more and more like mission impossible.

"Thank goodness that's over!" Gloria announced as Benita departed to capture images of Larry. "Before you arrived, she kept asking me where the family was. Can you imagine? The woman's never seen a wedding without a family before!''

Neither have most people, Maddy reflected, but smiled with what she hoped appeared to be sympathy.

Gloria chattered on as she lifted the wedding gown. "Isn't this smart? I thought it was stunning when I saw it in Las Vegas. That was before I had a man to go with it, in a manner of speaking.''

"You were lucky," Maddy said. She meant about finding Larry, but Gloria took it differently.

"Oh, there's always a decent wedding dress to be found if you search hard enough." As usual when she wasn't pretending to be a gracious hostess or loving soul mate, Gloria's face took on a disdainful expression that made her seem older and coarser.

"It's certainly beautiful." Assisting the bride in hiking the gown into place, Maddy wondered whether it would fit her own figure. Gloria had a thicker waistline and was slightly taller. But Maddy didn't suppose it would matter; she wouldn't be wearing it long. Just for eternity, when she had to walk down the aisle pretending to be a bride with everyone staring at her.

The thought of wearing the dress gave her a queasy sensation. Gloria had bought it to deceive and entrap an innocent victim. Besides, Maddy had the irrational sense that Gloria's pores oozed some kind of poisonous miasma.

Nonsense. The woman smelled like scented soap and hair spray.

Uttering a vulgarism, Gloria wriggled as she tugged the dress shut around her back. "I've gained weight. If Larry wouldn't keep stuffing things in my face, it wouldn't be a problem. He's always sticking something at me, a Danish or olives, as if I would enjoy eating it from his fingers! Can you zip me, honey?''

As she leaned over to comply, Maddy wondered why Gloria felt safe dropping her facade with her maid of honor.

Maybe it was just too difficult to pretend all the time. Or maybe the similarity in their appearances provided a false sense of kinship.

"Oof!" Gloria grumped as the zipper pulled the gown taut across her midsection. "I feel like a beached whale!"

Maddy stood back to get the full effect. "It looks terrific."

A slim underdress of white silk was overlaid by gauze embroidered with tiny rosebuds. The bustline dipped low enough to reveal Gloria's ample cleavage, and the see-through sleeves puffed out until gathered at the wrists with rose-garlanded cuffs.

Maddy held up her own subtly shaded lavender dress, which really wasn't all that wrinkled. "We should look good together."

"Tell me about *your* wedding dress." Gloria peered into the mirror, fluffing her hair. "I'll bet it didn't cost as much as this one, but you're younger—you can get away with cheap clothes."

The woman didn't appear to notice that she'd just insulted Maddy. Indeed, from the way Gloria was touching up her mascara and studying herself in the glass, her thoughts were only for herself.

That was fortunate, since it took Maddy a minute to remember that she and Jon were supposed to be married, so she presumably would have worn a gown of her own. "It was white," she said.

Gloria must not have expected much of an answer, because she didn't pursue the subject. "I can't bear to mash my hair down with a veil. Besides, what exactly am I keeping secret? Larry and I have been sleeping together since the day we met. It's not as if my face is a mystery to him. Heck, I should just walk down the aisle naked."

It amazed Maddy that the other woman could so calmly destroy her elegant image with every word she spoke. If maintaining appearances proved this difficult, no wonder Gloria killed her spouses the first chance she got.

How had she maneuvered Larry into endowing her with his worldly goods? Maddy assumed the task had already been accomplished, judging by Gloria's air of self-confidence.

A man as sophisticated as Larry Wicker should have known better than to revise his will or take out an insurance policy in favor of his new wife before the wedding. But Gloria probably knew how to phrase such a request so it appeared reasonable.

Or perhaps Larry hadn't made any will; lots of people didn't. In that case, Gloria might be counting on inheriting the lion's share of his property by default, including countless royalties yet to come.

Who would stand against her? There were no children, and apparently no other close relatives, since none were attending the wedding.

Gloria had chosen her victim wisely. Or maybe, as so often happened, luck favored the reckless.

In the meantime, Maddy still hadn't solved her problem. She was no nearer persuading Gloria to go to the motor home than ever, and now that the bride had donned her gown, the task appeared even more hopeless.

Maybe Gloria would have entertained the possibility of a last-minute tryst with Jon, but not with only half an hour left. Already people must be assembling in the lobby. The bride surely wouldn't risk a lifetime of wealth for a roll in the hay.

Maddy pictured Jon waiting impatiently in the motor home. He would be grumbling about the delay, perhaps growing angry as he wondered why Maddy hadn't done her part yet.

No, she thought, that was how her father would react in such a situation. Jon would simply lie on the couch with his hat tipped over his face, prepared to act when necessary but not wasting energy until that moment. He wouldn't get mad until he knew for certain that she'd failed.

"That's better." Gloria swung around, a circlet of rose-buds in her hair. She gave a girlish curtsey and giggled. "I do like it! But honey, you're not ready!"

"Oh, sorry." Pulling off her skirt and blouse, Maddy yanked on the lavender dress. It flowed over her body, every inch a testament to expensive tailoring and exquisite silk woven by the most aristocratic silkworms in China. Maddy's stepmother had brought it back from a trip to Paris.

At first, Maddy had worn it simply to please Lael, but then she'd decided it suited her even if it wasn't her usual style. Now she finished hooking it and slipped on her high-heeled sandals.

Gloria scrutinized her. "You need some powder. Your face is shining." She handed over the makeup.

Suppressing her unease at sharing Gloria's powder and lipstick, Maddy applied it to her face. At least the two of them wore the same color range.

A clock on the dressing table read fifteen minutes until two.

Maddy's palms felt sweaty. She had to act, but her brain wouldn't click into gear. In a few minutes, it would be too late. Once Gloria walked down the aisle, they'd never get her alone. Even if they did, there would be so many people circulating through the building and grounds, someone would be sure to notice something amiss.

She tried to send mental telepathy to Jon to come and grab Gloria himself, but knew it wouldn't work. Besides the obvious fact that he couldn't read minds, he would never make it out of the conference center with a screaming bride under his arm.

"Try some mascara." Gloria handed her a tube. "You need to darken your eyes."

Maddy obeyed purely by rote.

Ten minutes to go.

"Would you go check the lobby?" Gloria asked. "See if everyone's in place. Maybe we can start early."

"Sure." The word came out breathlessly. Unable to think of any ideas whatsoever, Maddy scooted back from the table and jumped up, too absorbed in her thoughts to notice where Gloria was standing.

It took a moment to register that the stool had bumped into something. By the time she realized she'd hit the bride, Maddy had landed on her feet and Gloria was jumping backward with an angry warning to watch out.

A sharp ripping noise announced the worst: Maddy's high heels had landed on Gloria's hem, and a long tear marred the gown from hem to midcalf.

A string of curse words burst from the bride's mouth, so foul she must have been collecting them for years.

"I'm so sorry!" Maddy cried. "Oh, Gloria! Let's see if we can pin it up!"

"You idiot! I knew I should have done without a maid of honor, but Larry thought it was such a good idea!" Gloria snarled. "Look at that mess! Did you say pin it? You think people won't notice a bunch of safety pins?"

That's when the idea came to Maddy, a weak one but the best she had. "I'm a pretty good seamstress," she said, which was a complete lie but sounded convincing. "I've got a sewing kit back at the RV."

Muttering furiously, Gloria swung around for her to unzip the gown. "All we need is white thread and a needle. I'm sure I've got that around here somewhere. Careful with the zipper! We don't need you to break that, too!"

Much as she resented Gloria's imperious tone, Maddy had to admit she'd been guilty of a terrible breach, even if an unintentional one. Carefully unworking the zipper, she followed Gloria's directions and opened a couple of bureau drawers until, sure enough, she came across a few sewing items.

So much for her great idea.

Maddy was trying to thread the needle without displaying her utter ineptness when the door opened and the photographer poked her head in. "Ready?" she asked. "I thought I should—what's going on?"

"We had a little accident," Gloria intoned sarcastically. "Would you please tell the guests there'll be a slight delay? I don't believe this! It's positively humiliating!" She glared at Maddy.

"I'm really sorry." The rip ran all the way through the mesh and the underskirt, Maddy saw as she took the garment in her lap. She'd seen her dressmaker whip out enough emergency repairs to know that she had to flip the skirt over and work from the underside, so she managed that maneuver with an air of calm expertise. "I'll just baste it."

She hoped she'd used the right word. Maddy knew that you could baste a turkey, but couldn't you baste a hem, too?

"I'll spread the word," Benita promised. "Don't worry. People are straggling in late—they always do."

As the photographer closed the door behind her, Maddy ran the needle through the fabric and pulled it out. The entire thread came with it. She realized she needed to make some kind of knot at the end.

This was getting her nowhere. Gloria had taken off the dress, but she was nowhere close to the motor home.

Well, Maddy decided, she might as well go for broke. If she didn't do everything possible, she had no chance of succeeding.

Gritting her teeth, and hoping that Jon would someday realize how much she was sacrificing in his behalf, she jabbed the needle into her finger.

"Ow!" No need to fake the cry; it came out spontaneously. So did three drops of blood, soaking into the front of the white fabric as if they had been aimed there deliberately. Which, of course, they had been.

"I don't believe it!" Not a trace of sympathy crossed Gloria's infuriated face. "Now you've ruined it for sure! Get away from there! Oh, my—this is the absolute pits. You clumsy little oaf!''

Sticking her finger in her mouth, Maddy sucked on it to stop the bleeding. The word *sorry* came out in a mumble, and then she said, ''We can get the spots out.''

''Not without washing the dress!'' Gloria cried. ''That's all I need, to march down the aisle with a big wet spot on my skirt!''

''I've got a quickie spot remover kit,'' Maddy said. ''It's fantastic. It even takes out wine, and it dries in a second!''

''Well, go and get it!'' Gloria snapped.

Maddy stared up at her wide-eyed. ''Do you want to sew the rip while I'm gone? Otherwise, maybe you should go.''

Gloria hissed out an exasperated breath. ''Unbelievable. You're the bridesmaid from hell, you know that?'' A glance at her own elongated nails resulted in yet another curse. It was obvious Gloria could no more wield a needle than she could control her temper. ''Isn't there a maid around here somewhere?''

She peered into the living room, then returned cursing furiously. ''There's never anyone around when you need them.'' She clicked her tongue angrily. ''What a laughing-stock I'll be! They'll all think I'm ridiculous. Besides, I'd never be able to find anything in your motor home.''

''My husband is there,'' Maddy said. ''We had sort of a quarrel a little while ago and he decided not to come.''

Gloria made a face. ''I can see why. What did you do, step on his cowboy hat?''

Biting back the impulse to frame a retort, Maddy picked up the needle and thrust it into the fabric again. It still didn't have a knot in it, and the thread pulled through again, but Gloria didn't notice. ''He's moody. But he likes you. I'm sure he'll help.''

''Well, all right,'' the bride growled. ''Don't tell anyone I'm gone. They're probably all inside by now, so with any luck they won't see me sneaking around.'' She pulled a pair of slacks and a shirt from the closet. "I'll go out through the French doors. Try not to destroy anything else while I'm gone, will you? That stain remover of yours better work, or you're dead!"

With those words, Gloria jerked on the clothes, slammed her feet into a pair of flats and marched out the back way. Maddy had no doubt that Gloria would happily have slain her at that moment for real.

But it didn't matter. Gloria was going to the motor home!

Then the doubts assailed her. It wouldn't work. Someone would spot Gloria and offer to make the trip for her. Or Gloria would change her mind. Or Jon would grab her and she'd scream, and he'd be arrested for assault.

Realizing she had better keep working on the gown just in case, Maddy managed to tie the thread into a knot on the third try. She began the repairs, trying not to notice the way the fabric puckered beneath her uneven stitches. She'd never appreciated before how careful and precise sewing had to be.

She would never take her seamstress for granted again, Maddy vowed silently.

As the minutes ticked by, her heart hammered inside her chest and her fingers kept slipping on the needle. At any moment she expected to hear an outcry, or for Gloria to return.

She tried to picture what was happening. Gloria would bang on the door impatiently and Jon would leap to answer it, marveling that Maddy really had carried out her part of the bargain.

Gloria would ask for the stain remover kit. Jon, not being entirely dense, would realize what was going on and offer to help search for it.

Next, Gloria would step into the motor home. And then? How would Jon keep her quiet while he handcuffed her? What would he say? Would there be a struggle? And once Gloria was tied up, what was to stop him from hightailing it out of the camp without waiting for Maddy?

Was it possible he would feel concern for her well-being and the embarrassment that would result when the police figured out who she was and the press got hold of the information? Or perhaps Jon didn't care.

Maddy's heart lurched as the inner door opened, but it was only Benita. "Where's Gloria?" she asked.

"In the bathroom." The lie leapt to Maddy's lips, maybe because it sounded so plausible.

"I need to get pictures of her wearing the gown," Benita said. "It's part of the package."

"We'll take them later," Maddy said. "We can pretend we're getting ready after it's over. She doesn't want to postpone the wedding another minute. I'm sure people are getting itchy."

"Oh, they're all right," Benita said.

Her mind finally clicking into gear, Maddy said, "Tell the person in charge of the music to wait five minutes and then start it. Gloria's got her hair and makeup done. It won't take a minute to put the dress on, and I'm almost finished." She kept one hand draped over the red spots.

"Well, okay," Benita said dubiously, and left.

Maddy stared down at the dress. Jon's plan called for her to substitute for Gloria, but now that the moment had arrived, she could see the flaws in it.

Everyone would notice that absence of the maid of honor. And then there was the stain on the dress; impossible to hide that as she marched down the aisle. Plus the veil, which Gloria had tossed across a pillow, was too thin to hide Maddy's face.

Worst of all, if Jon took off and stranded her, there would be no way to pretend innocence. Posing as Gloria would implicate Maddy beyond question.

She slipped the gown onto a hanger and carried it into the bathroom. Emerging a moment later, Maddy left the light on inside and closed the door. If anyone checked, it would appear that Gloria must be dressing.

Cracking open the bedroom door, she made sure the living room was empty. For a moment, Maddy contemplated scampering out the back way herself, but then Benita came in and gestured to her.

"Is she ready?"

"Almost," Maddy said. "She told me to go ahead, and she'd be right behind me." Seeing the other woman hesitate, she added, "Don't you need to get in position by the altar? You have to capture us coming down the aisle—we can't restage that, with the audience and everything!"

"I guess not," Benita agreed, and held the door open. "Aren't you forgetting something?"

"What?" Maddy's breath caught in her throat until she saw the photographer pointing to her bouquet. Snatching it from the bed, Maddy hurried out. "I guess I'm a little distracted!"

"I would never have noticed," the other woman said with a smile as they went down the hallway together.

There was still no sign of Gloria. Impossible as it seemed, Jon must have caught her.

Maddy's knees quivered and her hands felt cold. She wondered how Jon could make a living out of this kind of work, where a thousand things could go wrong at the last minute. One experience was enough to convince Maddy that she would never do it again.

Their approach must have been noticed, because the music wafting over the speakers changed from "We've Only Just Begun" to a wedding march.

Maddy scurried to the head of the aisle and took a deep breath. Across the lobby, at what seemed like a tremendous distance, Larry and Blair waited by the altar. Behind them, the minister stood with a bland smile plastered on his face.

In row after row of seats, faces turned to watch her. Tears glistened as, Maddy assumed, many of the women relived their own weddings. This event must have special meaning for them in light of the way they'd just reenergized their own marriages.

But this isn't real. It was a sham even before Jon and I got involved.

Clutching the flowers in front of her, Maddy stepped out. Count one, bring the other foot alongside, pause. Count two, bring the first foot alongside, pause.

She tried to drag it out as long as possible. Ahead of her, Benita ran forward, knelt and snapped a picture.

Larry Wicker sure is going to enjoy flipping through these for the rest of his life, isn't he? But at least he'll have a life.

"Isn't she lovely?" murmured a voice that Maddy recognized as belonging to Anne Stowe.

Ahead of Maddy, beyond the altar, glass doors revealed the patio and the woods beyond. She thought about the weekend, which had been so crammed with experiences, she could hardly sort them out. Jon, alternately arrogant and seductive, massaging her back and bringing her champagne. Frank and Lee, Bo and Sarita at their group session, listening to Maddy as if she actually had some wisdom to impart.

With a start, she realized that she'd changed. This weekend, Maddy had discovered new parts of herself: the part that wanted children, the part that got along with strangers who accepted her for herself, the part that couldn't resist making love to Jon no matter what might happen afterward.

She wasn't the same woman who had allowed her rebellion against her father to shape her life. She loved him, but she had to create her own future, and this weekend she had discovered that she was strong enough to do it.

Except that Jon was leaving, and Maddy didn't know what to do next. She kept visualizing herself in Texas with him, or having a family with him, or all those other things that could never happen. A great void opened in front of her, beyond this room, and she didn't know how she was going to fill it.

At last she reached the altar and stepped to one side, facing Blair. He gave her an admiring nod, and Maddy managed a smile in return.

Everyone turned to watch for Gloria.

The staff member manning the tape recorder knelt at one side, staring intently, his fingers twitching on a button. Benita heaved an exasperated breath and fiddled with her camera.

"Is she all right?" Larry murmured.

"She had a little accident with the dress," Maddy whispered back. "We had to stitch it up."

He chuckled. "I'll bet she's furious. That woman has quite a temper."

They waited, feeling the minutes lengthen and the audience begin to shift in their seats. In addition to the twenty-four people attending the conference, most of the staff had taken seats. Everyone sat politely murmuring to their companions, but Maddy could feel the tension rising.

Or was it only her own erratic heartbeat that she heard? Jon must have tied Gloria up by now. He'd be waiting for Maddy. Even now, he might be sitting in the driver's seat with one hand on the ignition, a leather-booted foot tapping impatiently against the gas pedal.

"I'll go check on her," Maddy said.

Larry stopped her with a hand on her arm. "I'll do it."

She couldn't let him. Once Gloria's disappearance was discovered, it would be too late to escape.

Maddy widened her eyes in mock horror. "You can't see the bride before the wedding! It's bad luck!"

Larry chuckled again. Obviously, it hadn't occurred to him there might be any serious problem. "Oh, all right, go on."

With little embarrassed nods to the right and left, Maddy hurried up the aisle. Benita started after her, but Maddy waved the photographer back. "She'll be along any minute!"

It took all her strength of will not to break into a run as she reached the corridor and headed toward the empty apartment.

Chapter Fourteen

As Maddy pushed open the bedroom door, she heard a shuffling noise that sent the blood roaring through her arteries.

Someone was inside. Who? How had they gotten here?

She stepped in, half expecting an infuriated Gloria to fly at her with nails drawn. Instead, Maddy stopped in shock at the sight of Jon, tensed by the French door. In his hand was a gun.

"What—" she gasped.

He lowered the pistol. "I'd nearly given up waiting for you."

But you came! You didn't leave!

Maddy tried not to show her flood of relief. "Never mind the details. Everybody thinks I'm checking on Gloria, so let's get out of here before they figure out something's wrong!"

Jon leaned outside and made a rapid check of the perimeter before waving her through. "Don't run," he muttered as she passed him. "We don't want to attract attention."

The challenge now, Maddy realized, was to circle the building and pass through the parking lot without anyone happening to glance out of the lobby. Since everyone was seated facing the other way, it didn't seem likely, but there was no telling.

"If we're spotted," Jon said, "pretend we're quarreling. Tell them Gloria's not ready, and you can't wait because I won't let you."

"Have you got her?" Maddy hurried with him around the far side of the building. For part of the way, they had to walk on bare earth, and her heels kept sinking into the dirt. She was glad now that she hadn't worn the wedding dress; it would have been just one more hindrance.

He nodded tightly. "She's a vixen, all right." A flick of his wrist called her attention to a long red mark where Gloria had scratched him.

"Where is she?"

"Hog-tied in the bathtub," he said. "That woman has quite a vocabulary."

"I'm surprised nobody heard her," Maddy said.

"I had the radio on." Jon peered around the side of the building. "They probably thought it was some rap song."

"All clear?" Maddy asked.

He gave the tersest possible headshake. "The florist's having a smoke."

"He doesn't have any reason to question us," she said.

"No, but he can sure point the finger...good, he's going inside. Wait just a minute, and then we'll—damn!" He pulled back abruptly.

"What?"

"Blair just came out," he said. "What the hell is he doing? He's supposed to be waiting by the altar."

"Maybe they discovered she's gone." Maddy couldn't believe Larry had decided to check on her so quickly.

"More likely, being a guard, he decided he needed to make sure everything's shipshape." Jon released a sharp, irritable breath. "You're going to have to go talk to him."

"Me?" Maddy's voice came out in a squeak. "I'm supposed to be in Gloria's room."

"Tell him you need something out of the motor home," Jon said.

"Like a stain remover kit?" she teased.

He gave her the edge of a grin. "Yeah. That was a stroke of genius."

"Thanks," Maddy said, and felt his hand on her back propelling her forward.

She stepped out, pretended a mild surprise as she caught Blair's eye, and then waved to him.

Curiosity creasing his face, the guard watched her approach across the grass. "What seems to be the problem?"

"She got a stain on the dress," Maddy said as she reached the parking lot. "I need to get a kit from my motor home."

"I'll walk you," he said.

She could hardly refuse, but this whole business was getting messier and messier, and time was running out. "I'd rather you went and told Larry what's going on," she said. "It's obviously going to be a few more minutes. Even the best stain remover doesn't work instantly."

She wondered what Jon was doing. Would he wait where she'd left him, or try to slip around the other side of the conference center? If he did, he'd surely be seen through the lobby windows.

All the while, Gloria must be busting a gut tied up in the bathtub, cursing her luck and her bridesmaid.

"I guess you're right," Blair said. "Maybe the staff could serve everybody champagne. That'll loosen them up."

"Great idea!" Maddy said. "Gloria's embarrassed about the whole thing. She wanted it to be perfect."

Blair shrugged. "Hey, the important thing is getting married and spending your lives together, not whether somebody's late to the wedding."

"Your fiancée is a lucky woman," Maddy said, and impulsively shook his hand. "I'm glad I met you."

"Don't get carried away—the weekend's not over," Blair joked.

"I know." Maddy assumed her best dizzy blonde expression, convincing enough to have gotten her backstage at a rock concert once when she was younger. "I'm getting sentimental already."

A shadow of something like regret passed across Blair's face. "Don't get too sentimental," he said.

"I know. It's just a Magical Marital Weekend like any other," Maddy said. "But it's been special for me."

"Well, you take care now," Blair said. "I'll see you in a few minutes." He swung around and strolled toward the doors.

The coast was clear. Now where had Jon gone?

Maddy hurried toward the motor home. One way or another, he would manage to meet her there.

Finding the door unlocked, she climbed inside. The motor home wasn't exactly shaking, but she could feel a slight vibration as she entered.

From the back came a muffled thumping. Gloria obviously hadn't given up trying to attract attention.

Maddy hesitated. Curiosity impelled her to check on her charge, but she wasn't sure she wanted to see the hate in Gloria's eyes. Besides, she couldn't help sympathizing with the woman, being trussed in such an undignified way.

A moment later the RV tilted slightly and Jon jumped inside. "Ready?" he demanded.

Maddy nodded, her throat constricting. Was it possible they might actually make their getaway unobserved?

Jon hopped into the driver's seat. "Come here. I want you sitting beside me."

"Why?" she asked as she kicked off her heels and stuck her feet gratefully into a pair of flats. She would have liked to change into jeans, but that wasn't as pressing a matter as her aching arches.

"If anyone comes after us, I might have to hand over the wheel." Jon waited until she came to the front before switching on the ignition. "Now hang on. Someone's likely to hear the motor starting and come check."

"I don't think they'll be concerned," Maddy said. "Blair's going to suggest that the staff serve champagne. They're expecting a fairly long delay."

"Anything that can go wrong, will go wrong," Jon muttered, and backed the rig out of the space. He must have disconnected the utilities earlier, Maddy realized; in addition, she saw that he'd put away the loose items that had been scattered around this morning.

What had he done with his pistol? From the bulge in his jacket, she guessed he must be wearing it in a holster. She wished he hadn't brought it. What was the worst that could happen if they got caught? Nothing worth shooting anybody over.

Every bounce of the RV as it reversed its way out of the parking bay reverberated through Maddy's bones. Someone would hear them, someone would get suspicious, Gloria would escape her bonds and raise the alarm. She imagined every possible snafu, and some that were probably impossible.

Beneath his Stetson, even Jon looked grim as he straightened the motor home and eased toward the driveway. This moment as they passed the conference center was the most difficult and dangerous part of their quest, Maddy realized.

When they started out, catching a murderess had sounded like a lark. Now Gloria had become a real flesh-and-blood person, and this wasn't a game at all.

Ahead of them, Maddy could see the parking lot with the florist's truck and the photographer's van sitting in front of the low building. No one was walking around and she didn't spot any movement inside the lobby, although the glass reflected so much light that she couldn't be sure.

"Can't you hurry up?" she asked Jon.

"I'm trying to keep the engine quiet," he retorted through clenched teeth. "Believe me, in this barge we can't outrun anybody. We've got to keep a low profile."

Maddy knew he was right. "I'm sorry." In the back, the thumping intensified; Gloria must realize they were leaving camp and meant to make the most of her last chance.

A ripple of light against the conference center made Maddy blink, and then she realized what had caused it. Someone was opening the front door.

Please let it be the florist. Or one of the staff who won't realize what's happening.

The door flew back and she recognized the dark, stern figure of Blair. He peered toward them, expression rigid with disbelief.

"Hey!" he called. "What's going on?"

Maddy rolled down her window and leaned out. "Jon wants to leave. I'm sorry. We're having this fight and—"

From the back of the motor home came a shriek that would have aroused the dead, had there been any nearby. Gloria must have worked her gag loose.

"What the hell?" Blair broke into a run.

Jon must have hit the gas pedal too hard, because the motor home choked and stalled. As he twisted the ignition key, Blair reached the side door.

He pulled it open; in their haste, neither Maddy nor Jon had thought to lock it. She turned to confront the furious figure stalking toward them. "We can explain all this."

"You'd damn well better." Blair reached for the gun on his hip.

Before she realized what was happening, Jon launched himself through the air and plowed into Blair, who collapsed backward with a groan. "Put it in drive!" Jon yelled. "Get us out of here!"

Maddy couldn't think straight. Part of her brain warned that they should stop now and simply tell the truth. But another shout from Jon sent her bolting into the driver's seat.

Behind her, the two men rolled on the floor, grunting and cursing as they struggled for possession of the gun. Maddy wrenched on the ignition and fumbled with the gearshift, finally putting them into forward.

They lurched toward the exit, the motor home jerking as if suffering spasms. From the bathroom, Gloria screamed bloody murder. She really did have quite a vocabulary.

Although she'd driven everything from a sports car to the Lexus, Maddy had never handled anything this big before. The rig moved stiffly, and she winced as a branch scraped across her window.

She wanted to shout to Blair to stop fighting and listen, but he obviously wasn't in any mood to obey. Besides, a glance in the rearview mirror revealed people pouring out of the conference center, staring in their direction.

Too many people. Too complicated an explanation. Too likely that she and Jon would end up in jail while Gloria marched down the aisle.

Better to take her to Texas. Better to get out of here. Better yet, to have a time machine and go back before Maddy got mixed up in this crazy business.

The driveway narrowed as it approached the bridge over the ravine. The motor home kept bouncing, even more than Maddy would have expected from the rough road, and then a peek in the right side mirror showed the side door wide open and banging.

And Larry Wicker was running toward them from the conference center, his eyes fixed on the open door.

Maddy didn't want him to catch them. Mostly, she didn't want to risk hurting Larry. Jumping onto a moving RV wouldn't be an easy task, and Larry was neither young nor athletic. But he would apparently go to any extreme to save his bride.

She stomped on the gas and they pitched forward. The side of the RV scraped along the bridge railing with a teeth-aching screech, and then to her dismay Maddy saw the railing give way.

Pieces of wood splintered into the ravine and the bridge shook beneath them. Why hadn't it been made stronger? Worse, she was having trouble controlling the motor home; the quivering of the bridge nearly wrenched the steering wheel from her hands.

Then they reached the far side and passed the guard gate. Thank heavens they were leaving Larry's campground at last.

She hadn't thought beyond this moment. Unfortunately, Maddy discovered a moment later, they'd leapt out of the frying pan and into the fire.

In her nervousness, she kept giving the RV gas, and it leapt along the narrow road. They would reach a wider road in minutes, and then there might be other traffic.

Gloria was shrieking so loudly, people must be able to hear her for miles. And despite Jon's larger size, Blair possessed a wily toughness that kept slamming them both around the interior, smacking into chairs and crashing against the foldout table.

Maddy winced, knowing they must both be bruised. But her main concern now was this rig, too big and too powerful to be halted quickly even when she pumped the brakes.

She had never held other people's lives in her hands before. She might occasionally drive her sports car over the speed limit, but never so fast that she felt out of control.

The motor home had not been designed as a getaway car. Veering onto the main highway, it rocked hard, threatening to fishtail. Maddy's arms ached as she clutched the wheel, hanging on for all she was worth.

Then she realized the terrible mistake she'd made.

Because of the angle at which the side road joined the highway, she had automatically steered in the easiest direction. That was downhill.

Now the force of gravity and the massive weight of the RV combined to plunge them forward, faster and faster. The brakes squealed but slowed them only marginally, and she couldn't jam them on for fear of going into a skid.

To their right, a ditch ran alongside the road. To their left, with almost no shoulder, the highway overlooked a sheer drop of hundreds of feet.

Behind her, Gloria had stopped screaming. Maybe she'd run out of breath, or maybe she finally had the sense to be frightened.

Blair and Jon were locked in a final test of strength. She didn't dare watch them, but Maddy could hear their labored breathing and feel the desperation with which they gripped each other's arms.

Around a bend, a car came toward them. She could see the driver's startled expression as he realized the motor home was speeding out of control.

Not quite, Maddy told herself as she held the rig steady, passing the car without mishap. She had to find some way to slow the RV: the speedometer read fifty, which was far too fast.

To her right, a slight berm ran between the road and the ditch. Pumping the brake, Maddy worked the wheel so the RV bumped the dirt lightly, twisting back and forth in a series of bone-rattling thumps that managed to reduce their speed by infinitesimal increments.

Behind her, Blair had gained the upper hand. Gasping, sweat running down his face, he lifted himself and held his gun pointed at Jon.

"Never!" came Jon's hoarse response. He sounded dazed, and Maddy guessed he must have banged his head during the fight.

"Just hand it over, man," Blair rasped, indicating the pistol in Jon's holster.

Maddy fought to slow the motor home further. She knew Larry might follow them in his car, or the police might pick up their trail at any moment, but she had to take that risk. If the motor home picked up speed again she might never be able to stop. Getting arrested would be better than plunging over a cliff and killing them all.

The impetus was waning. Another car came toward them, full of teenagers. Laughing and singing, they didn't appear to notice anything amiss as they went by.

Forty miles an hour, and reducing. Maddy allowed herself one quick look at the men.

She could see the gun wavering between them as Jon seized Blair's wrist. The cowboy might be down but he wasn't giving up. Stubborn to the end, he hung on with his full strength.

"Let me out of here!" came Gloria's voice through the vehicle. "I'll see you rot in jail and sue you for everything you've got, you little—" She then proceeded to call Maddy a series of names so foul that even a truck driver would have blushed.

Slower now. Thirty, twenty. Ahead of them, Maddy spotted a rest area and swung toward it. She needed level ground where they could stop while she tried to sort things out between Blair and Jon.

There was no sign of pursuit, but with the curving roadway, it would be hard to tell. By now Larry must have called the authorities, and she expected to hear sirens at any moment.

"Blair." Bringing them to a halt, Maddy turned in her seat. "We're not kidnappers, we're bounty hunters. Gloria's wanted for—"

Maybe it was the distraction of hearing her voice, or desperation at realizing they'd stopped, but Jon lunged upward and caught the pistol as Blair was on the point of wrenching it free. Maddy didn't see what happened next; it remained forever a blur in her memory.

That was when the gun went off.

WHEN HE FELT Blair slump on top of him, Jon knew there would be no going back.

He'd never been in this situation before, but he had to handle it. Even if he wanted to undo what had been done, he couldn't.

With a sense of deep sadness, he rolled away and eased Blair to the floor. Then he groped for a pulse.

He could feel Maddy's shocked gaze boring into him. From the back of the motor home, Gloria was demanding to know what had happened.

Jon took a shaky breath. "He's dead."

Maddy went white. "We have to go back. We have to get a doctor."

Stumbling to his feet, Jon felt as if the blood had drained out of him. He couldn't afford to give in to exhaustion. "Listen to me. You're in this just as deep as I am. Do what I tell you and everything will be all right."

"No, it won't." She hugged herself, shivering as if seized by a chill. "How can it?"

Even though he knew her reaction was normal, Jon steeled himself. They couldn't afford to give in to sentimentality now. Later, there would be time for regrets, but not yet. "Just sit still."

He went back and tightened the gag around Gloria's mouth, barely evading her attempt to bite him. The woman actually snarled, her lip curling back like a mad dog's. Not that Jon blamed her, but he had more important things to think about now than her discomfort.

"Move over," he said when he returned to the front. Barely waiting for Maddy to shift into the passenger seat, he took the wheel.

She reached for the cellular phone. "We have to call the police."

He slammed it out of her hand, more roughly than he'd intended. "I'll handle this."

"What do you mean, handle it?" Hysteria knifed through her voice.

"Look, I'm sorry." Jon switched on the motor. "I didn't mean to hurt anybody. You know that. It was an accident."

"People have to be notified." From the numbness of her tone, she was barely hanging on. "He has a fiancée."

"I told you, I'll take care of it." Jon headed out of the rest area.

"And Gloria. She heard the whole thing."

"She doesn't know what she heard," he said. "I've got an idea."

"What?"

"I haven't worked it all out yet." Before she could object, Jon pressed on. "I'm taking you home. You'll go into your house, and you won't tell anyone where you've been. No one here knows your real name, and there's no way to connect you with any of this."

Maddy stared at him in disbelief. "You can't pretend it didn't happen. Blair is dead!"

"And I don't have the power to bring him back, do I?" The distress on her face was almost enough to shatter Jon's nerve, but he forced himself to keep steady as they accelerated to the maximum safe speed going down the mountain.

He wondered how long it would take the staff to figure out that he'd cut the phone wires, and get to a cellular phone. At least one of the guests must possess one, probably Larry himself.

But they might not grasp exactly what had happened. Larry didn't know Gloria very well; a number of scenarios could present themselves. He might not be in such a hurry to notify the police and get his name and personal embarrassment spread through the newspapers.

At least, that was what Jon hoped.

"Besides," Maddy said, "someday I might run into Larry, or one of the guests. Or they might see my picture in the paper."

"So what?" Stuck behind a slow-moving parcel truck, Jon lowered the gear and battled his urge to sound the horn. "They can't prove it was you. Besides, what would they connect you to? I can fix it so no one ever knows what happened."

"But it's wrong," Maddy insisted. "And—and there's Gloria."

"I'll take care of her."

He heard a sharp intake of breath. "You aren't going to kill her, are you?"

What did the woman take him for? Couldn't she see that he'd never intended to harm anyone? "Of course not," Jon said. "If worst comes to worst, I'll let her go. She's not likely to report anything to the police, is she?"

"I guess not." Maddy didn't sound convinced.

"You don't want to go to prison and neither do I," Jon argued as the roadway began to straighten. "What purpose would it serve?"

"I can't—I can't keep this a secret," Maddy protested.

He could tell from her tone that she was weakening. He had to make her understand. "Have you ever seen the inside of a prison? Maddy, you have a hard time adjusting when there's nobody to paint your fingernails. You can't imagine the deprivations when you're behind bars."

"But I didn't do anything," she whispered. "I mean, not on purpose."

"I don't want to see you go to prison any more than I want to go there myself," Jon continued. "By the time you get out, how old would you be? Too old to have children, that's for sure. Try to picture it, Maddy."

"But Blair's girlfriend," she went on doggedly. "What about the children *they* planned to have?"

"We can't bring the man back," Jon said.

She calmed down finally, sinking into a morose silence. He didn't like to go near her home, but he could see she was in no shape to deal with a taxi. Besides, the fewer witnesses, the better.

At his insistence, Maddy gave directions to her place in the hills above Hollywood. With the thick foliage and narrow roads, the area felt almost as if they were still in the mountains, yet they were less than two miles above busy Sunset Boulevard with its restaurants, shops and offices.

Gloria had fallen asleep, according to Maddy, who went to check on her. It was a natural response to the rhythm of the motor home and Gloria's immobility, but it wouldn't last long. Dealing with that woman was going to be tricky.

They turned into a driveway and came around some bushes. The house that sprawled before Jon might have come from a magazine spread on movie star homes.

The Spanish-style building rambled across the landscape, flowering vines draping its many wings. The place must cover five thousand square feet; what the heck did one woman need with that much space?

One woman and a dingbat of a housekeeper, he reminded himself.

Along one side ran a row of garages. Jon thought he counted five, but there might have been one more around the back. He wondered how many cars the woman owned.

What a life Maddy had come home to. For one aching moment, he wished he could stay and share it.

Then reality caught up with him.

"Pack your clothes," he said. "Quickly. Don't worry if you leave stuff—I'll mail it to you. Then go inside. Tell your friend Bitsy we quarreled and you're upset about it. Then wait for my call."

"You'll—you'll let me know how it comes out?" Maddy asked.

He nodded shortly. "I promise."

Jon got out the suitcases and waited impatiently while Maddy threw clothes into them. He draped Blair's body with a blanket, shielding it from Maddy's guilt-stricken glances.

What if she had left some items back in Gloria's room? There were always loose ends, things a man couldn't anticipate, but he doubted her clothes could be traced. They'd be fine if Maddy could just keep her mouth shut.

As he helped her down from the RV and watched the tears glimmering in her eyes, Jon felt bad for what she was suffering. And he felt bad for the future that they might have shared—but which would never have worked out, he told himself.

From a storage compartment in back of the RV, he pulled the motor home's real license plates. He'd switched them before going after Gloria at the beach, using a pair purchased from a junk dealer. It was standard operating procedure in this business.

"Don't worry," he told Maddy. "Even if Larry reports Gloria's disappearance, they won't be able to trace my plates, will they? I promise I'll call. If there's anything you need to do, I'll let you know."

She took a long shuddering breath. "I can't believe this happened. It doesn't seem real."

"You'll get through it," Jon said. Stifling the urge to kiss her, he swung back into the motor home and drove away.

He could feel her watching him for a long time afterward. He had a feeling that, in some part of his mind, he would see that heartbroken look for the rest of his life.

Chapter Fifteen

To Maddy, her home didn't look the same. Perhaps it never would again.

The sprawling rooms with their expensive furnishings seemed extravagant signs of a wasted life, and her conscience warned that money and privilege couldn't shield her from natural consequences. She felt as if she were some stranger pretending to be Maddy Armand.

As she unpacked, Maddy couldn't stop visualizing Blair, so cheerful and easygoing. His eyes had shone when he talked about his fiancée and their plans for acquiring the local veterinary clinic.

She would give every penny of her inheritance, if only she could bring him back.

Several times, Maddy reached for the phone to call authorities, only to stop in confusion. If she turned herself in, that would mean betraying Jon.

What kind of man was he, anyway? Sitting on the edge of her waterbed, staring out at the koi fish pond in her private courtyard, Maddy wondered why she'd become so mesmerized by him.

Maybe it was the aura of danger that surrounded Jon, or the sense of restrained power, that had attracted her from the moment they met. She'd never known anyone who lived as he did, outside the usual reach of society, making his own rules.

Now she knew where such outlaw behavior could lead.

It didn't make her feel any better that she'd left quite a few things in the motor home, everything from underwear that she'd stashed beneath the kitchen sink to jeans that she'd folded into a drawer hidden beneath the bed. Jon had promised to send them, but Maddy didn't feel she deserved them, or anything else. She would tell him to give it all to the poor.

After a while, she heard Bitsy come into the house. Paper sacks rustled in the kitchen, which meant that Bitsy might actually have done some grocery shopping, although more likely she'd picked up cosmetics.

"Hello?" Maddy wasn't eager to announce her presence, but she didn't want to be discovered accidentally and risk frightening her friend. "It's me. I'm home."

"Hurray!" Bitsy bounced into the bedroom. She'd switched her hair color to pinky peach and her nails to midnight blue. Leaving that woman alone for a weekend was a dangerous proposition. "Did you catch your murderess?"

Covering her tracks must have become a habit, because without thinking, Maddy answered, "No, it was all a waste of time. That man is awful. Just awful!"

"Tell me about the big adventure! I've been dying of curiosity!" Bitsy gathered the remainder of Maddy's clothes and tossed them into a laundry hamper, which meant they would remain there until Maddy either washed them herself or took them to the cleaner's.

"There's nothing to tell." Maddy stood and closed the suitcase. "He seemed more interesting than he really was."

Bitsy made a face. "Too bad."

"So," Maddy said with an effort, "tell me what's been happening in your life."

It wasn't hard to get Bitsy talking; she always had a tale to tell. Her friends seemed to take turns doing foolish things that provided a never-ending source of gossip.

This time, Bitsy launched into a description of how one man lit a dozen bug bombs in an attempt to rid his apartment of cockroaches. The bombs set the apartment on fire, destroying his CD collection, clothes and sound system, and causing smoke damage to three other apartments. By the time the man was allowed back inside, the only thing he found were...

"Cockroaches," Maddy guessed.

Bitsy's jaw dropped. "That's right! How did you know?"

"They'll survive us all." Even the mention of the word *survive* gave Maddy a weird feeling, but she didn't want to think about it. "It's nearly six o'clock. Got anything for dinner?"

"Let's order pizza," said Bitsy.

That, at least, sounded normal.

THE NEXT MORNING, Maddy checked the *Los Angeles Times,* but there was no mention of Blair or Gloria. Apparently Jon had been right that, in the absence of hard information, Larry didn't want to risk embarrassment by reporting his bride's disappearance.

Where were Jon and Gloria now? Maddy wondered. What had he done with Blair's body?

She couldn't believe the death would go undiscovered, although she'd read about cases that remained unsolved for years. It didn't seem right. It wasn't right.

Jon had seemed so sure of himself. He said he'd never done anything like this before, but how did she know it was true? Maybe he was the murderer, and Gloria the victim. Why had she taken Jon's word for everything?

Because, she admitted to herself as she nibbled a piece of congealing toast, she'd fallen in love with the man. He excited her and outraged her and made her come alive.

For the first time in thirty years, Maddy Armand had given her heart, and she'd given in to an outlaw. She was lucky he hadn't murdered *her*.

All day, her brain replayed the events during that breakneck race down the mountain. She kept trying to figure out how she could have changed the outcome and saved Blair.

She thought about prison, and remembered movies in which gray-faced women endured untold hardship and degradation. Iron doors clanged shut in Maddy's brain, locking her away forever.

But wasn't that what she deserved?

As Jon had pointed out, they couldn't bring Blair back. But didn't his fiancée deserve to know the truth?

Bitsy persuaded Maddy to join her in nightclubbing that evening. The places Bitsy and her pals frequented didn't open until ten o'clock, and the latest hot spot turned out to be an empty warehouse rented in defiance of health and safety regulations.

Standing in a huge smoke-filled room amid hundreds of bodies gyrating to deafening music, Maddy felt more alone than she ever had in her life. And older, wiser and infinitely sadder.

With what little presence of mind remained to her, Maddy had insisted on bringing her own car. She excused herself to Bitsy and went home early, something the old Maddy would never have considered.

It was Tuesday afternoon when Jon called. Maddy could hear traffic in the background, as if he were calling from a pay phone.

"I've got it worked out," he said, tension straining his voice, "but I need your help."

"What do you mean?" Maddy's heart jumped into her throat. He couldn't expect her to take more risks. She didn't have the nerve.

"I buried the body yesterday, in the Arizona desert," he said. "Nobody will discover it, and if they do, they won't find any ID."

Maddy shuddered.

"You still there?" he said.

"Yes."

"Okay, now listen." A truck went by, and Jon had to wait before he could continue. "Gloria heard too much. I have to let her go. Here's the deal. In return for her freedom and a hundred thousand dollars, she'll not only keep her mouth shut, she'll call Larry Wicker and tell him she and Blair ran off together."

"What?" Maddy couldn't absorb this new twist. "Why would she do that?"

"Because that way, nobody will search for either of them," Jon said.

It was perfect. Jon had come up with a scheme that even Maddy couldn't poke a hole in. No body, no witness and an explanation that would turn aside any questions.

Everything except a way to bring Blair back to life.

"It's brilliant," she admitted.

"Except I don't have the money to pay Gloria," Jon pressed. "Hell, I'm broke. No bounty, no nothing. Can you scrape it up?"

"A hundred thousand dollars?" Maddy asked. It was a lot, even to her; but no more than Jon had sacrificed. "I guess so."

"I knew you'd come through." He gave her a bank account number. "Can you transfer the money here right away? I want Gloria to make that call before a general alarm goes out. Anything on the news in Los Angeles?"

"Not yet." Maddy tried to think. She didn't keep that kind of money in her checking account. Most of her inheritance was tied up in a trust, but it yielded several hundred thousand dollars a year in income, which she stuffed into various bank accounts until needed. "I, uh, I'll do my best."

"I'll put your clothes in the mail tomorrow," he added.

"Don't bother. Give them away or throw them away—I don't care."

"Look, Maddy." She could picture Jon as he spoke, his hooded eyes dark with concern. "I'm sorry this happened. I miss you. But what's done is done, and there's no going back."

"I know," Maddy said. She missed him too, although she didn't want to—missed the gentleness of his touch, the lazy amusement in his smile, the way he always managed to get the best of her.

Apparently Gloria had gotten the best of them both this time.

"You think you can get the money?" he asked.

Maddy sighed. "Yes. I'll get it transferred this afternoon."

He didn't answer for a moment, and she wondered if she'd said something wrong. Then he repeated, "I'm sorry."

"That makes two of us," she said, and hung up.

Maddy discovered that her hands were shaking. Nothing about this felt right, but she forced herself to collect her wallet and bankbook and get in the car.

The teller didn't seem to notice anything amiss as he followed Maddy's directions. Moving one hundred thousand dollars around was ordinary stuff at a bank, she supposed. As long as you didn't ask for cash, they had no reason to get suspicious.

As he presented her receipt, the teller said, "That's a beautiful ring."

"What?" Maddy glanced down at her finger. She'd forgotten about the dove nestled there. "Oh, thank you."

"My girlfriend and I have been looking for something like that," the man said. "Would you mind if I ask where you bought it?"

"A little place at the beach," Maddy said, and described the location. "But I'm not sure if they have any others."

Stepping outside into a day of pure summer sunshine, she realized she'd forgotten to retrieve Jon's ring. The least she could do, she supposed, was return to the shop and pay for it.

Still in a daze, Maddy drove to the beach. A hundred years might have passed since last Friday, yet everything appeared the same, she noticed as she parked. The same beach umbrellas, the same skateboarders, the same children building sand castles.

Trudging along the boardwalk, Maddy tried to remember her mood of the previous week. Had she really been so disgruntled at having nothing exciting to do? What an idiot she'd been!

A few steps later, Maddy halted. She clearly remembered the shop's location, but it wasn't here. She saw only a boarded-up store bearing no resemblance to the quaint emporium of a few days earlier.

This one had a plain front bearing the letters Custom Bikinis, Made to Order, faded almost to illegibility.

Where had the little old couple gone?

A wave of guilt rushed over her. She had promised to return the man's ring, and had failed. She couldn't go back on her word; she had to find these people.

Anxiously, Maddy prowled down the block until she found a phone booth. The white pages had been shredded but the Yellow Pages remained, and she spent fifteen minutes searching in vain for a gift or antique shop by the name of Curios for the Curious.

Inside a nearby restaurant, Maddy located some white pages and tried again. Still nothing.

The place was nearly empty, and she had no trouble buttonholing a waiter. "Do you know of a shop around here called Curios for the Curious?"

His young, freckled face creased as he searched his memory. "Gee, you know, that rings a bell but—I don't think so."

Thanking him, Maddy went outside. She asked shop-keepers at a couple of other stores, and got the same reaction, a kind of mystified puzzlement as if they vaguely recalled such a place but couldn't pin it down.

Maddy wouldn't even be able to repay that sweet old couple for their loss. She felt as if she'd done them a personal injury.

Standing on the boardwalk, motionless as a skateboarder whizzed past inches away, Maddy faced the truth.

She was tormenting herself about a missing ring, when what really mattered was that a man had been killed. She couldn't go on hiding. Neither could she betray Jon, but...

Plodding toward her car, Maddy realized she had to go back to the mountains and find the nearest police station. She would wait long enough for Jon to make a getaway, though.

He should receive the money today. The bank had been in Dallas, which she assumed Jon had picked because it was a large city and could provide anonymity. As soon as he paid Gloria, he'd be heading for parts unknown.

By Thursday, he'd be long gone. She didn't know how she could bear her guilty conscience until then, but she would manage it for Jon's sake.

THERE WAS NOTHING in the papers or on the newscasts Wednesday or Thursday. Maddy assumed Gloria must have phoned in her account by now, and felt sorry for Larry.

Maddy's planned confession would help him, too, she thought. But it wouldn't help her parents. She didn't even want to think about what their reaction would be.

She almost confessed everything Wednesday night, when her father called to say he wanted Maddy to join them in Texas the following week to celebrate the groundbreaking for a new shopping center. Lael came on the line, warm and welcoming, ready to smooth over any friction between father and daughter.

Maddy could only say, "Sure. I'll be there." Maybe it would even prove true, with no body and no witnesses and Gloria long gone. Maybe the district attorney would decide not to prosecute. Maybe the police wouldn't believe her. But she had to try.

She doubted now that Jon had given her his real name. The only one left holding the bag would be Maddy, and she had only herself to blame.

Bitsy noticed the change in her, but attributed it to an unhappy love affair. "You'll get over him," she counseled Maddy on Thursday morning, and then held up her newly painted apple green nails. "What do you think? Should I put stars on them?"

After Bitsy left for her Jazzercise class, Maddy wondered whether she should pack a suitcase. She wasn't sure how a person prepared to be hauled off to jail. Did they allow you to bring cosmetics? Fashion magazines? Chewing gum? As far as she recalled from prison movies, you had to wear ugly, baggy dresses and let your hair get stringy.

Well, it was a safe bet some photographer would turn up to snap pictures of the heiress being dragged off to jail. Instead of her usual casual clothes, Maddy put on a yellow blouse, a short skirt and medium heels. At least she didn't have to look like a lost cause even if she felt like one.

She would need a lawyer, of course. The only name Maddy had was that of an attorney specializing in wills and estates, but she supposed he could refer her to a criminal specialist.

Maybe she ought to take a lawyer with her, but that struck Maddy as cowardly. She didn't want to hide behind her money any longer.

Retracing the route Jon had driven with some help from a map, she reached the mountains by midafternoon. The sports car had no trouble zipping up the steep inclines, but then Maddy ran into a snag.

She had assumed it would be easy to find Larry's hideaway, but that didn't turn out to be true. Every intersection looked alike, and none of the road names were familiar. At the time, it had seemed as if they took the only route available, but now Maddy discovered that wasn't true.

She knew she must be in the general vicinity of the campgrounds, but an hour of fruitless circling left her frustrated. Maddy hadn't seen a single place to ask directions, and her map book didn't include many of the side streets.

It was with a sigh of relief that she took yet another turn onto yet another road that appeared out of nowhere, and passed a sign proclaiming Welcome to Mountain View.

Civilization at last!

She didn't need to find Larry anyway, Maddy reminded herself as she slowed her sports car. Surely there would be a police or sheriff's station in town where she could turn herself in.

She hadn't counted on the fact that Mountain View was a resort village, not a metropolitan suburb.

The winding main street revealed roughly a dozen commercial buildings, each situated at an angle based on topography. No urban developer had laid out this uneven tract, with its more or less Swiss motif marred by a modern glass front veterinary clinic plopped into the center of town.

No signs indicated where law enforcement might be found. Maddy decided to stop and ask.

She parked in front of the Mountain View Animal Clinic, an attractive low structure with a sign in the window reading Under New Management. That reminded Maddy that Blair's fiancée probably worked here.

The couple had planned to buy the clinic and operate it themselves. Apparently somebody else had beaten them to it.

Maddy sat behind the wheel, unsure how to proceed. She didn't want to risk encountering a woman she'd wronged, even if that woman was unaware of it. Yet Maddy's knees felt weak from the long drive and a lack of lunch, and she couldn't bring herself to start the motor and move on.

I'll just ask for a telephone. She knew people weren't supposed to dial 911 except in an emergency, but then, she *was* reporting a murder.

Knowing that in a few minutes there would be no turning back, Maddy got out of the car.

Despite the sunshine, the air carried a tinge of mountain coolness that proved refreshing. Maddy's stomach growled, and she gazed longingly at the Mountain View Café down the block.

Jail food was probably terrible. She wondered if they let you order take-out pizza. But now that she was here, she didn't want to delay, not even long enough to eat.

Inside the clinic, Maddy saw only a small boy waiting on a seat, holding a lizard. A placard on the counter said: Receptionist at lunch.

"Excuse me," she asked the boy, who looked about eight, "do you know if there's a phone around here?"

"There's one at my house," he said.

"Thanks, but that's not what I meant." To the left of the counter, a door led into unseen depths of the building. Although the public obviously wasn't meant to wander about, Maddy headed in that direction.

Before she reached it, a tall, dark-skinned woman in a white coat appeared in the doorway, examining a chart in one hand. "Bradley?" she said, and looked up, her eyes meeting Maddy's with a glint of surprise. "I'm sorry, I didn't know anyone else was here."

"I'm just looking for a telephone," Maddy said. She got the terrible feeling that this must be Blair's fiancée, but the woman didn't appear distressed. On the other hand, what was a veterinarian supposed to do, drag around like a basset hound because she thought her boyfriend had run off with another woman?

"I'm sorry, we don't have a public phone," the vet said.

Maddy felt her courage and her resolve bleeding away. It was now or never. "I have to call the police," she said.

"Has something happened?" asked the woman in alarm.

Maddy's throat went dry. How much should she explain? She didn't want to be the one to break the terrible news. "Possibly," she said. "It's important that I speak with someone right away."

The tall woman tilted her head as if thinking it over, then asked the boy to wait a few more minutes. "There's no police station in Mountain View," she told Maddy, ushering her into a corridor that ran behind the receptionist's station. "But there is a sheriff's station in the next town."

"That's fine." Maddy skirted a bucket of paint, and realized she was standing on a drop cloth. The building must be undergoing renovations on behalf of whoever had purchased it.

"Be careful. By the way, I'm Bev Leary. I'm the new owner here," the veterinarian said, holding out her hand. "Well, at least I will be when we close escrow. It all happened kind of fast."

As Maddy shook hands, curiosity tickled her brain. "You bought it yourself?"

"Well, my fiancé and I did," said Bev.

Oh, no; this was worse than Maddy had thought. Blair and Bev must have taken out a loan. Without him to help pay it off, the veterinarian would lose everything.

"Are you in shock?" Bev asked. "You keep staring as if you don't know where you are."

"I'm sorry." Maddy hugged herself. "I've had a rough time these past few days." *But not as rough as you're going to have when you learn the truth.* "Could I just use that phone, please?"

"Of course." The woman indicated a phone on the wall of the receptionist's cubicle. "But watch out for the wet paint. My fiancé's been . . ."

She didn't finish the sentence, because from the back of the building a man called, "Hey, honey, they were out of roasted chicken so I got fried! Hope that's okay!"

Before Bev could answer, a man in paint-spattered jeans and sweatshirt strolled around a corner into view, holding a large bucket of chicken.

It was Blair Chesley.

Chapter Sixteen

He and Maddy stared at each other in shock. It would have been difficult to say who was more stunned.

"Uh," was the first thing out of Blair's mouth.

"You're alive!" Maddy couldn't stop gaping. Her initial thought was that Blair must have recovered from his injuries, but it had been less than a week and there was no sign of a wound.

Besides, exactly whose body had Jon hidden in the desert?

"Excuse me?" Bev asked, taking in the exchange of startled glances.

"He's supposed to be dead," Maddy said. "I came here to report his murder."

"Dead?" The tall woman pierced her fiancé with a look. "Exactly what is going on here?"

"It's kind of a long story," said Blair.

Maddy felt her shock giving way to anger. "I don't know what's going on, either but—"

And then, suddenly, she did know.

One hundred thousand dollars. That's how much money she'd sent Jon.

Somewhere along the line, he must have found out that Maddy was an heiress. Thinking back, she could see it wouldn't have been difficult to guess. She'd made several slips of the tongue, her clothes were obviously expensive, and besides, Maddy's father was well-known in business circles.

Especially in Texas these days.

Fury boiled through her. Everything she'd shared with Jon, even their lovemaking, had been a sham. He'd used her, not just so he could catch Gloria, but so he could steal her money.

She'd sent him one hundred thousand dollars without question. The jerk had manipulated and conned her, and he'd used the oldest trick in the book: making her fall in love with him.

She wouldn't let him get away with it. Maddy could live without the money, but she couldn't live with the sense of unfairness. One way or another, Jon Everett—or whatever his real name might be—would regret he'd ever met Maddy Armand.

"He set me up," Maddy told Bev. "He and a man I thought was my friend. They made it look like Blair got killed and it was partly my fault. Jon claimed he needed one hundred thousand dollars to pay off a witness. I was so stupid, I fell for it, but my conscience wouldn't leave me alone so I came here to report it."

Bev's eyes narrowed and she planted her hands on her hips. "Blair Chesley, is that where you got the fifty thousand dollar down payment on this clinic?"

"Uh," Blair said again, his jaw working. His eyes darted toward Maddy in mute appeal, but she wasn't buying.

"Did you steal this woman's money?" If Bev had started breathing fire, Maddy wouldn't have been surprised.

Blair sighed. "Well, Jon said she's rich and she wouldn't miss it."

Maddy's cheeks burned. So that's how Jon had talked when her back was turned. The man had viewed her as a chicken to pluck right from the beginning. When she thought about the night they'd made love, it hurt more than anything in her whole life.

Bev turned to Maddy. "Miss, I'm sorry. I had no idea this man stole the money to buy this clinic. We'll cancel escrow and pay you back."

The small boy peeked around the doorframe. "Excuse me, is it going to take much longer?" He held up the lizard. "Bogey's kind of sick."

"I'm sorry, Bradley." Bev hurried over and bent down to inspect the creature. "Now, you tell me what's wrong." With an apologetic glance at Maddy, she said, "I'll just be a minute."

"That's okay." Maddy realized that, without knowing it, she'd been enjoying the scents of dogs and cats reminiscent of her stint at an animal shelter. From the rear of the clinic came a steady rustling and an occasional plaintive bark that made her want to run back and comfort the frightened creatures.

Blair stood shamefaced, with shoulders bowed. "What I did was wrong," he told Maddy. "I tried to make myself think it didn't matter, but it did."

"I've spent a horrible week!" she said. "I thought I'd helped cause your death! Do you know what that feels like?"

"I betrayed Beverly's trust," he answered. "That doesn't feel too good, either."

"Do you know where Jon is?" she asked.

He shook his head. "Long gone, I imagine."

"What about Larry Wicker? Does he know the truth?"

"I told him about Gloria when I got back," Blair said. "I covered up my part—said I fell and hit my head, and when I woke up you guys explained it to me. He called Texas and confirmed it."

At least that part had been true; Gloria *was* wanted for murder. Maddy felt relieved that at least she hadn't helped Jon shanghai an innocent woman.

By the time Bev finished advising the boy, Maddy had an idea. "Listen," she said when the veterinarian returned. "That money was just sitting in the bank, at a puny interest rate. Why don't we call it an investment in your business? Later, if you want to buy me out, you can, but meanwhile you make the payments and we'll be partners."

Hope leapt in Bev's eyes. "You're sure about this? You don't just feel sorry for me, do you?"

Maddy shook her head. "I used to work with animals, and I'd like to do something for them. I can see you're needed here—I'll bet there isn't another clinic for miles."

"About twenty miles," the woman admitted.

"We'll get a lawyer to draw up papers so everything's in order," Maddy finished.

After a moment's contemplation, Bev said, "It's a deal," and the two women shook hands.

"What about me?" Blair asked timidly.

"You're in the doghouse," answered his fiancée. "I mean that in every sense of the word. That wedding you wanted to move up? No chance. You're going to have to prove yourself trustworthy, Mr. Chesley."

He nodded, apparently relieved at not being banished entirely. "Fair enough. Honestly, Bev, I never did anything like this before and I never will again. That fellow Jon was a smooth talker and it seemed like a golden opportunity, but it was wrong."

"I'll vouch for his smooth talking," Maddy admitted. "And I let him persuade me to do something wrong, too, by not reporting what I thought was a crime. So I can't be too hard on Blair."

"Well, I can," said Bev, but a little smile played around the corners of her mouth as she said it.

ENTANGLED IN conflicting thoughts, Maddy grabbed a hamburger at the restaurant and then drove home. This time, she spotted the turnoff to Larry's property, and considered going to talk to him. But he'd probably already headed back to civilization.

Besides, since Larry knew the truth, there was no point in beating her chest and doing a mea culpa. The man no doubt wanted to forget about Gloria and the whole episode as quickly as possible.

Shivers of worry kept running through her out of habit, and Maddy had to remind herself that Blair was alive. Safe and sound, except for whatever punishment his fiancée chose to dole out.

She'd been so frightened. But she'd learned something about herself, that in the end she would do what was right.

The same could not be said of Jon Whatever-His-Real-Name-Was. Even if he'd told the truth about Gloria, he'd probably lied about everything else.

Maddy tried to remember specific things he'd said, but her memories ran together in a blur of sensations and images: Jon hauling her into the motor home at the beach; Jon bluffing their way into the couples weekend; Jon rubbing her shoulders during the massage-in.

She put a mental X through the picture of them alone in the RV. It had been a sham. The man had a heart of stone and a conscience of Swiss cheese.

Still, Maddy knew better than to call the police and report his confidence game. It would be a low-priority crime, and she doubted they'd find the man. Worse, the press might get hold of it. She could imagine the screaming headlines in the tabloids: Thief Of Hearts Cons Heiress. Or maybe A Fool And Her Money Are Soon Parted.

She would never live it down.

No, Maddy was going to play this smart. She would hire a detective and track the man, no matter how long it took or how much it cost. Then she would figure out a way to make him suffer.

A sense of satisfaction pervaded her, lasting until she exited the freeway. Then the glum reality of everyday life sank in: a traffic jam on Sunset Boulevard, a suspicious rattle in the sports car engine, the scent of exhaust and smog fumes turning the distant mountains to blue haze.

If she'd been restless before, Maddy felt hopelessly trapped now. She had tried to find meaning through adventure, and failed. What was she going to do with the rest of her life, anyway?

She still wanted to find Mr. Right and have kids. But every time she tried to picture the man of her dreams, a scoundrel in a cowboy hat kept getting in the way.

She hated that man. If sheer loathing could erode metal, Maddy would have been driving down Sunset Boulevard in a rusted-out hulk.

On the other hand, maybe her mood *had* affected the car, or perhaps their sojourn in the mountains had overtaxed its finicky heart. By the time she turned off Sunset into the hills near her home, the engine was whining perilously.

Although she had a housekeeper and a gardener, Maddy wasn't old-fashioned enough to hire a chauffeur. She would have to take the darn car to the shop herself. While the cost of repairs didn't faze her, she hated the smug look that came over the manager's face when he saw her, as if dollar signs were ringing in his eyes.

She was sick of being treated like a walking bank account. Didn't anyone have integrity any more?

Grumbling to herself, Maddy chugged toward her house. She had about half a mile to go when the engine coughed once and died.

Oh, terrific.

She twisted the key. The engine turned over and then sank into silence.

Maddy tried a few of the curses she'd learned from Gloria, but they didn't help. Afraid of causing an accident, she used gravity to back the car downhill until it rested on the shoulder. Then she dug the flip phone from her purse and took the auto club emergency number from the glove compartment.

The phone gave a weak blip and died.

Was the mechanical world rebelling against humankind, or were Maddy's habits of postponing maintenance and forgetting to replace batteries simply catching up with her?

She didn't know and she didn't care. Snarling low in her throat, Maddy kicked open the door and got out.

The road wound upward between high hedges. Narrow and devoid of sidewalks, it forced her to press hard right to stay clear of cars whizzing past with reckless speed.

Branches poked Maddy as she stomped along. A couple of bees dive-bombed her, apparently attracted by her yellow blouse, and only gave up a quarter of a mile later.

Her feet hurt in the dressy pumps, and the bushes scratched her legs. The way things were going today, Maddy grumbled to herself, she'd probably catch Lyme disease, hanta virus *and* the flesh-eating bacteria.

Her legs and back ached by the time she reached her driveway. She'd never realized what a long stretch it was to the house itself, nor how shaggy the oleanders had grown. Oleanders were poisonous, she remembered just as a leafy branch whacked her across the mouth.

By the time she got inside, Maddy thought, she wouldn't need a mechanic, she'd need the paramedics.

It wasn't until she rounded the final bend that she saw the intruder in her private parking lot. Sitting dead center in front of the house was a familiar motor home with Texas license plates.

JON FIGURED he had to be some kind of maniac to come back here.

He'd scored a double hit, the best of his life. A hundred thousand dollars bounty for Gloria, and the same amount from Maddy. Minus Blair's fifty thou, that left a nest egg that would put him on the road to a new ranch or, better yet, a business of his own. Something with vision, something that would stir and entertain people while keeping their Southwest heritage alive. Jon just wished he could figure out what it was.

And who he wanted to share it with.

He'd tried to create a mental likeness of Maddy-as-heiress that encompassed blond hair and blue eyes, garages full of cars and closets of expensive clothes. This ersatz Maddy glibly put Blair's death out of her mind while she lost herself in a whirl of parties and shopping.

It didn't fit.

He'd heard the distress in Maddy's voice. He knew she was eating herself up over this business.

Worse, he missed her. Jon couldn't figure it out; Maddy wasn't his type of woman. Too flighty, too sheltered, too unpredictable.

But she made him laugh. And she set him on fire. And she cared so deeply about everyone and everything. And when he'd more or less thrust the steering wheel into her hands, she hadn't panicked; she'd saved their lives.

Things hadn't gone exactly as Jon planned. He had figured to finish Blair off quickly, but the guard had played his part too well. The struggle had lasted until they were halfway down the mountain, during which time Maddy could easily have run them off a cliff.

Thank goodness for her presence of mind. But, Jon had tried to tell himself, she wouldn't miss the money, and she didn't expect to see him again, so what difference did it make if he tricked her a little?

Well, not a little. A lot.

He'd suffered for it, though. Two days of driving almost straight through, with Gloria making his life miserable, had been a punishment branded into Jon's memory. He'd never carried a prisoner that far, and knew he was skating on the far side of the law to do so. Also on the far side of his sanity.

There'd been the need for rest stops, and feeding her, and making sure the bonds didn't chafe too much, all the while enduring her curses and spitting. Once she'd punched Jon in the cheek, leaving a bruise, and another time she'd kicked him where the sun never shone. Only sheer willpower had enabled him to get the handcuffs back on. It had been the greatest relief of his life when he finally handed her over to the sheriff.

But he'd received the reward, and Maddy's money as well. After transferring it a couple of times to make it hard to trace, and shipping off Blair's portion, he should have been soaring in hog heaven. Instead, Jon had been seized by a compulsion to come back.

He just wanted to see Maddy one more time. He intended to explain, and to apologize. And, much as it galled him, to give back the money, along with the clothes she'd left in the RV.

She hadn't deserved the way he'd treated her. He might hate her father, but it wasn't Charles Armand who'd been seduced and abandoned. Jon might skirt society's conventions but he didn't hurt innocent people. At least, he never had before.

He maintained no illusions. Maddy would be furious. She would revile him, threaten to call the police, possibly tear up his check. He would simply write another one.

And he intended to return that ring, as well, the one in his pocket that sometimes felt as if it were fluttering. This time, Jon meant to leave no loose ends when he said goodbye.

He was gathering his nerve to go to the door when he spotted her in the side-view mirror. She hadn't noticed him yet; she was on foot, but not dressed for a hike. The woman was obviously frazzled, with dirt streaking across one cheek and her yellow blouse coming untucked from the short skirt.

Instead of a haughty frivolous heiress, Maddy looked like a woman who needed someone to take her in his arms and tell her that everything would be all right. And suddenly, Jon got an idea.

It beat handing her a check and driving away. It might even turn out to be his best idea yet.

MADDY RESISTED the urge to throw rocks at the motor home. With her luck, she would only break a fingernail.

Where was Bitsy to call the police? Where was the bolt of lightning that ought to come out of the sky and smash Jon Everett to burnt shreds of egotistic manhood?

Maddy halted, feet throbbing almost as hard as her pride. She watched with what she hoped was an expression of cold distaste as a lean figure in a Stetson leapt from the driver's door.

Jon paused a moment, sunlight dazzling across his gold-touched skin. She knew that hard body too well; she could sense the muscles tensed beneath the jeans and work shirt. What did he want?

"I know what you did," Maddy challenged. "I've seen Blair. He squared it with me, about his half of the money."

Jon hesitated, and she knew she'd surprised him. *I'm not as stupid as you think,* she reflected with a surge of confidence.

But he didn't stay motionless long. "Guess I only owe you fifty thousand, then," he said. That sounded promising, but there was something cagey about his smile, something Maddy didn't trust.

She found out why a moment later, when he raced toward her, spun her around and slapped the handcuffs on her wrists.

"Hey!" Maddy wanted to follow that word with a scream, but her throat had gone dry during the walk, and all she could do was cough.

"This is the only way I can get you to listen," Jon said as he hustled her toward the motor home. "The sooner you hear me out, the sooner I'll take them off."

"You think I'd believe anything you said?" she managed to gasp, before going into another coughing fit.

"Got a cold?" He hoisted her across his shoulder like a sack of potatoes and climbed into the motor home.

"Bitsy will be back any minute and she'll call 911!" Maddy gasped between choking noises, although she had no idea where her friend was and doubted Bitsy would have the presence of mind to do any such thing.

"Then I guess we'd better leave." Dumping her on the couch, Jon strode forward. A moment later, the motor home rumbled to life and began bumping its way out of the driveway.

"My car!" Maddy uttered. "It—broke—"

"We'll call Bitsy from the road," Jon said. "Hang on. I'll get you something to drink in a minute."

She didn't want something to drink. She wanted to go home and think nasty thoughts about Jon Everett, Maddy told herself. She wanted to pretend she hadn't enjoyed the feel of his body against hers and the masterful way he'd taken charge.

Masterful? Try arrogant! she reminded herself. What the heck did he expect from her, anyway?

She lost track of the turns they made, and it was at least half an hour later before Jon pulled the RV to the side and came to check on her. Maddy wished he didn't have a tender, amused glint in his eyes, as if he'd gotten the best of her again.

"Beer?" Jon took one out of the refrigerator. Maddy shook her head. "Cola? Root beer?"

"Perrier," she said.

He took a plastic cup from the cupboard and, switching on the water supply, filled it. "Use your imagination," Jon said as he held it for her to drink.

Some of it spilled on Maddy as she swallowed, but she was beyond caring. "There's no bounty on me," she said. "What do you want, a ransom?"

"Something better," he said. "Promise you won't run away, and I'll take off the cuffs."

Maddy weighed the merits of trying to flee. Even without the cuffs, she wouldn't get far; in a one-on-one confrontation, Jon outweighed and outmuscled her. She might as well hear him out. "Okay."

As he released the cuffs, she sat up straighter and saw through the window that they were shielded behind some trees in an industrial area. It wasn't the kind of neighborhood where she would want to run around on her own, anyway.

"Well?" she demanded.

Jon removed a check from his pocket and flashed it in front of her. It was made out to her in the sum of one hundred thousand dollars.

He ripped it to shreds and stuck the pieces back in his pocket. "I'll make you a new one for half that amount, since you've already got Blair's share."

"How did you talk him into it, anyway?"

"I sounded him out while you were dragging Bitsy's suitcases to the trailer." Jon produced a checkbook and began to write. "He was eager to help his girlfriend but not too keen on cheating anybody. I explained that we were just stealing back my own money." He tore off the check and handed it over. The amount was fifty thousand dollars, as promised.

Maddy took it with mixed feelings. "Your own money? You're one heck of a con man, Jon Everett."

"Not exactly," he said. "I want to tell you the whole story, too."

Maddy shrugged. "It's not as if I have much choice, do I?"

Jon didn't give a direct reply. "I knew who you were as soon as I heard your name." He sat down, stretching his tall frame out in the seat, his legs reaching nearly to the far side of the RV. "Your father cheated my family out of our ranch."

That stopped Maddy. She didn't know much about her father's business dealings, but he'd been ruthless for a long time. Only since he and Lael consulted Larry Wicker and he began to sort out his values had he eased up on the business dealings. "Are you sure about that?"

"Absolutely," he said, and began to talk more freely than he ever had before.

Against her will, Maddy found herself sympathizing with the hard-working ranch family beaten down by economics and nature, and finished off by her father. He hadn't exactly cheated them, she thought; what he'd done was perfectly legal. But not very ethical.

"I told myself that by tricking you, I was getting revenge on your father." Jon spoke quietly now, his expression reflective. "That wasn't fair. I'm sorry, Maddy."

Tears pricked beneath her eyelids. She didn't intend to cry, no matter what Jon said or did. "It's no big deal. I bought myself a weekend with a cowboy. So what?"

"Is that all I meant to you?" he asked.

No, you idiot, but that's all I'll ever acknowledge that you meant. "Why, what did you think?" she asked. "That you swept me off my feet and I fell head over heels like some— like some—country girl?"

"Don't knock country girls," Jon murmured.

"I won't. Only country boys," she snapped.

A chuckle warmed the air and dissipated the tension. "You're quite a spitfire, Maddy Armand."

"By the way," she said. "What's your real name?"

"Jon Everett." He made an apologetic gesture. "I didn't think fast enough that time."

"Well, Jon Everett." Maddy smoothed down her skirt, wishing it didn't reveal so much thigh. "Mind explaining why you just kidnapped me again?"

He nodded. "Now that you've heard the whole story, maybe you'll understand. I want to meet your father. I want to let him know the harm he's done. I want to make him understand that what he took isn't just a piece of land, it's a part of history and a part of my family."

Maddy brushed a stray twig off her blouse. "You don't need me to do that."

"Don't I?" he said. "You think Charles Armand will grant an interview to any cowboy who comes stomping into his office?"

Maddy had to admit he had a point. "So you want me to set it up for you?"

"Not formally." Jon's mouth twisted in concentration. "I want to catch him off guard—no executive assistant to brief him on my background, no lawyer to advise that he doesn't owe me anything. I figure the best way is for you to introduce me as your boyfriend."

Maddy's breath escaped in a hiss of frustration. "Give me a break! I'm supposed to let you drag me to Texas so you can read my father the riot act? For your information, I have better things to do. And for another thing, it won't help, because my father always hates my boyfriends. He wouldn't listen to you anyway."

Glee danced in Jon's eyes. "Then tell him we're getting married."

"What?"

"That ought to get his attention," he said.

"I wouldn't—I have no intention—" She was still sputtering as Jon's mouth closed over hers and he lowered her to the couch.

Chapter Seventeen

As Jon's arms slipped around her, Maddy felt the pressures and anxieties of the past few days form a lump in her throat. She began to shudder.

He drew back. "Are you all right?"

"I don't know," she admitted. "After everything that's happened, you can't expect me to just forgive you!" She saw his hand reach into his shirt pocket, and then he stopped. "What have you got?"

He retrieved the ring and handed it to her. "It's some kind of aphrodisiac. I can't explain it, but when we're both wearing our rings, we seem to lose control." He ducked his head apologetically. "I—well, I was tempted to use it and cheat. But I don't want to trick you again."

Under other circumstances, Maddy would have scoffed. But what Jon said clicked with her own perceptions, outrageous as the idea seemed. "Thanks. This doesn't mean you're forgiven, but...we'll see." She tucked the ring into her purse. "I'll return it, when I figure out where the store relocated."

He leaned back on the couch. "I've been thinking about you all the way back from Texas. Remembering every detail of the way you smell and look and feel. Do you know what that does to a man?"

"Teaches self-control?" she retorted.

He chuckled. "Among other things. Well, Maddy, will you help me?"

She would have liked to make Jon suffer, after what he'd put her through. On the other hand, Maddy's parents expected to see her in Texas anyway; she already had enough clothes on board; and this way, she could stick Bitsy with taking her car to the repair shop.

"Okay," she said. "But we sleep apart. And after I introduce you to Dad, you have no further claims on me."

"Done." Jon moved away. "Make yourself at home," he said, and got behind the wheel.

Maddy belted herself into one of the rear seats as they hit the road, wanting to stay away from Jon while she sorted her thoughts. She couldn't figure out why she'd agreed to go with him. She didn't trust Jon Everett, but neither could she deny the huge burden that had lifted from her shoulders.

He wasn't just using me. He cares about me, at least a little.

She didn't know why that should matter. Jon wasn't the kind of man Maddy could settle down with. She didn't intend to raise her children in a series of campgrounds or to interrupt their schooling to chase one escaped criminal after another.

But there was something about the sight of Jon's erect back as he steered the motor home that made Maddy feel safe and warm.

And she wouldn't mind giving Daddy a surprise. Maybe just once her father wasn't going to have the last word.

IT WAS THE SECOND NIGHT on the road, in a trailer park in a town that looked like a hundred other towns, that Maddy and Jon made love again.

They had finished cooking hamburgers over an outdoor grill, the smoke keeping the mosquitoes at bay. On one side of them, two elderly couples could be seen through the open window of their RV, playing cards. From the sound of their voices, they were ragging each other about their moves with a mixture of affection and competitiveness.

On the other side was parked a motor home driven by a family of Swiss tourists. Maddy had heard them exclaiming in German over the flatness of the landscape, the low prices in the stores and the strange, subtle colors of the desert vista.

Jon disposed of the trash while she washed dishes, and then he got out a harmonica. Sitting atop the RV's steps, he played his way through "Comin' Round the Mountain" and "Red River Valley."

The Swiss people came to watch, and applauded when he finished. Some Japanese tourists drifted over, feet tapping to the strains of "Home on the Range" and "Clementine," and smiling as they listened.

By the time he finished, Maddy felt as if the entire world had united on their doorstep. She'd never imagined it was possible to meet such an international crowd in such an unlikely setting.

Later, it didn't feel right to force Jon into a sleeping bag when the folded-out bed was at least marginally big enough for them both. And it felt very right indeed to snuggle against him, and slip out of her nightgown, and feel his skin press against hers.

Their lovemaking was gentler this time, but the climax just as powerful. Maddy fell asleep in Jon's arms, feeling as if she belonged there. Temporarily, at least.

JON HADN'T BEEN BACK to Vaughan's Gap in the five years since his family lost the ranch. Although he knew plans were under way to build a regional mall, he hadn't expected to see much change yet.

But as they pulled off the highway and approached the once sleepy town, he almost thought he'd taken the wrong exit. This place scarcely resembled the village where he'd grown up.

The drought had ended, and rains had turned the landscape green. The ranches he passed looked more prosperous than in the old days, the fences newly painted, the cattle fatter.

But it was Vaughan's Gap itself that had been transformed. No longer cracked and weed-pierced, the main road had been widened and repaved. A McDonald's had sprung up outside town, followed by a modern strip of shops including a laundry, a beauty salon and a video gallery.

Farther into town, Vaughan Avenue sported an expanded department store, spruced-up facades, restriped parking and a new hotel, Vaughan's Inn. Even on the side streets, as far as Jon could see, new houses were rising from what had been vacant lots.

In the old town, he'd known almost everyone. Kids went through school together; families intermarried until almost everyone was at least a third or fourth cousin; and no one asked for identification for a check.

Now he saw a street full of strangers, and more cars than pickup trucks. Charles Armand and his development plans had changed more than just one ranch.

Jon had believed that he'd cut all emotional ties to this town, but now he realized it wasn't true. It made his spirit leap to see the old church repainted and its bell tower restored. He took pride in the central park, where new benches gleamed and up-to-the-minute play equipment provided a child's delight of slides, tunnels and swings.

"This is where you grew up?" Maddy asked.

Jon nodded. "We lived on the ranch mostly, but during the school year sometimes my brother and I would stay with cousins in town. That made it easier going back and forth to school."

"It's pretty," Maddy said wistfully.

"Where did you grow up?" he asked.

The answer wasn't unexpected: "Los Angeles." Then she added, "But we weren't really a part of the neighborhood. Dad was busy making money, and Mom would travel with him sometimes and I stayed with a housekeeper. A whole series of them, actually. It was okay, I guess. But not homey like this place."

Homey. Yes, Vaughan's Gap was definitely homey, but it wasn't home, not any more.

On the other side of town, they spotted the local headquarters of Armand Inc., a sprawling industrial building on what had been the site of Vaughan's Feed and Equipment. A couple of luxurious houses on the grounds must be occupied by executives, Jon supposed.

He felt his blood pressure begin to rise. According to Maddy, her father would be in town now. Right there, across a broad parking lot in that industrial building, lurked the long-hated Charles Armand.

Jon had never actually met the man; he'd seen plenty of the fellow's lawyers, though. He'd formed a mental picture of Charles Armand as resembling the greedy Mr. Burns on "The Simpsons," but now, glancing at Maddy beside him, he didn't suppose that image fit. Her father must be at least halfway human to have produced a child like this.

There were no guards and no parking restrictions. Jon left the motor home in a patch of shade and they walked toward the main lobby.

"Dad will be surprised to see me," Maddy murmured. "I never told him when I was arriving."

She sounded tense. Jon touched her shoulder, and felt the stiffness in her muscles. "The two of you don't get along, I gather?"

"He wants to run my life," she said. "Or at least, he used to, until he met Larry Wicker. That's why I wanted to save Larry from Gloria, because I felt I owed him something."

In the lobby, they found a table-height model of what the regional mall would look like. Jon walked around it, trying to picture these structures rising on what had been the Everett Ranch.

He liked the design. It suited the landscape, and the mix of restaurants, movie theaters and shops would no doubt attract people from a wide area.

Still, Jon reflected, there was something missing. In fact, he mused, Charles Armand was overlooking a tremendous opportunity to make his mall special and important to the area. If somebody didn't wise the guy up, the last remnants of the proud pioneer heritage of Vaughan's Gap would vanish into the blandness of Anywhere, U.S.A.

Two men walked by wearing business suits, pausing to glance at Jon's cowboy hat and jeans. They didn't sneer; they merely looked curious, as if they might like to stuff him and put him on exhibit.

They also spared appreciative glances for Maddy, who wore a flowered sundress she'd bought the previous day. Fresh as a flower, Jon thought, and tough as a weed.

A wall directory guided them to the executive office, where the secretary politely asked their business.

"I'm here to see my father," Maddy said. "Charles Armand."

"Oh!" The woman stood up and shook Maddy's hand. "I'm so pleased to meet you! Mr. Armand was hoping you'd arrive soon!"

As she bustled off, Jon removed his hat and thumped it against his leg to knock a dent from the crown. The woman hadn't even asked his name; he might as well have been Maddy's pet poodle.

Then Charles Armand came out.

Although in a way he'd been anticipating this moment not for days but for months and years, playing and replaying scenarios in which he confronted his family's nemesis, Jon found he wasn't prepared.

For one thing, the guy didn't resemble the cartoon Mr. Burns at all. The man who swept Maddy into a bear hug had a warm, round face and an unruly thatch of graying hair that made him resemble an overgrown schoolboy.

For another thing, Charles Armand was gazing at his daughter with unalloyed delight. "You actually came! Lael said you would, but I wasn't so sure."

"Daddy." Maddy squirmed out of the hug. "There's someone I'd like you to meet." She turned toward Jon. "This is Jon Everett, my, uh…" She stopped short of a lie, then waved her hand in the air so her father couldn't miss seeing the ring.

A bittersweet expression came over Charles's face as he clapped Jon's shoulders. "Well, well. You're not the sort of man my little girl usually dates, but maybe that's a good thing. Your name sounds familiar. You're not—" He paused in confusion.

"Everett Ranch," Jon said.

"You put up quite a fight, my attorney told me." Charles frowned in confusion. "But how did you and Maddy link up?"

"Kind of a coincidence," Jon said. "Could I talk to you alone, sir?"

"Certainly." To Maddy, Charles said, "Your stepmother is in the cafeteria having lunch. I know she'd be thrilled to see you."

"Sure." Maddy gave Jon a little wave. "Good luck."

"Thanks," he said. He had the feeling he was going to need it.

LAEL ARMAND ROSE to greet Maddy with a smile of welcome. "I'm so glad you're here," she said as they hugged. "Have you seen your father?"

"Yes. He's having a discussion with a, uh, friend of mine." Maddy couldn't bring herself to deceive Lael. She hadn't felt right about tricking her father, either, but she'd promised Jon.

As Lael filled her in on the details of the planned groundbreaking, Maddy wondered what was going on in her father's office. She would have given a lot of money to have a hidden microphone.

Were they arguing? Did her father detest Jon the way he'd loathed her other "young men"? She wouldn't tolerate it, Maddy told herself. Even though she and Jon weren't really engaged, she wouldn't allow her father to belittle him.

An hour later, after they'd eaten and Lael had shown Maddy around the building, they ran into Charles and Jon in the lobby. The men were studying the model of the shopping mall intently, Jon pointing out something as Charles listened.

Maddy had never seen her father demonstrate such respect to a younger man before, let alone someone he thought was involved with his daughter.

Then her father looked up, his warm gaze enveloping Lael and Maddy. "Honey, this fiancé of yours is quite a fellow."

"Fiancé?" Lael regarded Maddy questioningly. "Why haven't I heard about this?"

"Well, it's—kind of informal," Maddy said.

Her stepmother took Maddy's left hand between her palms. "I did kind of wonder about the ring."

"It's a friendship ring," she said.

"Well, it's beautiful."

"Take it from me," said Charles Armand, "if you've got any sense, Maddy, you'll snap up this young man."

Jon wore an expression of angelic innocence. Maddy wanted to punch him.

She couldn't believe her family had switched over to his side. They had no idea what this rogue was capable of. He'd lied, he'd cheated her, he'd kidnapped Maddy twice and Gloria once, he'd—he'd—

Just exactly what had he done to put that beatific smile on her father's face?

"Mind explaining what this is about?" she asked.

"Jon has some terrific ideas." Charles tapped the glass encasing the model. "He saved me from making a major mistake."

"Oh?" Maddy wondered what Jon had proposed, and what might be the motive behind it. She'd expected him to confront her father, not subvert the project.

If Jon had some swindle in mind, she wouldn't stand for it. She might quarrel with her father, but she wouldn't be a party to cheating him.

Then she realized her father was talking about redesigning part of the mall. Something about local history, a children's museum with interactive exhibits focusing on the region's history and Native American heritage.

"Plus Jon has pointed out the opportunity for attracting customers by scheduling entertainment," Charles went on. "I hadn't thought about an amphitheater for country music concerts. He says there are some local bands worth featuring along with the big names. Plus book signings for Texas authors. The publicity opportunities are endless."

Maddy had to admit, the package sounded impressive, but what lay behind it? Jon had come here as a man on a mission. That mission had not been to put feathers in Charles Armand's cap.

"And here's the best part!" Charles clapped a hand on Jon's shoulder, which was something of a reach, since the younger man stood at least eight inches taller. "I'm going to hire my son-in-law to oversee and operate the entire project! The fellow I've got running it is fine for the business end of things, but he's got no head for promotion and, well, that human touch."

"Just a minute." Maddy held up both hands, feeling like a traffic cop trying to stop a runaway truck. "He's not your son-in-law."

"He will be!" announced her father.

"I told you, nothing's definite." It had never occurred to her that Charles might actually want her to marry Jon. The very idea made Maddy bristle. "I've never let you run my life, Dad, and I'm not going to start now."

"You're the one who brought him here!"

"And a darn fool idea it was too!" she snapped.

Before she could continue, Jon took her elbow. "I think your daughter and I need to continue this discussion in private."

"What my daughter needs is to stop acting like an over-grown adolescent!" roared Charles Armand.

"Now, dear," murmured Lael. "Remember what Larry Wicker always says."

"I *am* breaking barriers! And the next barrier I'm going to break is my daughter's neck!" But he said it ruefully.

"Larry told you to stop trying to control the entire world," Lael continued. "And that includes your family."

Jon steered Maddy out of the lobby before she could decide which of several insults to hurl at her father. "It was a pleasure meeting you, Mr. and Mrs. Armand. We'll talk again soon."

"Soon!" Maddy sputtered as they crossed the parking lot. "Well, Mr. Jon Everett, you can talk as much as you like, but *I'm* going home."

"Darn right you are," he said, and piloted her to the motor home.

"I don't live here!" she defied him as she went up the steps.

"Home is where you hang your hat."

"I don't have a hat!"

He plopped his Stetson on her head. "Now you do."

It slipped down her forehead, half covering her eyes. "Too big," Maddy said. "But it smells nice."

He pressed her into one seat and lounged in another chair opposite her. "Your father and I have come to terms. It seems he's been looking for me."

"Why?" she demanded from beneath the brim. "Did you abscond with the deed or something?"

"It appears he had second thoughts about his ruthless dealings, something to do with Larry Wicker encouraging him to reevaluate his life," Jon said. "He sent extra payments to my parents and my brother, and he wanted to buy me off as well."

"Take the money and run." Maddy tipped back the hat. "Jon, what's your game? You're not going to manage some mall—I know you too well. Let Dad give you the conscience money and then go do whatever it is you do when you're not complicating my life."

"Marry me." Jon said the words in a level tone, almost casually.

"Do I look as if I've recently taken leave of my senses?" she demanded.

His slow, assessing gaze took in the disheveled Stetson, the hair bunched to one side and the defiant expression. "Yes." He leaned forward and rubbed his fingers lightly beneath her chin. "See, I've got this problem. I love you, crazy lady. Come share my life of poverty and lawlessness."

Maddy remembered her fantasy of having children and a home. There'd been a vague, shadowy husband in there, too, she felt almost certain. Also a housekeeper and a beautician.

"Can we bring Bitsy?" she asked.

Jon began to laugh. "We can bring an entire caravan of Gypsies," he said. "Just say yes."

Maddy allowed herself for the first time to imagine spending the rest of her life with Jon. It meant freedom, unpredictability, and yet security, too. Her children might not grow up in a big house and they might not attend an exclusive school, but they would have fun and excitement. And love.

"You're on," she said.

"Is that a yes?" Jon queried.

"Done."

"I prefer the traditional response."

"Okay, you got it," Maddy said.

"I haven't heard it yet."

"What do you want?" she asked. "You want me to surrender, is that it?"

"More or less," Jon said. "Humor me. Let me savor the moment. I'm sure it won't happen often."

"Yes," Maddy said.

"Louder?"

"I hate you!" she shouted.

The biggest, slyest grin she'd ever seen spread across Jon's bronzed face. "Here's the best part. After we get married..." He paused and faked a yawn.

"What?" Maddy asked suspiciously.

"We don't have to live in a motor home," Jon said. "I'll be working for your father and we'll build ourselves the best house Vaughan's Gap, Texas, has ever seen."

"You want me to marry you and live in a big house and let my father run *both* our lives?" Springing to her feet, Maddy tossed the hat aside. "Well, Mr. Everett, here's another traditional response. No, no, no!"

"Once would make the point," he said mildly.

On the verge of storming out, Maddy remembered that she didn't want to have to come back for her clothes. "Go away and let me pack." She began poking behind the seats for a suitcase.

It didn't surprise her when she felt Jon's hands catch her waist, or when she found herself transported to the couch, or when she discovered that somehow he had wedged himself atop her and was kissing her.

That was what a rejected lover was supposed to do, after all. And she liked Jon. Okay, loved him, maybe, a little. Wouldn't mind sleeping with him again. Maybe sticking around for a while.

"But I can't marry you," Maddy said.

"Why not?"

"Because my father would approve."

He started to laugh. "How horrible."

"You have no idea."

"As Larry would say, break the barriers." Jon began unzipping the back of Maddy's sundress.

"We already broke those," she said.

"That's not the barrier I mean," he said. "Think about it." He lowered her bodice and began kissing the tops of her breasts.

"How can I think while you're doing that?" Maddy felt a moan escape from deep within her.

"Okay, think later," Jon said, and then they both stopped talking for a good long time.

Afterward, lying in Jon's arms, Maddy felt the power rippling through his body as he cradled her. No one would ever control Jon Everett, and that included her father. He must have decided to work here because it was what he truly wanted.

It didn't matter where they lived or what kind of work Jon did, she realized; they would define their own lives and their own marriage. Nothing else mattered, not her father's opinion, nor Jon's line of work, nor whether she had Bitsy or somebody else to do her nails.

She supposed their kids would enjoy growing up next door to a mall. What kid wouldn't? And they'd get a chance to enjoy the outdoor life of Vaughan's Gap, to learn to ride and camp and lasso. She could picture them now, a brood of tiny figures wearing cowboy hats, toddling into the sunset swinging lariats.

"Yes," Maddy said aloud.

She felt rather than saw Jon's smile as he snuggled her tighter, his large body curling around her smaller one.

Oh, well, it wouldn't hurt to make her father happy, just this once.

Chapter Eighteen

The people of Vaughan's Gap would never forget the wedding of Madeleine Armand and Jon Everett. It took place in the old church at one o'clock on a sunny September afternoon.

The church was fragrant with orchids. Rumor had it that an entire Malaysian rain forest had been stripped of the flowers, although more practical citizens suggested a denuded greenhouse in Mexico.

A new organ, donated to the church by Charles Armand, was played with earsplitting effectiveness by a slender young man who had recently made his debut at Carnegie Hall and thought he was still there. The choir loft shivered beneath the weight of an octet of gospel singers, and tiny lights glittered like stars in the branches of potted trees and across the arched ceiling.

A double-size mobile home had been set up outside as the bride's dressing room, since no one could expect her entourage to fit into the small chamber usually reserved for that purpose. No one criticized the heiress for having a hairdresser on hand, along with a seamstress and a makeup expert. But it was difficult for the honest citizens of Vaughan's Gap to understand why the manicurist had to run alongside her through the vestibule, applying last-minute hearts to her glittering nails.

The rings had been custom designed. According to an article in the local newspaper, the bride's diamond had once belonged to a rajah, but his beloved left it behind when she absconded with a soldier of fortune.

There was no maid of honor, possibly because the bride couldn't pick one of her many friends to rise above the rest. A cleaning lady reported that the bride had said, "Besides, somebody might do to me what I did to Gloria," but nobody could figure out who Gloria was.

The bouquet was made of orchids and roses, the gown designed of gold mesh over white silk and pictured the next month in *True Bride's Monthly Magazine*. Delicate sandals of white-and-gold silk peeped from beneath the skirt, and hardly anyone believed the cleaning lady's tale that the bride had initially demanded in-line skates.

In any other setting, the bridal chapeau might have aroused comment, but the residents found themselves flattered rather than amused by the white cowboy hat with its short veil. The bride wore her blond hair loose about her shoulders, topped with one small braid on each side.

No one understood why the bride chose to have both sets of parents stand by the altar and to march down the aisle alone rather than on the arm of her father, but it was probably one of those modern innovations that hadn't reached Vaughan's Gap yet. Besides, the way that lady with the nail polish crouched alongside doing touch-ups right to the last moment, it almost appeared as if the manicurist were giving her away.

In time, the details would be forgotten. But no one who attended the wedding—and almost the whole town crammed into that church—would ever forget the expression of delight on the groom's face, or the modest way the bride bit her lip when she saw him, as if she couldn't quite believe her good luck.

Of course, it was possible that the mothers of the bride and groom, Lael Armand and Suzanne Everett, missed some of those details due to the tears in their eyes. But they could review the whole thing later in matchless close-ups on a film shot from three cameras and cut together by one of the best film editors in Hollywood.

MADDY HAD PUT HER FOOT down when it came to the reception. Her father wanted to rent a hotel in Los Angeles and invite his business associates, celebrities and anyone else on the Hollywood A-list.

As far as Maddy was concerned, her new home would be Vaughan's Gap, and that's where they would hold the reception. Her father could invite anyone he liked, but most of the guests would be townspeople and relatives of the groom.

She hadn't counted on the fact that the Vaughan's Inn lacked a banquet room, and the only space available was in the community recreation center. A large room used for Mommy 'n' Me classes and square dancing sessions was pressed into use, and decorated within an inch of its life by a florist imported from Dallas. If you ignored the scuffed linoleum and the sliding glass doors opening onto the swimming pool, it didn't look half bad.

The band was local, and made up in enthusiasm for what it lacked in polish. Maddy looped her long skirt over one arm and joined Jon in a square dance.

She didn't know the steps, but it wasn't hard to follow the others. The tricky part was tearing her eyes away from the groom.

Jon had set aside his cowboy garb for a tuxedo. Tailored to fit his broad shoulders and lean frame, it gave him an air of sophistication and command.

Or it might have, if he hadn't looked so uncomfortable in it.

"Only for you," he'd muttered to Maddy the first time he tried it on.

She was looking forward to stripping it off him as soon as custom allowed the two of them to retire. For the past six weeks, to avoid gossip and spare the feelings of Jon's warmhearted but conservative parents, Maddy had stayed with her father and Lael. Amid the whirlwind of parties and preparations, she and her husband-to-be had found themselves reduced to stealing kisses when they thought no one was looking.

It had been almost enough to make her consider chucking the whole wedding and eloping. Almost, but not quite.

Now, at last, they faced the prospect of a week alone together. Jon had remained mum about the honeymoon destination, but Maddy's father had dropped broad hints involving south seas, palm trees and blue lagoons.

Hawaii, she thought. Or maybe Tahiti. Fiji, anyone?

Maddy didn't know when she'd been so happy. She loved parties, and this one had all her favorite foods—no wonder, since she'd selected the menu—as well as her favorite people.

After the square dance, her party friends from Los Angeles joined the Vaughan's Gap residents in a conga line, everyone laughing as they snaked through the room. In one corner, Lael and Mrs. Everett toasted each other with champagne. In another corner, Bitsy flirted with Jon's brother, who looked handsome in his marine uniform.

Maddy wished it could last forever. But then Jon whispered in her ear, "Isn't it time to leave?"

"I'll go change," she whispered back, and hurried away.

For traveling, she'd selected a black suit with a colorful scarf-collar, a flippy little skirt and low heels. Comfortable enough for an airplane ride, and sophisticated enough for any destination.

Lael had packed Maddy's suitcase, after consulting with Jon about the secret destination. Now that the moment of truth approached, Maddy found herself tempted to peek inside, but her new mother-in-law joined her before she had a chance.

"I'm so glad Jon found you." Suzanne Everett was a tall woman with bone structure that would have made a model envious. She wore her graying hair swept back in an elegant French twist. "You're what he's needed to settle him down."

Maddy smiled. "My father feels the same way about Jon, that he's settling me down."

"You'll be good for each other." Mrs. Everett gave her a hug. "And I'm pleased that the two of you will be in charge of our old ranch, even if it isn't a ranch anymore. It feels good to keep it in the family."

"I've never been part of a tradition before," Maddy said. "But I guess that happens when you get married, doesn't it? You become part of a whole chain of things."

"It can be a bit intimidating," agreed her new mother-in-law. "I remember feeling proud and a little intimidated when I realized a marriage wasn't just my husband and me, but his parents and our children and someday our daughters-in-law and their families, and then our grandchildren. We all get knit together and sometimes that makes for a bit of friction, but the beauty of it is that when you need someone to lean on, we're here for you."

Maddy's eyes prickled. She wondered if it was the dry air, and then she realized it was tears. "I'm proud to be part of your family," she said.

"Oh!" Suzanne tapped her arm. "I heard someone calling for the bride to toss her bouquet!"

Outside the community center, Maddy found a crowd of giggling young women waiting. Standing on the top step, she tossed the flowers and watched them grab for it. Bitsy made a leap worthy of an NBA champion and nabbed it in mid-air.

"Wow!" said the former housekeeper, who had recently landed a job with a new nail salon in Beverly Hills. "This is great! I'm going to have it shellacked!"

Having changed from his tuxedo into jeans and a western-style shirt, Jon beamed at their guests as he escorted Maddy toward a waiting limousine. "Whoa!" he said as a chauffeur opened the door. "Who ordered this?"

"I did!" Charles Armand stepped from the crowd, proffering a travel agency folder. "I said I had a surprise for you, didn't I, Jon? Here's two tickets to Hawaii, and a week at my favorite hotel. Have fun, you two!"

Maddy reached for the envelope, but Jon plucked it from her fingers and handed it back to her father. "Thank you, sir, but my wife and I prefer to honeymoon in our own way."

"Hawaii *is* my way," Maddy said.

"Too crowded," murmured her husband.

Now, there was a sentiment she could understand. "I see what you mean. But where—?"

"And too conventional," Jon added, waving the limousine away. It drove off, leaving Maddy feeling bereft. But Jon was right; how could they do anything so ordinary as go to Hawaii on their honeymoon?

"What did you have in mind?" she asked.

"Independence," said Jon. "Adventure. Solitude. Romance."

"A cruise?" she asked hopefully.

"Solid land," he corrected, adjusting his Stetson. "Where's your suitcase?"

"Here!" Lael turned it over. "Have fun, you two!"

There was neither a car nor a taxi in sight. "We aren't walking, are we?" Maddy asked. "I didn't bring my in-line skates."

"You won't need them," said Jon. He whistled, and Maddy heard the one sound she hadn't counted on and would never have associated with a honeymoon, in this life or any other.

Hoofbeats.

They came around the bend at a canter, a mounted cowhand leading a gleaming black stallion and a golden mare. Across their backs lay thick packs that appeared to be sleeping bags.

"Oh, no," Maddy said.

"Oh, yes." Jon caught the mare's reins as the horses pulled up. "Here you go, lady."

"Camping?" she said. "Not even a tent?"

"There's no rain in the forecast," said Jon. "And I'm bringing my rifle, so we'll have fresh meat."

"You think I'm going to—you're going to shoot—me, cook?" Maddy finished.

He poked her lightly. "Honey, everybody's staring."

And they were, the entire town and her friends from L.A. and a bunch of dirty-faced children who had materialized from a nearby playground. She could see little smiles on their faces, at her expense.

This was a battle she couldn't win. Not now, anyway. Certainly not here. On the other hand, Jon hadn't tasted her cooking yet. He also hadn't seen Maddy's temper when she didn't get her coffee on time.

And heaven help him if he actually shot an animal. She'd have to bandage it, feed it and cart it home until it recovered. Now that she was part-owner of a veterinary clinic, it was the least she could do.

"Well, let's go," said Maddy, and flung herself at the horse. It took a good bit of pushing on Jon's part, but she landed upright in the saddle.

"What changed your mind?" he asked as he swung onto the stallion.

"The spirit of adventure. What else?" said Maddy, and kicked her horse into a gallop. At least, that was her intention. In reality, the mare sighed and ambled forward at a slow walk.

Lael Armand watched them go with a twinge of guilt. She'd known Jon's intentions when she packed Maddy's clothes, but she'd honored his request not to reveal a thing to her husband or her stepdaughter.

She wondered if Charles might be angry, but he wrapped an arm around her waist as he watched his daughter depart. "They can always use the tickets later," he said. "You know, I think this fellow is just the man my daughter needs."

"And you know what?" Lael said. "He's exactly what she wants, too."

A block away, Jon took them off the pavement onto a dirt path and headed toward backcountry. Maddy didn't need to know that their destination included a furnished cabin with a fully stocked kitchen and a whirlpool spa. He'd meant what he said: he wanted to be alone with her. They had six weeks of separation to make up for.

Maddy herself was trying to adjust to the horse's rocking pace. She could feel a run starting in her stocking, and one of her nails had chipped when she mounted. But it didn't matter.

Glancing down, she smiled at the sight of her diamond glittering in the sunlight. She would have been just as happy with a smaller one, or a simple gold band, or...

She frowned at the ghost of a memory. Hadn't she been wearing some other ring, one that she had meant to switch to her right hand? She could have sworn it had been on her finger until she started down the aisle; in her excitement, she'd forgotten about moving it. But then it had vanished.

And hadn't there been another ring in her purse? She wondered if it had vanished, too. In fact, she had the strangest feeling the rings had existed only to bring her and Jon together. But that was a ridiculous thought.

Overhead, two doves flew by, dipping low and then wheeling into the sunlight. Maddy's heart flew with them, bright and free.

Then Jon turned in the saddle and their eyes met, and she forgot about the rings and the doves, and never thought of them again.

ARIEL CUPPED THE RINGS in her palm. The moment they'd reappeared, she knew exactly what had happened to Maddy and Jon, and so did Tuck.

"I told you love would work itself out." He gazed through the shop window at the beach. They'd both awakened this morning with the sense that it was time to return to this location, and so they had. Fortunately, the vacant store had remained unoccupied, and their traveling curio boutique fitted perfectly into place.

"We were lucky," answered his wife. "That thief didn't put it on. Otherwise, who knows what might have happened?"

"I tell you, the magic won't let itself be misused," replied Tuck.

"You can't be sure." Magic had fallen out of favor in their world, and both of them were rusty in its use. That was why they'd come to this new world, to see if there was a place where people still dreamed and hoped and made room in their lives for wonder. "Are you satisfied now?"

"Are you?" he asked.

Ariel sorted through the images newly arrived in her mind, of Maddy and Jon squabbling and laughing, battling and falling in love. "I'd hate for the magic to end here."

"So would I," said her husband. "Perhaps we'll try it again soon."

Ariel wasn't sure. But she didn't say no. She needed to give it more thought.

With a tender glance at his wife, Tuck lifted the man's ring from her palm and slipped it on his finger. "Ready?" he said.

Ariel gave one last, wistful glance out the window. This brash modern world invigorated her, but she preferred the thatched cottages and slower pace of home. "Ready," she said, and put on her own ring.

At sea, an arch of violet and red brightened the sky. Sunbathers and surfers turned to stare at this early sunset, then realized it wasn't twilight but midafternoon.

Someone speculated about northern lights. Someone else mentioned navy jets. A few people suggested it might be special effects for a movie.

No one noticed when the curio shop vanished. No one saw the old store returning, with its sign painted out and its windows boarded. They were too enraptured with this sudden phenomenon, this rainbow without rain that reverberated inside each watcher like subliminal music.

As they watched, each person on the beach found himself remembering something long forgotten, a face or a moment, a treasured toy, a special day in childhood. The memories came so vividly that they might have been occurring for the first time, and then without warning they faded.

A collective sigh wafted from the beach, and then the surfers began to cut across the waves again, and the children to build sand castles, and the sunbathers to stretch out across their towels.

Only one little girl noticed a ruby red twinkle far off, like a taillight headed for a distant planet. She thought it might be a falling star, and wished to find a penny in the sand.

When the light disappeared, she poked at the sand glumly with her plastic shovel. A copper gleam drew her eye to a penny so shiny it must have fallen there straight from the mint.

"Look!" she cried to her mother. "I got my wish! It's magic!"

The mother glanced away from her novel. "There's no such thing as magic, sweetie."

"Yes, there is," said the little girl, and tucked the penny into her mother's purse where it wouldn't get lost. Someday, she thought, the ruby star would come back for her, and bring the magic with it.

And maybe it did.